UP

BY
ETHAN STONE

BY ETHAN STONE

~Print Edition~

ONE

ANOTHER DAY, ANOTHER DEAD BODY.

I flashed my badge to the uniformed officer standing guard and stepped under the crime scene tape. The wind from nearby Elliot Bay had me pulling the collar up on my coat as goosebumps raced over my flesh. The rising sun did little to alleviate the chill.

"Hey, Detective Tao." Dr. Jill Trencher, King County Medical Examiner, glanced up. The corpse lay on its back, jeans pulled halfway down, arms and legs tucked alongside the body, and eyes wide open. It appeared to be male, but I wasn't sure. The lack of breasts pointed to one fact but there wasn't any male genitalia either. No male or female parts. Just dried blood where something should've been.

"What do we have, Jill?"

She stood. "White male. Mid-twenties."

I kneeled, eyeballing the body and mentally cataloging the young man's features. Short, light brown hair, eyes the shade of a dull penny. Squat, muscular body. "Time and cause of death?"

"I'd say around midnight for the time of death. As for the how, there's a wound on the back of the neck," she replied. "I suspect the killer severed the spinal cord. Would've been fairly quick and fairly painless."

"Even the castration?"

"From the looks of it, that occurred postmortem. I'll be able to tell you more when he's on the table. The crime scene unit has already been and gone. We're just waiting on you. Took you a little longer than normal to get here."

I stood and scowled. "I was home, in bed, where I still should be." No need to tell her I hadn't been alone, or who had been in my bed. "I'm *not* the detective on call."

"That would be his fault." Jill pointed behind me.

Turning, I faced my partner, Detective Jamey Nolan.

"Why aren't *you* at home with Chelsea?"

He rolled his eyes and stuffed his hands in his pockets. "I happened to be at the station when the call came in from Harbor Patrol. Sounded like an interesting case so I took it."

"Am I supposed to thank you?"

"Guess you'll just have to deal with it, huh?"

I snorted, unable to argue. Not that I was all *that* upset. A man murdered and castrated could indeed be a fascinating case and a fresh change from the gang killings Jamey and I had been investigating lately.

"Are you guys done?" Jill asked. "Can I get the body out of here?"

I took out my phone and snapped a picture of the victim's face.

"Yeah, are you finished whining, Tao?" Jamey asked.

Smirking, I replied, "Not even close, but I'll save it until we're alone."

Jamey and I stepped away and watched as Jill and her assistants removed the corpse.

"So, why *were* you at the station before the ass crack of dawn?"

Jamey didn't answer. Instead, he turned away and stared out at the bay. I stepped next to him and put a hand on his shoulder. "You and Chelsea having problems again?"

Jamey glared at me, but it wasn't like I was wrong.

"You know us. It's always something."

"Wanna talk about it?"

He glanced over and shook his head. "Not right now."

"Well, if you do, just let me know."

Jamey waggled his eyebrows and flashed a cheesy grin. "I wouldn't want to interfere with your plans."

I elbowed him in the gut, and he pretended I'd hurt him. As far as I knew, Jamey was the only one of my co-workers who knew I was gay. I hadn't told him. He'd figured it out shortly after we began working together five years ago. Not surprising, really, not with his twenty-six years of experience as a detective. It hadn't bothered him a bit. In fact, he liked, no, he *loved* ribbing me about it.

"If you'd been worried about messing with my plans, you wouldn't have taken this case."

His eyes got large, and he put a hand to his mouth. "Did you have what's his name over again?"

"If you mean Haro, then yes, he stayed last night. We were both asleep when the call came in."

"That's like, what, the fourth time he's slept at your place?"

"Sixth, actually," I said. When Jamey winked, I added, "And don't get any ideas. This is strictly no-strings-attached." Haro and I had a lot in common—namely, conservative, old-school parents who wouldn't handle having a gay son well.

"Yeah, but I know sometimes those types of relationships can turn into more."

I side-eyed him. "Even if settling down with a guy was in the cards for me, what makes you think I'm in any kind of hurry to do that?"

He patted my cheek. "I just want my best friend to be happy. Figure one of us should be." Sadness took over his face again, and I wished I could do something to help him out. "I need coffee. What about you?"

"Definitely. I didn't have time since I was so rudely woken up this morning."

"Quit your whining."

We strolled toward the nearest Starbucks. Living in Seattle meant there was basically one on every corner.

"I'll whine if I want to, jackass. I was hoping for a morning BJ."

"Shut up, Peter. You know I don't want to hear about your sex life."

"That's because you're jealous. It's probably been months since you got any."

Normally, that would've brought on a retort from Jamey, but instead, he fell silent. This wasn't the time or place to push it, otherwise, I would've demanded he tell me what was bothering him. Instead, we waited in silence to cross the street.

There were three people ahead of us at the coffee shop and, apparently, the person at the counter had never ordered before because he seemed baffled by all the choices.

"What are your thoughts on the body?" I asked.

Jamey glanced around, then whispered, "Maybe this isn't the best place to discuss a dead guy who had his junk cut off."

I shrugged, not truly caring who overheard.

When we finally got to the register, Jamey ordered for the both of us. "Two venti Pike's Place Roasts. Extra shot of espresso in one." He leaned in closer to the cute young woman at the register. "My buddy needs that extra shot because someone disturbed his beauty sleep."

She giggled and regarded me. "Doesn't seem like he needs too much beauty sleep."

Jamey sniggered, and my face heated.

"I'll be right back," I said, to get out of the situation. I turned and hurried into the bathroom. I could still hear Jamey laughing as the door shut.

I didn't really have to piss, so instead, I splashed cold water on my face and waited a minute before returning to the lobby. Jamey had taken a seat in the corner and was still grinning from ear to ear. I was about to join him when our names were called. I took the drinks from the barista and thanked him. As I crossed the room to sit with Jamey, I glanced at the names on the cups.

His name had been misspelled *Jamie*, which wasn't unusual. My name was correct, but below it was a phone number and the name *Lisa*. I glanced back at the cashier. She winked and waved, and once more, I couldn't control the blush. This set Jamey off into another loud laugh, and it took every ounce of control to not throw the hot java on him.

"You are such an ass," I murmured as I sat across from him.

"So you gonna call her?"

"Bite me," I snarled, trying not to let him know I did find it a little bit funny. Just a little bit.

"She's going to be devastated."

"Even if she was my type, she's at least ten years younger than me."

"Oh, that's right, I forgot about Darren. You like older men." His eyes widened, and he slapped a hand to his mouth. "I'm sorry, Peter. I shouldn't have brought him up."

The mention of my ex-boyfriend erased every bit of the lighthearted mood. It was as if the skies had turned from clear and blue to dark and cloudy with a snap of the fingers.

"Can we discuss the case now?" I took a sip of coffee, enjoying the jolt it sent through me.

"Of course." Jamey pulled out a pad of paper and reviewed his notes.

"Let's start with castration," I said.

"I'd rather not."

I rolled my eyes. "You're not funny. We could be dealing with a Lorena Bobbitt."

"Lord, don't give Chelsea any ideas." When I shot him a scowl he held up a hand. "Sorry, I'll be serious now." He straightened up.

"This type of mutilation doesn't happen all that often. It could be a Lorena Bobbitt-type event," I said, referring to the case of a battered woman cutting off her abusive husband's pecker. "I'd say the killer blamed our victim for something sexual. Rape, molestation, abuse.

"The victim could be a surrogate. Australia had a serial killer who lured men into dark alleys, stabbed them, and then cut off their junk. The guy was acting out vengeance on a man who'd raped him as a child."

"It's way too early to try and label this a serial killer."

"I wasn't saying that." I took a sip of my coffee. "I was just thinking of cases where castration had occurred."

"And why do you know about a serial killer in Australia, for fuck's sake?"

I shrugged and tugged an earlobe. "Serial killers interest me."

"You need a different hobby, Peter. You shouldn't be taking this stuff home with you. Home should be a sanctuary away from death and murder."

"Oh, please," I retorted. "Take your own advice. Remember the Bartley murder? You took the files home every night."

"Yeah, and Chelsea was furious for months. You want some advice, Peter, don't do what I do."

"You've been married for a long time. You got hitched at nineteen for Christ's sake and you're still together. You must've done something right."

"Yeah, I married a woman who's given me far more chances than I deserve." He was quiet for a moment, then tapped his notepad.

I waited for him to expand on that, but he didn't, so I returned our focus to the case. "We can hypothesize about why this guy was murdered all we want, but let's start with identification. We won't have any reports back from forensics for days, weeks, or even months so we need some good old-fashioned police work."

"Canvass the area?"

I nodded and stood. "You ready?"

"Yup."

We were at the door when the cashier called out in a singsong voice. "Bye, Peter."

I waved and stepped outside where Jamey was cackling again.

"You are such an ass."

He put an arm around my back. "Yeah, but you love me for it."

WE WANDERED AROUND THE ELLIOT BAY PARK NEAR where the body had been located then on to the Bell Harbor Marina. Our first walk through was simply to get a feel for the place. Jamey and I had done it often enough we didn't need to speak. I noted where the homeless sat or slept, the restaurants and shops nearby, and how many boats were moored and what kind. When we reached the end of the dock, we stopped at the marina office.

"Can I help you?" An older fellow at a desk stood when we entered.

"I'm Detective Nolan and this is Detective Tao," Jamey said. "Seattle Homicide."

"Is this about the body they found?"

"Yes. We're searching for any information that could help us. Have you, by chance, seen this man?" Jamey pulled up a picture of our victim on his phone and showed it to the guy.

"I ain't seen him before," he answered.

"We believe he was killed around midnight," I said. "Was there anyone working last night?"

He shook his head. "Nah, we don't work twenty-four hours a day here. Pretty much nine to five. Boats are supposed to be tied up for the night by dark for safety reasons."

"What's your maximum capacity?"

"Fifty," he replied. "And I'm barely half full at the moment."

"You got anyone staying onboard?"

"Two, off the top of my head."

"One's the Cobalt A40, right?" Jamey asked.

He jerked his head back. "You know your boats. You're right. Mason Patel owns it. He's only here for the weekend, thank God."

"Why is that?"

"He's a young party boy. Likes to make a lot of noise. Usually, I get complaints from other people. Thankfully, I'm not full at the moment. He makes a mess, though he usually does have it cleaned up himself."

"Who's the person living onboard?"

"Deanna Harmon," he answered.

"We'll need to speak to both of them."

Jamey knew the location of the Cobalt so the guy gave us the slip number where the woman was staying. Jamey left a card, and we exited the office.

"So how'd you know the make and model of the boat?" I asked.

"My dad has one."

Jamey came from money, though he never acted like it. He'd grown up a spoiled rich boy and expected to follow in his father's footsteps. Jamey's father, James Howard Nolan the third, ran a prestigious investment group and Jamey, James Howard Nolan the fourth to be precise, was the firstborn. Fortunately for me and the people of Seattle, Jamey had decided to become a cop instead, and for that, he was considered the black sheep of the family.

My partner was worth millions and could buy whatever he wanted at a moment's notice. He'd used the money to build Chelsea the house of her dreams, but other than that, he lived like every other cop on a shitty salary.

"It's beautiful." I wasn't easily impressed, but the forty-foot sport yacht was impressive.

"You should feel how it handles on the water. So powerful."

"Why don't you buy your own? Lord knows you could, and it's not like you ever spoil yourself."

"I've considered it lately," he said, twisting his wedding ring. "Especially now that I've…"

"Now that you've what?" I asked.

"Never mind. Let's see if this guy's here." He cupped his hands over his mouth and yelled, "Hello, the boat. Permission to come on board?"

A moment later, a head popped out from below deck. "Huh? What do you want?" His dark hair was a total mess, and his eyes were bloodshot.

"Are you Mason Patel?" I asked.

"Who the fuck's asking?"

"Seattle Homicide."

Jamey and I flashed out badges, and the guy's eyes flickered with fear as he emerged from below.

"Did I do something wrong, officers? I kept the noise down last night, and I only had a few friends over."

"Permission to come aboard?" Jamey asked again.

"Uhh, yeah, of course."

Jamey easily hopped over the water, but I was more cautious. Even so, I nearly fell on my ass when my feet hit the wet floor of the boat.

"Are you Mason Patel?" Jamey asked again.

"Yeah. You need my ID or something?"

"That won't be necessary," I said. "We just want to ask a few questions. It's not about anything you did."

"Oh, good." He sighed and ran a hand through his hair, not that it helped at all.

Jamey began, "There was a murder around midnight last night. Where were you?"

"I had about ten friends over, and we were right here, on my boat." Ten? That was his idea of a few friends?

"Did you happen to see this man?" Jamey showed Mason the victim's picture.

"Doesn't look familiar. But I wasn't checking out guys, if you know what I mean?" He grinned. "There was a couple babes here last night, and I was pretty focused on them."

"Did you see anyone last night besides your friends?"

He shook his head then stopped. "Wait, I almost forgot. There was this one chick I noticed when I did a beer run around eleven. When I left, she was up by the office, but when I came back, I spotted her down by the end of the dock just kind of staring out onto the water."

"Did you talk to her?" I asked.

"I tried," he said. "I asked her if she wanted to come party. She didn't say anything. Just shook her head and turned her back to me."

I narrowed my eyes. "What did she look like?"

"I didn't get a real good peek at her 'cuz she had a hoodie pulled over her head. Not very tall. Maybe five-five at the most. Small and petite, just the way I like 'em." He smirked.

Jamey nodded and winked conspiratorially. "Anything else you can tell us about her?"

"She had red hair. I could see it under the hoodie."

I handed Mason my card. "Call me if you think of anything else."

He took it, then asked, "Hey, should I be worried that whoever killed that dude is gonna do it again?"

"I'd suggest only spending time with people you know," Jamey said.

"How the hell am I going to meet new ladies that way?"

Jamey shrugged. "This guy had his dick sliced off."

Mason's face blanched, and, for a moment, I thought he might faint.

"Just be careful," I said before Jamey and I hopped off the yacht.

When we were out of earshot, Jamey doubled over and began chortling. "Did you see his face when I said the victim's cock had been cut off?"

"He damn near shit his pants." I chuckled and waited for Jamey to get himself under control.

"Wonder if this redheaded chick is Deanna Harmon," I said.

"Let's go find out."

Harmon's boat was nice but not nearly as impressive as the one we were just on. A twenty-seven footer that had to be at least ten years older than Patel's.

"Can I help you?" a female voice from behind us asked.

Jamey and I both turned and showed our badges at the same time.

"Detectives Nolan and Tao," he said. "We wanted to ask you a few questions. Are you Deanna Harmon?"

She nodded.

She was definitely not the young, redheaded female Patel had seen. This woman was in her sixties with short dark hair.

"Have you ever seen this man?" Jamey asked, once again using the image on his phone.

She examined it through bifocals then shook her head. "He doesn't look familiar. Why're you asking?"

"He was murdered around midnight last night."

"Oh," she gasped and put a hand to her chest.

"Where were you at that time?"

"Midnight? I'd have been in bed for three hours by then. I'm no youngster. I don't stay up late at all."

"Did you see anyone suspicious this morning or before you went to bed last night?" I asked.

"Nope, not that I can recall."

We asked a couple more questions then left a card with instructions to call if she remembered anything.

Jamey and I walked back up the dock.

"The redhead's our sole lead at the moment," I said. "Not much to go on. It's not like we can put out a BOLO for a petite female ginger."

"How would a small woman overpower the victim?" Jamey asked. "The victim isn't huge, but I assume he could've held his own against a woman."

"Jill said the knife in the throat would've been quick. She could've surprised him. If he died quickly, all she had to do was open his pants, do a slice and dice, and be gone. It appears the body wasn't moved."

"I don't know." Jamey grimaced and gave a slight shake of his head. "I'm having a hard time imagining a woman doing this. I'm not closing my mind to the possibility, but my money's on a man. Maybe our victim was involved with another man's girlfriend and the boyfriend took his revenge."

I shrugged. "We could play *what if* for hours. Until we have more information, I'm going with the redhead as a possible witness at least."

Bell Harbor Marina was home to a couple restaurants and shops, so Jamey and I hit every single one, showing a picture of our victim and inquiring about a female redhead. Since most places closed at eleven at the latest, there weren't many people around the harbor at the time of the murder. Those who were hadn't seen a thing, of course.

When we returned to the Elliot Bay Park where our cars were parked, I noticed two people, homeless judging from their clothes, sitting on a grassy spot about one hundred feet from where the body had been located. A woman with stringy blonde hair was sitting up while a man slept next to her. One of the things I learned from working with Jamey was that speaking to street people was often one of the best ways to get information. Most of the time, they were ignored, but that didn't mean they weren't watching or listening to everything around them.

"You going to talk to them?" Jamey asked.

I nodded.

"I need to use the bathroom," he said. "I'll be right back."

Walking up to the woman, I got down on my haunches, and asked, "Can I ask you a question?"

She gawked at me and flashed a meth-mouth smile. "You can ask, but that don't mean I gotta answer."

I showed her a picture of my victim's face. "Have you seen this man?"

She squinted but shook her head. "Don't look familiar to me. But I ain't been staying around here for long." She nodded to the sleeping guy at her side. "He's here most of the time."

"Do you think you could wake him?"

"Manny." She whacked his head and he jumped up.

"What the hell?"

"This cop's got a question for ya."

Manny scowled at her then turned to me. "Yea? Whatya want?"

"Have you seen this guy?" I flashed him the man's picture.

He stared at it then nodded. "Yeah, dude was here was last night. He was walking around, pacing like something was wrong, ya know?"

"Did you talk to him?"

"I asked him if he had a cigarette, but he said he didn't smoke. Gave me a five, though."

"He didn't say why he was down here?"

Manny shrugged. "Didn't ask him. But I'd say he was meeting someone. He eyed anyone who came by and kept glancing at his watch."

"Did you see him with anyone else?"

"Nah. I left to grab some food. When I came back, he wasn't here anymore."

"What time was that?" I asked.

He scrubbed his face as he thought about the question. "Eleven."

"How long were you gone?"

"Half an hour, maybe."

"And there wasn't anyone here when you got back?"

"Nope."

"Did you happen to see a small redheaded woman?"

Same answer.

"Did you sleep here?" I asked.

Manny shook his head again. "Decided to go find a place with some shelter. Wasn't sure if it was gonna rain or not so I found a buddy with a tent over on Sinner's Row." That was one of many homeless encampments in Seattle. "When I got back this morning, I saw all the cops. Is that why you're here?"

"Yes, this guy was murdered."

The woman sucked in a breath. Manny closed his eyes for a second like he was sending up a prayer.

I handed both of them my card. "Find me if you remember something *or* if you hear something that would be useful."

Jamey returned, holding two bags from the Bell Street Deli. "You guys like roast beef and ham sandwiches?"

They nodded simultaneously and Jamey handed them the bags. "There's cookies and chips in there too. And a couple cans of Pepsi."

"Thanks, man," the woman said. "Normally, the cops harass us."

Jamey waved a hand. "Those are the assholes."

Manny opened the sandwich wrapper and took a huge bite. He mumbled a thanks through a mouthful of roast beef, turkey, lettuce, and tomatoes.

"Call me if you hear anything," I said. "Anything at all."

"It doesn't have to be about this case, either," Jamey added. "Even if you need help. We're here."

They waved and continued scarfing down the food.

"That was nice," I said as we trudged away.

"Hey, I got more money than I can spend in a lifetime. Why not spread the love? Besides, they won't forget that. You never know when a simple act of kindness will pay off."

We got to our cars. "See you at the station. I'm sure the chief is aching to talk to us and see what we got."

"Unfortunately, it's a big load of nothing."

"Yeah, that conversation's gonna be fun."

He rolled his eyes. "Not so much."

Sure enough, the minute Jamey and I entered the squad room, Deputy Chief Carmen Slight was hollering for us to get to her office. Jamey and I exchanged smirks then marched in.

"Shut the door, Tao." Slight did not appear to be happy. Not that she ever seemed happy. She had a mean case of resting bitch face. Not that she was a bitch, she just appeared to be one with her pinched mouth and angry eyes.

"What's up, Chief?" Jamey asked.

She glared at him. "I'd love to slap you silly right now, Nolan."

"What did I do?" He raised his palms and gave her the sad puppy dog eyes.

For a moment, I thought she was going to smile. Instead she snapped, "Do you know what it's like to have Detective Shepherd Adley in your face the first thing in the morning? The minute I stepped into my office, he's in here yapping about protocol and infractions and bullshit like that."

I was trying to hold in my laughter but a snigger came out. Slight glared at me, and I recovered my composure. I relaxed when she returned her attention to Jamey.

"Why in the hell did you take this case when it was Adley's turn in the rotation?"

"Do you want a bullshit reason or the truth?" Jamey asked, almost causing me to lose control again.

"The truth, Nolan."

"I was at the station at three o'clock this morning," he said, his voice completely serious. "Does that tell you anything?"

Slight's pinched expression eased off. "Things okay, Jamey?"

He shook his head. "No, but I don't want to talk about it. Let's just say I need a case I can throw myself into. I'm sorry it pissed off Adley, and I'm sorry you were collateral damage. I should've cleared it with you."

She waved a hand. "Whatever. It's done. Tell me what you got."

"Not much, I'm afraid," I answered. "We canvassed the area, spoke to the people at the marina, including two visitors staying in their boats."

"One guy noticed a redheaded woman." Jamey crossed his arms. "He didn't get a good look at her because she was wearing a hoodie, and he was more interested in the party on his boat. The other person staying there didn't see a thing. Same with everyone we spoke to at all the local establishments."

I took over. "I did speak to a homeless man who spotted the victim just before midnight. He sleeps in the area occasionally, so I'm hoping he'll hear something."

"The homeless are an excellent resource," Slight said. "I wish more detectives utilized them."

Jamey shot me a wink. We'd just scored a few points with the chief.

"What are we releasing to the press?" Jamey stepped closer and leaned against her desk.

She crossed her arms. "I'd like to keep as much to ourselves as possible. I don't want his family learning he's dead on the news."

"We can go that route if we don't have an ID soon," I suggested.

"I agree," Slight replied. "And definitely keep the fact that the guy is missing his dick away from the press. We'll say that an unidentified male body was found near Elliot Bay Park and Bell Harbor Marina. Give as little information as possible for now. Hopefully, it's not such a slow news day that the reporters will be begging for more facts. Okay, keep me informed," she said by way of a dismissal.

Jamey and I strolled over to our desks, which faced each other in the back corner of the squad room.

"I can't believe you got out of that ass chewing," I said.

He grinned. "I went with the truth. Carmen knows me well enough that it worked."

"So things truly are that bad?"

"Yeah."

"Do you…"

"No, I don't want to talk about it."

I put my hands up in surrender. "I'm here for you when you're ready."

"Thanks, Peter."

Some people aren't crazy about modern technology, but I believe it's a boon for law enforcement. Since so many different departments handle various aspects of cases it could be difficult to stay up to date on all the information without it. However, thanks to our network, I could open the case file on the computer, and, provided every department did its job, I could learn what had been done.

CSU had taken the victim's fingerprints but there hadn't been a match yet. That didn't mean anything because it could take up to a week to get a match *if* he was in the system. A photo of the man's face was also taken and run through a facial recognition program. No results there, either.

I'd started searching through missing persons reports, just in case the computer missed something. A couple years before, there had been a dead body in the morgue with no identification. The detective had relied on facial recognition but the photo on the missing person file had the man with a mustache, which he had shaved prior to being killed. The body sat in the morgue for a month before a family member provided a different picture. The shit had really hit the fan on that incident.

We were now supposed to search through the missing persons files, look at the photos, and not just rely on the computer. It was a mundane but necessary task.

"How about I take M through Z?" Jamey asked.

I took him up on the offer, but barely managed to get through H before it was time to call it a day. If we'd had any leads on the case to follow up, we would've stayed late, but with nothing, there was no reason to.

"You going home?" Jamey asked when I stood and grabbed my coat.

"After I pay Jill a visit and see if she's got anything. What about you?"

"I'm almost done with the S files," he replied. "I'll leave when I finish with those."

"Okay, I'll be home tonight if you want to stop by."

He lowered his voice to a whisper and hunched conspiratorially, "No guests tonight?"

"Nope, his ass needs a break."

Jamey chuckled and scurried back to the computer.

The ME's office was only a few blocks away and on my way home, so stopping by wasn't a big deal.

"Christ, Tao, you think I'm a magician?" she teased when I arrived.

"Yes, actually." I winked.

"Well, I am damn good." She beamed from ear to ear. "I found a red hair on him and sent it to the lab. Of course, I also took several vials of blood and sent them off for tests. I haven't completed the autopsy, but I can give you the preliminary results. Cause of death was severing of the spinal cord, just as I'd suspected. He was stabbed between the cervical vertebrae."

"Can you tell me anything about the murder weapon?"

"Appears to have been a standard blade. It went at least two and half inches deep, which is one and half more than was needed to do the job."

"Overkill?" I asked.

She shrugged. "Or the killer just didn't know how deep he had to go. The neck isn't that thick and the spinal cord is just inside the skin there."

"Can you tell me anything about the victim?"

"I'd say he's got money. His outfit cost a small fortune. The jeans are Gucci. Those cost six hundred, minimum. Another six hundred for the Ferragamo loafers."

"Any tattoos or birthmarks? Anything that can be used to identify him?"

She shook her head. "Afraid not. Looks like you'll have to get out and do your job," she teased.

I playfully flipped her off. "You worry about your job and I'll do mine, Dr. Trencher."

TWO

I'D BARELY SAT DOWN AT MY DESK AND taken my first sip of coffee when Jamey's phone rang. He answered before it could ring again.

"Yes, ma'am," he said. "We're on it." He set the receiver down and stood. "Let's go, man. We got a DB at Gas Works Park."

I sighed. "Nolan, you *did not* just take another case, did you? We have one, remember?"

"I'm pretty sure this one is connected to the case we caught yesterday."

I set my java down and regarded him. "How so?"

"Guy's missing his junk."

Gas Works Park had once been an industrial park manufacturing gas from coal, but the import of natural gas made the complex obsolete. In the seventies, the place was made into a public park with the boiler house converted to a picnic shelter. The former exhauster-compressor building was now a children's play barn, with a maze of brightly painted machinery.

The entire park, including the parking lot, was secured, otherwise it would've been full of tourists and stay-at-home mothers with their kids. The body was on the outside of the boiler house toward the back. On my first glance, I had no doubt the two cases were connected. The deceased, a man, was missing his genitals. Jill was already there, examining the body.

"Except for the...uhh...guy's junk being gone, are there any other connections to the body from yesterday?" I asked Jill.

She turned the victim's head to the side and pointed to a hole in the back of his neck. "Looks like the same cause of death to me, Detective."

"Damn."

Other than their wounds, the two men didn't have much in common. The first one had been white, young, and fit, while the second victim was African American and older, at least fifty, with a shaved head. Not in decent shape at all. He had a large belly that covered part of the bloody mess at his groin. What other aspects they shared I couldn't begin to figure out until I had their names. Hopefully, that would come soon.

"Time of death was likely between one and four a.m.," Jill said.

Two CSU officers were scouring the area so Jamey and I tried to stay out of the way. However, when the body was removed, I ambled up to get a closer peek at where the corpse had been. I didn't find anything on the ground, but I spotted something on the wall a few inches away. I examined it closely without touching it—a red hair.

"Jamey, check this out."

He came over and squatted next to me.

"Wasn't a red hair found on the first victim?" I asked.

"Yeah, but that doesn't necessarily mean anything," he said. "This is a public building. That hair could've come from anyone."

"Including our killer, right? Won't hurt to have it analyzed and compared to the other one." I plucked the hair with a pair of tweezers and dropped it into a paper evidence bag, then handed it to a CSU officer.

Jamey and I checked out the scene for a bit longer before heading back to our car. Since the park had been closed off to the public, most of the vehicles were the official kind—ME's van, police cruisers, and an ambulance. There was one car that seemed out of place—a white 2013 Audi Infiniti.

I made a beeline back to our vehicle with Jamey right behind me. "You think that car belongs to our victim?"

"I'd say it's a good possibility." Using the onboard computer, I ran the license plate.

"Tyrone Osceola," I said, reading the DMV record aloud. "Fifty years old."

Jamey checked out the photo. "That's our guy, though he's gained at least thirty pounds since that picture was taken."

"We've got an address in Hawthorne Hills." At least with this guy, we had a name and a place to start.

On the way to Osceola's place, I used my Bluetooth to call Molly Whitmore, the homicide department's current assistant. She was a uniformed officer who'd gotten into trouble and was being punished with desk duty. She was still a fine cop and was excellent at digging up information.

"How can I help you, Detective?" she asked.

"I've got an ID for the newest victim," I said, and told her how I'd found it. "I'm on the way to his place. Can you do a quick search and get me some preliminary info?"

"I'm on it."

Ten minutes later, Molly returned the call.

"Speak to me."

"Tyrone Osceola is an executive at Boeing. Married. Wife's name is Fiona. No children. I have more, but those are the bullet points."

"Great. Now get me everything you can find on the missus's place of employment. Phone number. Local relatives. All that."

HAWTHORNE HILLS WAS AN AFFLUENT RESIDENTIAL AREA WITH houses valued at a million bucks, at a minimum. These weren't cookie-cutter houses—each one was distinct. The Osceola house was three stories high with a large front yard and a stone pathway to the front door.

There was no answer when I rang the bell, but as we were

leaving, a middle-aged woman in a pink camo sweat suit slowed at the end of the path and jogged in place.

"I haven't seen either one of them for two days," she called out.

We strode down the path and stopped in front of her. "That long?" I asked.

She nodded as she continued jogging in place. "Well, I haven't seen Fiona since their big fight."

Jamey leaned against the fence. "They had an argument?"

She snorted. "Screaming match right here on their front lawn for the whole neighborhood to see."

I took out my notepad. "Could you make out what they were saying? Do you know what they were fighting about?"

"'Fraid not," she answered. "And believe me, I tried."

I got her name, number, and address then handed her my card. "Call me if you remember anything or if either one of them comes home." I knew Tyrone wouldn't be returning but I didn't want the neighbors to know just yet.

"Sure thing." She waved, turned, and jogged off.

"You want to stick together and interview the neighbors or split up?" I asked.

"You take this side of the block, and I'll take the other."

The Osceola home was basically in the center so I had three on one side and two on the other. I trekked to one end and worked my way back. The people I spoke to included a twenty-two year old guy, a retired woman, and a lesbian couple. There was no answer at the other two houses, but I left my card in the door, asking them to call. The young guy didn't even know the Osceolas and hadn't seen the spectacle. The retired woman and one half of the couple had witnessed the altercation. Their recollection of the event varied somewhat when it came to precisely what Fiona said but they agreed when it came to the intent of her anger. She had been furious that her husband had cheated on her.

Jamey spoke to four of the neighbors, two of who watched the fight and whose accounts matched those of the people I interviewed.

"So we have a woman scorned," Jamey said. "You think she's the killer?"

"That's a plausible hypothesis. He cheated on her and she went crazy by cutting off his junk." We returned to our vehicle. "But how would that tie in with our first victim?"

"Without an ID on him it's hard to say," Jamey replied. "Unless…" He sat in the driver seat and worried his bottom lip.

"What are you thinking?"

"What if Osceola played for your team?"

"You mean maybe the first guy was Osceola's boyfriend?" It was a possibility, but it was all supposition until we learned more about Osceola and located Fiona Osceola.

"Maybe someone at Boeing can give us some clues."

OSCEOLA'S ASSISTANT WAS A WOMAN AROUND THIRTY YEARS old with the unfortunate first name of Sprite. She was shocked when we informed her of her boss's death and instantly burst into tears. Jamey put an arm around her and comforted while I waited patiently for her to get her shit together. He had always been better at that type of personal interaction than I was.

"Are you aware of any marital problems between them?" Jamey sat beside her while I remained standing.

She nodded then paused. "I overheard several arguments between them."

"What were they fighting about?"

"I don't know. I tried *not* to eavesdrop." The way her face flushed combined with her refusal to make eye contact told me she wasn't being one hundred percent truthful. Jamey and I exchanged knowing glances, and he patted her back.

"You look like you could use a break. Why don't you and I get some air while my partner speaks to Mr. Osceola's boss?"

"Of course," she replied and picked up the cell phone on her desk.

A few minutes later, I sat in a lush mahogany chair in the office of Paula Carson, a thin woman who had her gray hair pulled back in a tight bun, giving her face a severe appearance. It didn't appear as if she smiled often.

Her expression barely changed when I told her Tyrone Osceola was dead.

"That's unfortunate," she said. "Tyrone was an excellent employee. He was well liked by both his superiors and the staff who worked under him. He'll be a hard man to replace."

"Is there anyone who might have wanted him dead?" I asked. "Any interoffice squabbles that could've become serious?"

She straightened her back and crossed her arms. "I assure you, Detective Tao, we run a tight ship here. Any interpersonal issues are dealt with immediately. We have an excellent conflict resolution program."

I leaned forward, putting my elbows on my knees, and shot her a bright grin. "I have no doubt about that, Mrs. Carson. However, nothing can run at one hundred percent *all* the time. Surely, there have been problems."

She tapped her chin, then said, "Well, there was an employee who caused a problem when Tyrone fired him. He claimed his termination was personal and not based on his job performance. His claims were unfounded."

"Can I get that person's name?" I asked.

"Russell Burch," she replied. "My assistant will get you his phone number and address."

"That would be excellent." I clapped my hands and rose. "Thank you so much for your time, Mrs. Carson."

I swear the old lady cracked a smile at my gratitude, and it appeared to have been the first one in decades.

Jamey and I met up in the hallway after I got Burch's contact information.

"Did you get anything out of Ms. 7 Up?"

He snickered. "Her name is Sprite, jackass. But, yes, she did open up to me. She confirmed Osceola had been cheating on his wife with at least one, maybe two women."

"Confirms our one theory so far, though that'd shoot down our idea that the first victim was Osceola's lover. Unless the guy played for both teams."

He scratched his chin. "Did you get anything?"

I filled him in on Burch. "Figured we could go chat with him next."

Back in the car, I called Molly to see if she had anything on Fiona Osceola.

"I have her cell and home numbers. I left messages requesting a return call on both voicemails," she said. "She's unemployed and her parents live in town. I called them as well. Her mother claims not to have seen her in a week. I didn't say anything to them about Osceola's death, just said Fiona might be a witness to a crime. I'd suggest interviewing them in person."

"Gee, Officer, I would've never thought of that myself," I replied, heavy on the snark.

"Oh, I'm sorry, Detective Tao. I didn't mean to—"

I chuckled. "I'm messing with you. You're doing a fine job. Anything else on Mrs. Osceola?"

"No, sir."

Jamey elbowed me after I ended the call. "That was mean. You know she's on edge."

"Yeah, but it was a little funny."

RUSSELL BURCH ANSWERED THE DOOR WEARING A DIRTY T-shirt and a ratty pair of sweatpants. "What do you want?" he snarled.

Identifying ourselves didn't cool his surly attitude, but his reaction to learning Tyrone Osceola was dead did throw me for a loop.

"He's dead?" Burch's eyes got wide then he burst out laughing. "Couldn't have happened to a better fella." His reaction changed when he realized we weren't sharing his mirth. "Wait, you don't think I killed him, do you?"

"Perhaps we could discuss this inside," Jamey said.

Burch stepped aside and we entered. The place was a disaster area. Newspapers, pizza boxes, and dirty dishes covered every surface.

"Excuse the mess," he said. "My wife and I are having…issues. Losing my job didn't make it any easier."

He cleared a spot on his couch and Jamey sat a few inches away from him while I remained standing. "We were told you weren't happy when Osceola fired you."

Burch glowered at me. "Who wouldn't be pissed at being sacked? But I would've taken it better if it had been based on my job performance instead of…"

"Instead of what?" Jamey asked, his voice soft and gentle.

"The man slept with my wife," Burch snapped. "He fucked her, and I confronted him when I found out. Not on the job. I kept it away from the workplace. I went to the hotel room he was meeting her at. Surprised him when I showed up instead of her."

I strolled around, checking out the mess, while Jamey asked the questions.

"What happened?"

"I called him a bastard for having an affair with a married woman. He acted like it wasn't a big deal at all, and that truly pissed me off so I punched him."

"You had a fight?"

He snorted. "Not exactly. There were two hits: me hitting him and him hitting the floor. He didn't fight back at all. Just told me to get the hell out of the room."

"Then what happened?" Jamey asked.

"I left. The next day at work, I put in a transfer to a different department. Even if I had to work with him, I would've been professional. I've been at Boeing for twelve years. This was my career, you know? But a week later, Osceola fired me for missing a deadline."

"You didn't miss it?"

Burch shrugged. "Yeah, by one hour. And the project wasn't even due for another week. We had plenty of time."

"You think he fired you because of the confrontation in the hotel?"

"Well, that, and the fact that Tina, my wife, ended things with him. He apparently thought they had a future together. I don't know if he thought she'd come to him if I didn't have a job or what."

"Where is Tina right now?"

"In San Jose with her parents. She hasn't even talked to me for weeks."

I picked up a picture of Burch with a redheaded woman. "Is this your wife?"

He stood and came over to me, taking the frame out of my hand. He ran a finger over the glass, gazing at it wistfully. "Yes, that's her."

"Where were you last night?" I questioned.

"I didn't kill him." He set the picture down and clenched his fists. "I may have wanted him dead, I may even take a little joy in the fact that he's dead, but I did not do it."

I repeated my question. "So where were you last night?"

"Home alone." He sighed. "Watching movies."

"Don't suppose anyone can verify your alibi?"

He glared at me. "No, like I said, I was home *alone*."

Jamey stood and came over to us. "How did you watch movies?"

Burch cocked an eyebrow, but I had an idea where Jamey was going.

"What I mean is, did you rent them from somewhere or did you do pay-per-view?"

"On demand thru cable," he replied.

"Well, if we get access to your account, we can find proof of when the movies were requested."

"Sure, whatever I can do."

"Where's your bathroom?" I asked. Burch pointed down a hallway, then turned to Jamey to give him the access information.

In the restroom, I put on rubber gloves and picked up a hairbrush entangled with ginger locks. I retrieved a few and put them into a small evidence bag, then slipped the bag into my pocket. I flushed the toilet and ran the water to complete the fib and returned to the living room.

"Okay, Mr. Burch," Jamey said. "We'll get back to you if we have any more questions."

"I'm not under arrest or anything, am I?"

"Not yet," I growled, "but don't think about leaving town anytime soon."

Once we were in the car, I asked Jamey, "What do you think? Burch could be our man. He certainly had motive. Hacking off Osceola's cock could've been revenge for banging his wife."

"He's our best lead so far, but I'm not convinced. I need to check out his story with the cable service, though that's hardly the strongest alibi. I also got Tina's contact info. We'll need to find out if she truly was in California at the time of the murder. I assume you snagged some of her hair in the bathroom."

I nodded. "You do know me well, partner. I know it won't hold up in court, but we can have it compared to the red hairs found at the scene. If it matches, we can use that to move forward."

"And if it doesn't?"

"Then we're no worse off than we were before."

OUR NEXT VISIT WAS TO HAROLD AND HELENA Beemer, the parents of Fiona Osceola. She obviously came from money because the

Beemer house was three times as large and valuable as Fiona and her husband's.

The Beemers were somewhat put out to be visited by cops after they'd already spoken to one on the phone. However, Jamey happened to have met them at a party thrown by his parents. He managed to sweet talk them into speaking with us. While he schmoozed with them, I excused myself to use the bathroom and searched a few rooms afterward.

I'd just stepped into the fifth bedroom on the second floor when a woman wearing a maid's outfit caught me.

"Who are you?"

I showed her my badge. "Sorry, I'm just being nosy. I'll never afford a place like this on my salary."

She smiled. "It's too much house for anyone. They don't use a quarter of the rooms anymore."

"They don't have visitors?" I asked.

"Not for a while. Last year, Mr. Beemer's cousin visited, but that's it."

"What about their daughter?"

"Fiona?" She frowned and shook her head. "She hasn't even stayed for a night since she married Mr. Osceola, and that was at least twenty years ago."

"So you haven't seen her lately?"

"The last time she visited was at least three weeks ago."

I thanked her and returned to the living room.

"If you do see your daughter, please tell her we need to speak to her as soon as possible," Jamey said as he shook Mr. Beemer's hand.

"I'll do that, and please tell your father I said hello."

"You got it."

In the car, I said, "I don't think Fiona's been around. The maid hasn't seen her in three weeks."

"Yeah, the Beemers claim it's been two weeks since they even talked to their daughter. They weren't aware of any marital problems either."

Molly located me as soon as Jamey and I got to our desks. She was a thin, young African-American woman with almond-shaped brown eyes. She had a hard set face because she didn't smile often. I joked with her occasionally, but she either didn't get my sense of humor, or just didn't think I was all that funny.

"I've got names and numbers for several of Fiona Osceola's friends. I've been monitoring her social media accounts but she hasn't posted anywhere for several days."

"I'm going to verify Burch's alibi," Jamey said.

"Give me Tina Burch's info and I'll call her."

He retrieved a scrap of paper from his pocket and handed it over. Then I sat and examined the list of names Molly had collected. "Where did you get all this?"

"Facebook, mainly," she answered. "I checked out her friends list then dug up their information."

"Did you call any of them?"

"I was just about to do that when you arrived."

This was the part of police work I wasn't so fond of—the monotonous phone calls and computer work. I preferred the person-to-person interactions, which was why I liked having Molly's help. I considered things like checking social media accounts boring, though that was where we often found clues.

"Excellent. I'll take one half and you take the other. I have one other call to make before I start."

"Yes, sir."

"Officer Whitmore, please don't call me sir. Peter is fine, or Detective, if you're not comfortable using my first name."

"I'm sorry, sir…I mean Detective Tao. I'm an army brat so manners and respect were drilled into me from early on."

"I understand," I replied. "But I don't consider myself your superior, and I like being on even ground with the people I work with. So just try to take it down a notch or two."

"I'll try." She nodded then strode to her desk.

I dialed the number for Tina Burch and expected to get voicemail, so I was surprised when a woman answered.

"Is this Tina Burch?" I asked.

"Yes. Who is this?"

"Detective Peter Tao, Seattle Homicide."

"Homicide? Did something happen to Russell?"

"No, your husband is fine," I replied. "However, Tyrone Osceola is dead."

"Oh, my God," she gulped. "Are you sure?"

"I'm afraid so. He was murdered."

She gulped audibly again. "Did Russell…Russell didn't kill him, did he?"

"He claims to be innocent but my partner is checking his alibi right now. Where were you last night?"

"Me? Why are…You don't think I killed Tyrone, do you?"

"We have to check everything, Mrs. Burch. I'm sure you understand."

"Yeah, I guess so." She sighed. "I've been in San Jose for almost a month now."

"Have you had any contact with the victim during that time?"

"He called me a few days ago. Told me his wife found out about us and said he wanted to be with me."

"What did you say to him?"

"I wasn't interested and told him so. He tried to change my mind at first, then he got angry. Mean."

"How so?" I asked.

"He told me there were plenty of other women and I was nothing special. Tyrone said he could find someone to replace me with a snap of his fingers. I hung up on him and haven't heard from him since."

"Where exactly were you last night?"

"At my new job," she said. "I'm the nighttime clerk at the San Jose Marriott. I can prove I was there easily enough, if you need me to. I'll call my boss and ask him to give you whatever you require, provided you let him know I'm not being accused of anything."

"I can do that." She gave me the name and contact information for her supervisor and I ended the call.

Jamey set his phone down at the same time. "I don't think Burch is our man. Their records show when the movies were ordered. Three in a row, one right after the other, during the time Osceola was killed. They weren't ordered in advance, either—done right from the remote at the time."

"I didn't think he was our guy anyway," I said before filling him in on what I'd learned from Tina Burch.

"We still need to locate Fiona Osceola, but I have my doubts a woman could've done these murders."

"Because of the blood?" I asked. "That's a bit sexist, isn't it? Women can be just as deadly as men. There've been several female serial killers. Not just Aileen Wournos, either. Nannie Doss killed a handful of husbands and several family members. And there was—"

"Christ, Peter, I don't need another history lesson. I get your point."

"I'm just saying we can't discount our killer being a woman. I'm more inclined to think a woman did it due to the sexual element of the cock being removed."

Jamey sat. "I hear ya, man."

Tina Burch's supervisor corroborated her alibi and provided electronic check-in information and security footage. She definitely wasn't Osceola's killer.

I spent the rest of the day calling Fiona's friends, none of whom had heard from her for at least a week. A couple of them confirmed Fiona learned about Tyrone's infidelity and had left him. No one had a clue where she currently was. I also got a call from one of the neighbors, who repeated the story I'd already heard.

It was an hour past our normal quitting time before I went home, leaving Jamey at his desk.

I'D SHOWERED AND WAS DEBATING WHAT TO EAT for dinner when my doorbell rang. I checked the peephole. Jamey stood there with a huge grin on his face and bags of Chinese take-out in his hands.

I opened the door and gestured for him to come in. "What's up?"

"What, can't a guy bring food over for his best friend?"

"Sure," I replied. "But I have a feeling that's not the case here."

When Jamey set the food on the kitchen island and turned to face me, the smile had disappeared. "You got me. I need to talk."

"About you and Chelsea?"

He nodded and took a seat in a tall chair close to where he'd deposited the bags. I grabbed a fork and a container of sesame chicken. Jamey used chopsticks but, ironically, I'd never mastered them.

I took a few bites, eyed my friend for a moment, then said, "Spill it, Nolan."

He sighed and set his food down. "I fucked up, Peter."

"What's new?" I chuckled, but he met my gaze with an intense expression.

"No, I *really* messed up this time. Horrendously. I don't think I can fix it this time."

"What did you do?"

Jamey stared at the counter and traced a design only he could see. "I cheated on Chelsea."

My eyes wide, I stared at him. "You had an affair?"

"No."

I relaxed for a second. He knew how I felt about cheating. I had no patience for anyone who did that.

"It wasn't an affair," he said. "It was one time."

Ugh. So he *had* cheated. But only a single occurrence not a regular event.

"With multiple women."

I slammed my food down so hard some chicken tumbled out. "What the fuck were you thinking?"

He avoided my gaze and chewed on a fingernail.

"Chelsea is an amazing woman. She's beautiful and puts up with your shit. And years ago she forgave you when you kissed that damn rookie officer. How could you do something to hurt her? Why would you—"

Jamey clenched his fists and pounded the counter. "Damn it, don't you think I've asked myself those exact questions? Don't you think I've beat myself up for the shit I've done?"

I took in a deep breath and tried to calm down. He needed a friend, not a lecture. "Okay, I'm sorry. I'll just listen, no judgment."

Rolling his eyes, Jamey said, "Yeah, right. You've already judged me, but I don't blame you, not after what happened with Darren."

"I'm your friend. I'm here for whatever you need. If it's just a sounding-board, that's fine." I didn't like putting Jamey in the same box as Darren but just the mention of my ex's name set me on edge. I'd been hurt badly and, if I was being honest, I hadn't recovered.

He took a few bites of pork fried rice but acted like the food tasted horrible. "There were at least six women, mostly one-night stands. I don't have an excuse. Well, not a good one, anyway. I know what I told myself but looking back, it's truly shitty reasoning."

As if there's any good reason to cheat on your spouse. But I didn't say that.

"Chelsea and I haven't had sex in months, but even before that, we hadn't really been close. The times we did sleep together there was no passion. I've missed sex and just wanted to feel desired again. Yeah, I know that's a shitty reason to step out on my wife, but that's how it started. I found a woman, married as well, who wanted the same thing."

"And once you did it the first time it was easy to do it again?" I asked.

He nodded. "It became a habit. Finding these women and arranging a time and place. I enjoyed it, but I also felt guilty. Especially afterward. God, Peter, I felt horrible, but I still kept doing it."

"How long has this been going on?"

"A couple months."

"Chelsea knows?"

"She does now. Last week she found a pack of condoms in my coat. We haven't used rubbers for years so there was no reason for me to have them. I didn't even try to lie. Just came clean and told her everything."

"I assume she didn't take it well?"

He snorted. "Of course not. Why would she? She was hurt, then angry. Cried then screamed and even slapped me."

"And now?"

Tears streamed down Jamey's face as he peered at me. "She left me. She's staying at her sister's place, but I don't think she'll ever come back to me. I can't believe I did this." He buried his face in his hands and cried loudly.

As angry as I was at my friend, now wasn't the time to condemn him further. Right now he needed comfort. I strode over, wrapped my arms around him and squeezed. Jamey melted into my arms and I held my friend as he wept. After a few minutes, he straightened up and wiped the tears from his face.

"God, sorry for being such a crybaby."

"You don't need to apologize, man. I'm not going to think less of you for breaking down."

"Thanks," he said. "But I've been doing a lot of this crying shit at home alone. What I need is a couple hours' distraction."

"You want me to kick your ass at Fallout 4?"

He snorted. "What the fuck ever. You're going down."

THREE

GETTING UP IN THE MORNING WASN'T THE EASIEST because Jamey and I had stayed up until midnight playing. I'd offered him the couch but he declined even though I could tell he didn't like the idea of going home to his large, empty house.

I drank my breakfast in the form of dark coffee and grabbed my newspaper from the front porch. After flopping down in my comfy leather recliner I put my feet up and scanned the front page and settled on a headline that read:

Married Businessman Outed Thanks to Hackers

The article stated that Bryce Carrick, CEO of SeattleCarrick, a huge tech firm, had been yanked out of the closet thanks to his membership on a website called *Ashley Madison*. The site name sounded familiar but I had to check out a sidebar to refresh my memory.

Ashley Madison was a website dedicated to extra-marital affairs. It provided a place for married men and women planning to cheat on their spouses to find each other. Their motto was 'Life is short, Have an affair.' The site had recently been hacked by the group called Anonymous and Carrick's membership exposed.

There was a picture of Carrick, and I gaped at the page. He was one of the most handsome men I'd ever seen. Silver-gray hair on top of his head matched the scruff of facial hair. Beautiful hazel eyes and a warm smile completed the look. I'd always been drawn to older men, but this guy took my breath away. There was something special about him.

My doorbell rang, pulling me out of the haze, and a moment later, Jamey stuck his head in. "You decent?"

"Never. But I am dressed."

He chuckled and came in holding up a Krispy Kreme bag. "Hungry?"

"Donuts?" I cocked an eyebrow. "Way to reinforce a stereotype."

"Well, if you don't want one…" He acted like he was going to throw the donuts away.

I bounded up and grabbed for the bag. "I didn't say that. What kinds did you get?"

He grinned and set the food on the counter. "Glazed maple, powdered strawberry-filled, and a new one—salted caramel latte."

"Sounds horribly unhealthy," I said. "I'll take it."

He chuckled and handed me one of the fattening treats with a napkin. I took a bite and could practically feel the cavities forming. I returned to the newspaper as I ate the donut.

"Have you heard of this site, *Ashley Madison*?" I asked.

Jamey choked on a bite. "Umm," he mumbled. "Why are you asking?"

"Bryce Carrick was a member."

"Oh, I heard about that from my parents," Jamey said. "He was kicked out of his own company."

"Why?" I asked.

"Because of *Ashley Madison*," Jamey answered. "The stockholders got him removed on some kind of morality clause. Guy lost his job *and* his wife."

"Bunch of hypocrites," I murmured. "How many of those stodgy old geezers cheated on their wives?"

"It's not just that he cheated, it's that he did it with men."

"Still hypocritical even if what he did was disgusting." Obviously, I had nothing against men hooking up with other men, but *married* men doing it was something else. Gay men ended up married to women all the time, though I didn't know why that happened in this day and age. My parents had been pressuring me to get married since I was eighteen, but I refused, without ever telling them why. I couldn't ever tell them the truth—that I was gay. But I wouldn't marry a woman to appease them either.

I firmly believed that marriage is a contract that should mean something, whether those involved were gay or not. Men who cheat are assholes, regardless of whether they cheat with men or women, but for some reason, I found married men who cheated with men even more reprehensible. They'd entered into the marriage *knowing* they preferred the same sex, and that was a betrayal from the start.

I put the paper down, glanced at my watch, and then stood. "Time to go. You want to take the same car? You're welcome to hang out here after work. We can order pizza, and I can try to earn my dignity back after the ass kicking you gave me last night."

"You sure?" He cocked an eyebrow. "I'm not looking forward to being home, but I don't want to interfere with any plans."

I punched his shoulder. "Bite me."

"Sorry, man, not my thing. That's Harry's job."

"Haro," I corrected. "And he does *not* bite me. I'm the one who does the biting."

"Whoa, TMI!"

As soon as Jamey and I entered the squad room, Molly ran up to us, her excitement apparent by the gleam in her eyes. "Where have you been?"

I tapped my watch. "We're fifteen minutes early."

"Sorry, I'm just so—I have something to tell you." She followed me to my desk, tapping her fingers on a file folder.

"Jesus, Molly, how much coffee have you had today?"

"Only three cups."

"Three? How is that possible?"

"I've been here for two hours," she admitted.

I pulled off my coat and set it on the back of my chair then sat. She stood there, shifting from foot to foot.

"Okay, what is it you're so eager to tell me?"

"I identified the first victim."

I glanced up at her and her eyes widened. It seemed as if she was going to explode at any moment.

"Excuse me?" Jamey asked. "Did you say—"

"Yes," she squealed, "I did it. I got the victim's name."

Molly handed me a file and I opened it. Jamey dashed around the desk and read over my shoulder.

Julian Ramsey, twenty-four years old, of Portland, Oregon. No criminal record. His DMV photo matched the face of the man in the morgue.

"Why didn't we catch this before?" I asked.

"There's no missing person report," Molly said. "He's a businessman who travels a lot. His wife wasn't expecting to hear from him for a couple more days. The guy's worth millions."

"That age and a millionaire?" Jamey sat at his desk, leaned back, and put his feet up.

"He's some kind of tech genius. Created an app when he was twenty that he sold to GE. Every year or so he comes up with something new. That's why he was in Seattle. Apparently, he had meetings with several companies."

"How did you figure this out?" I asked and propped myself against my desk.

"It hit me that he had to be from out of town or there'd likely be a missing person report. He wore Gucci jeans so he had to have money, and that meant he was most likely staying at one of the nicer hotels, so I started with the most expensive one and worked my way down."

"You made cold calls?"

"Affirmative."

"Wow, that's initiative," I said.

She beamed and held her chin high. "I called them all and sent them our victim's picture. The clerk at The Sorrento recognized him. The victim checked out the morning he was killed."

"Interesting," Jamey murmured and exchanged a prideful look with me.

"Once I had a name, I went from there and called his wife, Alma."

I asked, "Did you tell her that her husband is dead?"

Molly shook her head. "No, I said he was a witness to the crime and we were trying to contact him."

"Give me her number, and I'll contact Portland PD and have them do the notification," Jamey said and reached for the phone.

After Molly handed him the number, I pulled her aside. "I was serious about what I said. That was some excellent police work. I'd say you have the instincts of a detective."

"You think so?" She grinned from ear to ear.

"Yes, I do, and I will make sure the chief knows."

Her face blanched. "Don't do that if it'll put you on the shit list with me."

"Don't worry." I patted her back. "You'll earn everyone's respect back. It just takes time."

She blushed then hurried back to her cubicle, head held high.

Jamey was done with his call when I sat down.

"Portland PD is sending two officers out right now," he said. "They'll have her call me right away."

"Okay, I'll keep trying to locate Mrs. Osceola."

I logged onto Facebook and located Fiona Osceola's profile. As much as I hated doing this type of investigation, I knew it was necessary. There weren't any new posts, but I scrolled down further, trying to search for clues about where she might go if she wanted to hide. Peripherally, I was aware of Jamey's phone ringing and him saying Ramsey's name. I also checked Osceola's Instagram, where she had the requisite shots of food, something I'd never understood. She ate a variety of foods at restaurants all over Seattle. She didn't seem to have a favorite Chinese, Mexican, or American eatery but when it came to sushi, she always ate at The Blue C. I'd just opened their site when Jamey spoke to me.

"Alma Ramsey is a mess, which is to be expected. She ID'd her husband through the photograph."

"Did you get anything helpful?"

"Yup. Ramsey had appointments with several local companies over the past week. SeattleCarrick, EMC, Artefact, Amazon, Zillow, PopCap, Big Fish Games, Microsoft, and Wizards of the Coast."

"That's an odd group." I leaned on my desk, propping my head on my hand. "Video games, retail, real estate, and computers."

"Apparently, his new program has a variety of applications," he said. "Oh, there was one more company. Boeing. Specifically, he had a meeting with Paula Carson."

"Tyrone Osceola's boss?"

"Yup."

I wouldn't have pegged the stone-faced woman as a killer but people could be surprising. The fact that both victims knew her could be a coincidence, but I didn't like to believe in coincidences.

While I considered the new information, and Jamey used the restroom, I finished the task I'd been working on—checking out Blue C Sushi. Turned out it was housed at the Grand Hyatt in downtown Seattle. If Fiona ate there that often, she might choose it as the place to stay when she went into hiding.

"Looks like we're headed back to Boeing," Jamey said. "You want me to handle the interview?"

"Nah." I shook my head. "Paula knows me. She'd be more likely to open up to me."

"Paula, huh? On a first-name basis." Jamey snickered. "You aren't thinking about switching sides?"

"If I was to do such a thing," I said, "it wouldn't be for her. She's a bit on the cold side."

Jamey stood and grabbed his coat. "Whatever you say, Romeo. Let's go."

I rose and held up a finger. "Give me a minute." I went up to Molly's desk. "I have an assignment for you."

"Absolutely, Detective."

"Contact the Grand Hyatt on Pine Street and see if Fiona Osceola is there. I have reason to suspect that might be where she's hiding."

"I'm on it."

PAULA CARSON DIDN'T MAKE US WAIT EVEN THOUGH she had three people in line ahead of us to see her.

"What can I do for you, Detective Tao?" she asked with what had to be her version of a smile.

I plastered a grin on my face as I shook her hand. "Well, I'm in kind of an odd situation here, Mrs. Carson."

"Ms.," she corrected. "I'm not married but you can call me Paula. And I'll help however I can."

Jamey and I entered the office and sat while she leaned against her large dark granite desk. "Okay, Paula it is," I said. "We have a murder victim who we believe was killed by the same person as Tyrone Osceola."

"Really? How so?"

"Same MO," Jamey replied. "That's all we can say."

She shot him a slight scowl then turned her attention back to me.

"Yes, same MO. But we also have reason to believe you knew this man as well."

Her brow furrowed and she cocked her head sideways.

"Julian Ramsey."

She pursed her lips then shook her head slightly. "I don't recognize the name."

I pulled up Ramsey's picture on my phone and showed it to her. Her eyes widened and she nodded.

"Oh, yes." Her face hardened until it resembled her stone desk. "I remember him."

"How so?" Jamey asked.

Even though he was the one who spoke, she directed her response at me.

"I had a meeting with him four days ago." Under her breath, she snarled, "Cocky little bastard." Raising her voice, she said, "He thought he could include me in a bidding war for some technology he swore could change how we do business."

"You weren't interested?"

"He wasn't specific about what his invention did or why it would be so innovative. I guess he thought I'd be intrigued based on his past endeavors. But I don't play games." She straightened her already straight lapel. "I had him escorted out when he refused to answer any of my questions. I wasn't going to blindly bid on something without proof."

"So you weren't thrilled with him, were you?" I asked.

"No, he annoyed me by wasting my time. But I barely gave him a second thought once I threw him out. I have way too many other things going on."

"I'm sorry I have to ask this, but where were you the night before last and the one before that? I need to exclude you as a suspect. As of right now, you're the sole link between both murdered men."

If that information concerned her, she didn't show it. She waved a hand. "No problem, Detective. The night before last I slept in my office. Security can verify that. I'll give you access to whatever you need."

"And three nights ago?"

Paula steepled her fingers in front of her lips. "Oh, yes. I left the office at eight and had a meal at Emory's on Silver Lake. They have the best seafood in the area. You should check it out sometime." She batted her eyes at me, and I had to force myself to continue smiling. Next to me, Jamey coughed, but I knew he was stifling a laugh.

"And after the meal?"

"I went home. My doorman can corroborate."

"Thank you, Paula. I appreciate your time. Like I side, I'm sure this is nothing but a coincidence, but I still need to verify your alibis."

"Absolutely. I'll have my assistant escort you to the security office and give you all the phone numbers you need."

I extended a hand, and she gripped it with both of hers. "Thank you for your time."

"My pleasure, Detective."

We left Boeing thirty minutes later after security had corroborated her alibi for the night of Osceola's murder. I'd check in with the restaurant and her building, but I doubted she was the killer.

"She was pleasant," Jamey said when we reached the cruiser.

"Oh, shut your mouth. I just took a page out of your notebook and turned on the charm."

He sniggered. "I didn't realize you had any."

I glared at him. "You know you would've done the same thing. Sometimes my rude cop routine works, but it wouldn't have with her."

"I'm not disagreeing with you. I'm proud of you. Took you long enough to figure out that lesson."

"I'm gonna check in with Molly." I retrieved my cell.

"I was just about to call you, Detective," Molly said after I greeted her. "The concierge at the Grand Hyatt didn't want to divulge any guest information, but I got him to admit Fiona Osceola is currently staying there."

"Awesome job, Officer. We're heading over there right now."

As Molly had told us, the concierge at the Grand Hyatt was reluctant to help us. However, Jamey turned on his megawatt smile and charmed the guy into confirming Fiona was staying in room 327. The guy even provided a keycard in case we needed it.

A few minutes later, we stood in front of room 327, and Jamey knocked so loud people three doors down could have probably heard him. When there was no answer, Jamey did it again. I was about to use the keycard when a tall man wearing nothing but a towel answered the door.

We showed him our badges. "Is Fiona Osceola here?"

He scrunched up his face then turned and yelled back into the room. "Hey, is your name Philomena?"

"Fiona," I corrected.

"Whatever." He shrugged and grinned. "I don't usually bother with names."

"Who is it?" A female voice called from inside the room. "Is that my dumbass husband?"

"Husband?" the hunk asked.

"Yeah, sorry," she replied. "Tell him to come in."

He shrugged again and glanced at us sheepishly. I pushed past him and into the room. The woman in bed jumped and covered herself with the sheets.

"Who the hell are you?"

"Detectives Tao and Nolan," I said. "We need to talk to you."

The half-naked dude strutted by, and said, "I'm gonna take a shower."

"Did my husband send you?" she asked.

"I'm afraid I have bad news for you." I especially hated shit like this. "Your husband is dead."

Fiona's eyes bulged out before she burst into tears and buried her face in her hands. "Dead? Oh, my God! Tyrone!" she wailed.

When she calmed down, she pulled on a bathrobe and sat down with us to talk. She cried as I described how and where his body had been found.

"Who would do this?" she asked.

I eyed her for a moment. "We're hoping you can tell us."

She clutched her chest. "You don't think I had anything to do with it, do you? I loved him."

Jamey snorted. "Yeah, you loved him so much you wasted no time taking a guy to bed."

She scowled. "Tyrone cheated on me first."

"Is that why you moved out?" I asked.

She nodded. "I was going to come back. I just wanted him to realize what he was missing." She grabbed a half-empty bottle of water from the night stand and took a drink. "This wasn't the first time, either. He had an affair with a woman when we first married. I forgave him, and we worked through it. He swore he would never do it again."

"How'd you find out?"

"I visited that website and put in his email address. Didn't actually think I'd find it. I was so pissed when his profile came up."

I arched an eyebrow. "What site?"

"I think it's called *Caught*. It lists the people who were members on that adultery site."

Jamey's jaw dropped. "Are you referring to *Ashley Madison*?"

She snapped her fingers. "That's the one."

"Just to be clear," I said. "Your husband was a member of *Ashley Madison*?"

She nodded and wiped at her face.

"Where exactly were you two nights ago between midnight and six a.m.?" Jamey asked.

"With me," the hunk said as he came out of the bathroom. This time he wore a pair of pants. "Same place she's been for the past three nights. I didn't know she was married, not that it matters. We both knew this wasn't anything serious, right?" He eyed Fiona and relaxed when she nodded.

"I need some information," I said then led him a few feet away.

"I'm going to go check out the hotel security footage," Jamey said.

"Okay." I glanced at Jamey and noticed his whiter than normal face. "You okay? You don't look well."

"Huh? Oh, I'm fine. Just tired. I need some coffee."

I shrugged and turned back to my witness. "What's your name?"

"Chad Pruitt." He retrieved his wallet and handed over his driver's license. "For the past three nights, I've been coming over here after work."

"What have you been doing?"

He scoffed. "What do you *think* we've been doing?"

"Anything in addition to sexual intercourse?"

"Room service and movies," he replied. "That's pretty much it."

"Where did you meet?"

"The bar downstairs. I bought her a few drinks, and she invited me to her room. I spent the night, and she said I was welcome to come back." He quirked the corner of his mouth. "So I did. She didn't want any kind of commitment. I would've been a fool to pass that up, right?" He winked at me like we were buddies.

"So you never knew her name? Or her husband's name?"

"Nope. Didn't ask and she didn't tell. Why are *you* asking?"

"Tyrone Osceola, her husband, was murdered."

He gasped. "Damn, that sucks."

"Spouses are usually the first suspect," I said. "Quickly followed by lovers."

He put up his hands. "Dude, I had nothing to do with a murder. I didn't know she was married. Hell, you saw me at the door. I didn't even know her name was Philomena."

"Fiona," I corrected.

"See!"

I didn't see him as a suspect, but I had to be sure. I asked him for his number. "I may need to ask follow-up questions." He gave the digits without reservation and vacated the room without even pulling his shirt all the way on when I said he could leave.

The widow Osceola was still sitting and crying. She should've been my number one suspect but I didn't see her as a killer. She may have had motive for the second killing, but not one for the first, not as far as I knew. Besides, according to Chad, she had been with him both nights.

I showed her a picture of Julian Ramsey. "Have you seen this man?"

She shook her head. "Who is it? Is he a suspect?"

"No, but he may be connected to the case."

I was asking Fiona some follow-up questions when Jamey returned. "Security footage shows that she hasn't left the motel for four days. It also showed her boyfriend coming and going each night."

It was possible she had hired someone to off her husband, but her grief and surprise seemed authentic. Additionally, I trusted her when she said she didn't know Ramsey. To believe Fiona was behind her husband's murder would mean she was responsible for Ramsey's as well. I just did not see that being the case.

"Am I still a suspect?" she asked.

"No," Jamey said, "but we might have more questions down the road."

BACK AT THE PRECINCT, I ASSIGNED MOLLY THE job of verifying Paula Carson's story while Jamey and I worked a few other angles.

I examined Osceola's financials, including his bank accounts. There weren't any questionable purchases that I could see, but there were several two hundred and forty-nine dollar payments to *Ashley Madison*. I'd hoped to find charges to hotels where he'd had his indiscretions, as they could've led to a description of his lovers, but I was out of luck. No such payments appeared in his statements.

While I pored through paperwork we now had access to thanks to Fiona, Jamey contacted people at the various companies Julian Ramsey had been in town to meet with. By the end of the day, he hadn't uncovered anything new.

"His appointments with Wizards of the Coast and PopCap were scheduled for after his death," Jamey said. "He missed his appointment at Zillow the day he was killed. The guys at EMC and Artefact said the same thing Paula Carson did but they were both willing to participate in a bidding war. Ramsey was supposed to get back to them. Big Fish Games basically told Ramsey to fuck off."

"Who's left?"

"SeattleCarrick, Microsoft, and Amazon. I haven't gotten around to calling the last two but it's too late now. No one answering this late would've been the people Ramsey was meeting with. I was told Ramsey met with Bryce Carrick, but talking to him is going to be difficult."

"Because he's no longer with the company," I filled in.

"Exactly. No one at the company knows where he is, or, if they do, they're not saying."

"Sounds like something we'll have to check out in person tomorrow."

He nodded.

"You ready to go?" I asked.

"Yeah, just give me a minute. I need to pay a quick visit to the tech division."

"Why? Something to do with the case?"

"Nah. Something personal. Nothing major. I'll meet you at the car."

I was curious but didn't press him. I waited in the car for ten minutes before he got in.

"You gonna tell me about it?" I asked.

"Not right now. Maybe later."

I shrugged and started the car. We grabbed two pizzas on the way home and ate them in my living room as we watched *Fatal Attraction*.

"God, you'd think this movie would be enough to stop any guy from cheating. Dumb assholes." I regretted the comment as soon as I said it and felt Jamey's gaze on me. I tried to ignore it and focus on the movie.

"You got something to say?"

I glanced over and attempted to act innocent. "Huh?"

"Is there something you feel the need to say to me about cheating?"

"I didn't mean you. Not you specifically, anyway."

That didn't help things and Jamey's face reddened even more. "You wouldn't understand."

Now it was my turn to be pissed. "Is there something to comprehend about you putting your dick where it doesn't belong? Or anybody doing it, for that matter? It's wrong and it hurts people."

"People have their reasons, Peter. You really shouldn't be so judgmental."

"What sort of reasons could there be to break your marriage vows? I don't think there could be any justification for such a thing." My appetite gone, I tossed a slice in the box on the coffee table, leaned back on the couch, and crossed my arms.

"Why do you have to be such a prick?" he snapped. "Things are either black or white with you. Right or wrong, no in-between."

"We're not talking about me right now. We're talking about you and guys like you who can't keep it in their pants."

He leaped to his feet so quickly the food in his lap spilled on my hardwood floor. "You have no idea what it's like to be in a relationship for as long as I have. Hell, you don't have a clue what it's like to be in a relationship. Period."

I stood and got in his face. "True and you know why."

"Yeah, I do know. It's because you're scared. Scared of coming out. Scared of putting yourself out there."

"I did put myself out there one time. Look what happened!"

"How long are you going to use Darren as an excuse? Yeah, he hurt you but that doesn't mean you should hide out from men for the rest of your life. And it certainly doesn't give you the right to judge me or my actions. I know I fucked up. I don't need you riding my ass and making me feel even more guilty."

His words hit me and my anger faded. I regretted what I said. My body deflating, I said, "I'm sorry, Jamey."

The tension in his body didn't ease. Instead, he turned and grabbed his coat. "I'm going home. I need to be alone."

"You sure? You can stay. I'll keep my mouth shut."

A forced smile spread across his lips. "I doubt that."

"I'd try."

"Nah, it's okay. I need fresh clothes anyway. I'll see you at work tomorrow."

And with that, he was gone. I cleaned up the mess and put the leftovers away.

A couple hours later, I was getting ready to go to bed when my cell beeped. I had a text message from Jamey.

Can you come over? I need to talk and I'm drunk.

I texted back. *I'll be there in half an hour.*

THERE WAS NO ANSWER AT THE DOOR WHEN I knocked so I used my key and stuck my head in.

"Jamey?" I stepped in, shutting the door behind me. "Hello? Anyone home?" I wasn't too worried by the lack of an answer. I figured Jamey had passed out. I made my way down the hallway to the room Jamey used as his office slash man cave.

The door to the room was partially closed, but I pushed it all the way open and called out his name again. No answer, so I entered, expecting to see him passed out on the brown leather couch. He wasn't, so I ambled in farther and spotted his feet on the floor on the other side of a large entertainment center. A fifty-inch television loomed over him looking like a big dead eye.

"Geez, Jamey, get off the floor." I turned the corner and froze, my heart leaping into my throat. Jamey lay on the floor, his pants at his knees and his genitals cut off. "Oh, Jesus Christ." Bile rose in my throat as the coppery smell of blood hit my nostrils. I covered my mouth and fought the urge to vomit. I grabbed my cell and dialed 911. After identifying myself, I ordered an ambulance. "Officer down. I repeat, officer down."

The operator asked me to stay on the line but I dropped the phone and rushed to my friend. I wanted to kneel and take him in my arms. Embrace him for the last time. But I didn't want to mess with any evidence. I did, however, sit and take his hand. I felt for a pulse though I knew he was already gone. His skin was still warm, and for a moment, I could pretend he was still alive. It felt good to hold his hand for what I knew was the last time. I sat so I could see only his upper body, not wanting to see the grotesque mess below his waist.

How could someone do that to another human being? And why? I'd seen a lot of dead bodies in my career, but I'd always managed to keep a professional distance. Officers had to, otherwise the job would eat them up.

But I couldn't do that now, not when my partner, my friend, had been murdered. I was going to do whatever it took to find the killer.

"Goddamn it, Nolan. This wasn't how you were supposed to go out." We'd discussed our deaths and our preferred ways of biting it. Jamey's first choice had been to die old and happy with Chelsea in his arms, but his second choice had been to go down in a blaze of glory as he took out a bad guy. I agreed. As a cop, that was a noble way to die. "We were supposed to have more years together, man. Many more. I still had a lot to learn from you."

I heard a noise at the front door, but I couldn't bring myself to leave Jamey. I couldn't let him go. Everything that happened next happened in blurry chunks: voices in the room; a hand on my shoulder; my name being said again and again. It took a lot of strength to focus on what was going on around me.

"Detective Tao, you need to let his hand go." A somewhat familiar female voice penetrated the fog.

I turned and gazed into the face of an EMT I knew. Couldn't remember her name, though, so I glanced at the nametag on her chest. Valerie.

"He's dead," I muttered.

"I know." Her rounded face softened with understanding. "We need to check him out though."

"Don't do anything to disturb the body," I said as I found my voice. "Can't lose evidence."

She nodded. "I understand, Detective. We just need to check for his pulse."

"Okay." With her help I rose and stepped out of the way, leaning against the wall. Valerie and her partner checked his pulse several times before announcing the time of death.

I headed outside and stood near the front door. In minutes, the place was going to be swarming with people. Needing to keep the scene preserved snapped me the rest of the way out of my fog of mourning. That could come later. When two patrol cars pulled up, I began barking orders.

"Get crime scene tape up around the entire property. Don't let anyone past unless they're CSU. I don't want anyone trampling the scene."

"Yes, sir."

I held my ground and refused to let other cops past the sidewalk. Most of them just wanted to see Jamey's body, and I wasn't going to let him be gawked at like a tourist attraction. I pissed off a few guys, but I didn't give a shit. I was in the middle of arguing with a lieutenant in charge of the SWAT team when Chief Slight arrived. Lt. Schlesinger was trying to use his position to order me around but Slight put him in his place.

"Detective Tao is right, Lieutenant. There's no reason you need to see the body. You won't be handling the case so either get out of here or make yourself useful and help keep other people away." Despite the late time, neighbors had begun crowding around the house.

"Um, yes, ma'am," he sputtered.

I lifted the crime scene tape for the chief and we strode up the walkway.

"I know this is tough, Peter, but tell me what happened."

"I got a text from him to come over. He was drunk."

"Do you know why he wanted you to come over?"

I wiped my face. "We had a fight earlier."

"About?" she asked.

"Nothing work related." As if that would reassure her.

"Where's Chelsea?"

"Oh, fuck," I murmured. I'd actually forgotten about her because I was so focused on everything that was going on at the house. "She's not here. Staying at her sister's place, I think."

"I'll send some uniformed officers over there. Do you know the address?"

I didn't but it was in Jamey's phone.

Slight put her hand on my shoulder. "I'll get it. You stay out here."

"Can you have the officers bring Chelsea here? I'd like to be the one to tell her."

She nodded and slipped inside. Jill and a CSU crew showed up next.

"Is it true?" she asked. "Detective Nolan…Jamey's dead?"

I nodded. "It appears to be the same killer as the others."

"Oh, my God." She buried her face in her hands.

I wrapped my arms around her and hugged her for a moment. Then I stepped back, cupped her face, and made her look me in the eye. "I know this is tough, Jill. Trust me, I understand. But we have jobs to do. Jamey needs us to find his killer, and that means we have to be at one hundred percent."

She sucked in a breath and nodded. Then she swiped the wetness from her cheeks, straightened up, and said, "You're right. Thanks."

CSU assumed I was the one in charge and asked me for a quick rundown before they entered.

"The victim is one of our own, guys. Detective Jamey Nolan. His murder is connected to the case he and I have been working."

"The victims with the missing genitalia?" one guy asked.

"Yes," I confirmed. "That means the killer was inside the house. Which is one thing that's different from the other murders. Evidence collection needs to be perfect. Incredibly thorough. Nothing is too small. We'll need exclusionary prints from his wife and family members. That includes me. Bag and tag strands of hair, every piece of DNA. Search for shoeprints inside and out."

They didn't need the directions, they were more than capable, but it felt good to be doing something. And they knew I wasn't trying to step on any toes. They immediately went to work, and I stood around, still rather gob smacked at the fact that my partner and friend was not only dead, but the victim of a serial killer.

I was staring off into space and jumped when Chief Slight tapped me on the shoulder. I turned to face her, and she handed me my phone, which I'd dropped earlier. "I just sent two officers to speak to Chelsea and bring her here."

"I want this case, Chief. I *need* to work it. If you take me off it, I swear I will—"

She cut me off. "Don't worry, Peter. I have no intention of removing you. The fact that you cared about Jamey is what makes you perfect because you'll do what is needed to find the killer."

"Thanks."

"You have every available resource at your disposal. Just let me know what you need, and I'll get it."

I thanked her again. "I'll let you know. Right now I can barely think. I have to hold it together for Chelsea. She's going to need me. Hell, I might have to call their kids too."

"You'll be up late, so come in whenever you need to tomorrow. Get some sleep and come in refreshed."

"I doubt I'll be able to sleep, but I appreciate everything."

"Like I said, whatever you need, you got it. Overtime, extra resources. Anything." She squeezed my shoulder. "Okay, I have to go speak to the commissioner and the mayor. Let them know what's going on."

Jill came out a few minutes later. "He's got the same stab wound in the back of his neck as the other victims. There isn't much doubt it's the same killer."

"Are you done with the body?" I asked, hating to think of my friend in such a way. "I'd like to get him out of here before Chelsea gets home. She doesn't need to see him like that."

"The EMTs are loading him up right now."

Just in time, or so I thought. They wheeled Jamey out as a red Ford Fusion pulled up with a police cruiser right behind it. Chelsea bolted from the car before it was even parked and ran toward the cart. I stepped in her way. "You don't want to see him. Not like that."

"Oh, my God," she murmured with a hand over her mouth. "It's Jamey, isn't it? They wouldn't tell me, but I had a feeling."

"I'll tell you everything," I said. "But not in front of everyone."

"Can I see his face, at least?" Her voice and hands trembled.

I nodded at the EMTs and they pulled back the blanket to show his face. She cried out and wrapped her arms around herself while I embraced her from behind. Her sister Daisy jogged up, and Chelsea turned into her arms.

I put a hand on Chelsea's shoulder, but she flinched away. "Let's talk over here." They followed me to several chairs on the back porch, and I flashed back to the times we'd had barbecues—drinking beers and playing lawn darts. We'd never be doing that again.

"What happened?" Chelsea asked. "Who did this?"

"I don't know who killed Jamey, but I swear to God I will find him." I reached out to take her hand but she pulled away before I could touch her.

"Is it connected to a case?"

I hesitated, because I wasn't sure how much I wanted to tell her but figured she'd hear about the genital mutilation sooner or later. "I can give you *some* details but it's pretty gruesome."

She rolled her eyes and glared at me. "I've been a cop's wife for more than two decades. I can handle it."

I paused to take a deep breath. "Jamey and I have been working a case with two dead males. Both men had their…penises cut off."

Chelsea and Daisy gasped in unison.

"Was Jamey…Is that what happened to him?"

I nodded, and she burst into tears. Daisy reached over and squeezed her hand.

"Did the killer come after him because of the investigation?" Chelsea asked.

"That's a line of inquiry I'll be following." Though I would be digging into it, I didn't think that was why Jamey had been murdered. We weren't even remotely close to identifying the killer, so I didn't know why he would want to come after either one of us. My gut told me Jamey being a victim of the serial killer we were investigating was a coincidence. Again, I didn't usually believe in such things, but I was sure there was some connection I hadn't found yet.

Chelsea was quiet for a few minutes then stared at me and asked, "You knew, didn't you?"

Knowing she was referring to his cheating, I whispered, "Yes."

"You knew the entire time." She smacked her lips and shook her head in disgust. "Of course you did. You boys in blue always stick together."

"No. He *just* told me the other day."

She gestured as if she was swatting away a fly. "I find that hard to believe, Peter. He talked to you *a lot* more than he did to me."

Putting a hand to my chest, I said, "I did not know until just the other day. I was furious with him. Hell, we argued about it."

"It doesn't matter when you knew." She sniffled and straightened her shirt. "You wouldn't have told me, and don't insult me by saying you would've."

"C'mon, we're friends, too, Chelsea. I love you."

She narrowed her eyes and glowered. "You would *not* have told me." Her voice was ice cold as she enunciated each word slowly and clearly.

I couldn't deny her claim, though I wished otherwise. Jamey was my friend, and I would've held his confidence. "I'm so sorry he hurt you like that."

A single tear dropped down her face, and she swiftly wiped it away. "I don't understand why he did it," she said. "Our marriage wasn't perfect but if he'd just come to me and shared his feelings, we could've worked things out."

"That wasn't Jamey's thing, though, was it?"

"No, it wasn't." More tears came and this time she let them flow. "I was furious at him, still am, but I still loved him. We may have been able to fix things."

"I believe Jamey would've done whatever it took to make it work. He was angry at himself and how he hurt you. He regretted it so much."

"That doesn't help much. It's too late now." She let out a mournful sob, and Daisy held her through it while I waited to ask questions I really didn't want to.

In any other case, the wife would be the first suspect, but I didn't see that here. Chelsea wasn't a killer, and she was still in love with her husband. I had no doubt she and Jamey would've eventually reconciled. Regardless of how I felt, I still needed to exclude her as a suspect.

"Where were you tonight?" I asked.

Daisy glowered at me and snapped, "You don't think she did this, do you?"

"I'm sorry," I replied. "But I have to ask."

"Of course he's suspicious." Chelsea held her chin high. "Jamey would've been. He never could put his cop hat away. He was always on the job no matter what we were doing."

I was about to apologize again when she stopped me.

"I was with Daisy," she answered curtly. "We played games with the kids tonight and watched a movie."

"Don was there, too," Daisy said, referring to her husband. "You can talk to him and the kids tomorrow."

"Thank you."

"Are we done here?" Daisy asked. "She's exhausted and we need to contact the kids."

"Oh, dear," Chelsea scrubbed her face. "I have to call my children and tell them their father is dead."

"Do you need me to do that?" I asked.

She jerked her head back and forth. "You do your job, and I'll do mine. I'll call Jamey's parents, too."

"Okay." We all stood, and I went in for a hug but she put a hand on my chest and stopped me. Without another word, they turned and strode away.

I hung around the scene for a bit longer, not leaving until the crowds had vanished. I headed home, though I wanted to get working on the case immediately. Unfortunately, there wasn't anything I could do. It would take time for Jill and CSU to have any results. If I went to the station, all I'd be doing was waiting around. I figured I could do that just as easily at home in the comfort of my recliner. It was after three a.m. when I left.

At home I turned on the TV and watched a DVR episode of *The Flash*. The sight of a huge talking gorilla should've kept me awake but I dozed off.

For a minute after I woke, I thought—hoped—it had been a nightmare, but then reality hit me, and I remembered my partner and friend was dead.

Grief weighed on me, and I wished I could take the time needed to mourn Jamey, but I had to keep my head on straight. Focus was needed, and I couldn't do that if I allowed the sadness to overtake me. It wasn't easy to put my emotions aside, but it's what Jamey would do if the situation were reversed.

With barely three hours sleep I was tired but Jill might have something for me by now so it was time to get to work. I stood in the shower and let the hot water cascade over my body until it ran cold. I was somewhat rejuvenated but needed more, so on my way to Jill's office, I stopped at Starbucks and ordered a Pike's Place Roast with two shots of espresso. The barista didn't hit on me this time, but I chuckled at the memory of the one who had. It was Jamey's reaction to the young woman giving me her number that was most humorous.

Jill was at her desk when I arrived. She rose when she spotted me and flew into my arms. "I'm so sorry about Jamey," she said. "I know that doesn't help much. I wish I could do more."

I pulled out of her embrace. "You doing your job is the only thing I want from you."

"Of course," she said and straightened her shirt. "I examined the wound on Jamey's neck as well as the genital mutilation. It's different from the first two murders."

What the hell?

"Are you saying it's not the same killer?"

"Oh, no, not at all." She tucked her hair behind her ear. "I'm just saying it's a different knife."

I pressed a palm to my heart. "Thank fuck. I don't think I could handle that."

She grabbed a tablet and pulled up images of the necks of all three men. "The entry point is the same on all three. I'd say the person isn't very tall, most likely between five foot four and five foot six." She touched the first picture and enlarged it to show the wound better. "The murder weapon appears to be a steak knife. Six inch blade with a one inch width."

Scratching my head, I said, "I thought you said the murder weapon was different with Jamey."

"It *was* different, but it was the same type of knife."

"Then how do you know it's not the same one?"

"Both knives had serrated blades but the one used on Jamey was different." She closed the pictures on her tablet and brought up two digitally created images. "I created these based on the marks on the inside of the wound. The knife used on the first two men created marks slanted to the right while the one used on Jamey had left-slanted striations."

"But you're positive it's the same murderer?" I asked for reassurance.

"I can't be one hundred percent sure, but I'd say yes. There's too much in common to suggest otherwise. What're the chances two different killers would use the same method—the same *unusual* method?"

"Add in the genital mutilation and it's even more unlikely."

"Exactly," she said. "You didn't release that information to the public, did you?"

I shook my head.

"Oh, I almost forgot to tell you. There wasn't any DNA on the hair found at the first scene, but there was on the one from the second scene. I'm running it for a match right now. I'll let you know if there's a hit. We also found something interesting on Jamey's couch." She set the tablet down and pointed at a paper evidence bag. Contrary to what was seen on television and movies, law enforcement doesn't use clear plastic bags. That led to degradation of DNA, obviously something we didn't want to happen.

"What is it?"

"A red hair," she replied. "His wife isn't a ginger, is she?"

"Nope. I'll check with her to see if she knows anyone who is."

I thanked Jill for the information and headed to the precinct.

Molly sat at Jamey's desk but leaped to her feet the second she spotted me. "I'm sorry, Detective. It won't happen again."

Furrowing my brow, I asked, "Why are you apologizing?"

"For sitting at Detective Nolan's desk."

I waved a hand dismissively. "Don't worry about it. Feel free to use it. It will help having you close since you're going to work this case with me."

"What?" She sputtered. "I'm helping you?"

I removed my coat and put in on the back of my chair before sitting. "Yes, you are. Chief Slight said I could use whatever resources I want."

"And you want me?" Her eyes widened. "Why? I'm doing desk duty because I got in trouble."

"So what? You messed up. Who hasn't? I know I have. Detective Nolan certainly screwed up more than once. You have excellent instincts, and I think that can help me in this case. I want someone I can trust and, right now, that means you." I pointed at her.

"I don't know what to say."

"How about thank you?"

"Thank you." She beamed from ear to ear. "Thank you very much."

"Now sit down so we can discuss the case."

She sat in Jamey's chair, put her hands together, and peered at me.

"The fast pace of the killer worries me. Four nights and three murders. If he keeps going at this pace, we could have a dead body every other day or so."

"Most serial killers don't move this quickly," she said. "Even Ted Bundy spaced his victims out more until the Chi Omega murders."

I ogled her, and she blushed.

"I've studied serial killers. I find them fascinating."

I chuckled. "I knew there was a reason I liked you." I tapped the desk a couple times. "What's your take on their dicks being hacked off?"

She put her hands behind her head and leaned back. "Genitalia mutilation usually has a sexual connotation. The castration was done after death, correct?"

I nodded.

"So torture isn't the point. The killer didn't make them suffer. If he'd wanted to hurt them, he would've cut off their dicks while they were still alive. Since the purpose of the maiming wasn't to cause pain, I think it's a statement. The killer probably believes the victims did something wrong with their cocks."

I regarded Molly for a moment but didn't speak. Eventually, she got uncomfortable with the attention and asked why I was staring at her.

"Just amazed at how in sync we are. I agree with everything you just said."

She beamed and held her chin high.

"Do you have any thoughts on how the killer is choosing his victims?"

She bit her bottom lip for a moment. "To answer that, we have to examine the similarities and connections between the three men. We know there's a business connection between Osceola and Ramsey."

"But as far as we know the two men never met," I said. "Ramsey met with Osceola's boss but her alibi is solid."

"Anything else the victims have in common?" she wondered aloud.

"All three were wealthy."

She pursed her lips. "Detective Nolan had money?"

"Yeah, his parents are über rich. Jamey was worth millions, not that he ever lived like it."

"Interesting, but I'm not sure how that helps us. You can't spit in Seattle without hitting someone with money."

"True. So there has to be some other commonality. And we need to find it as soon as possible." I actually knew of one thing Osceola and Jamey had in common—they had both cheated on their wives. I didn't see how that could matter since the city had to have dozens of men and women who'd cheated on their spouses. Now if Ramsey was an adulterer as well, that would be a different matter. I was reluctant to share something about Jamey's personal life if it wasn't pertinent to the case.

"What do you want me to work on today?" she asked.

"Follow up on Ramsey's meetings. Jamey talked to everyone but the people at Amazon, Microsoft, and SeattleCarrick. I'll give you access to the files on the server so you can read Jamey's notes. Let me know if I should speak to anyone in person. Trust your instincts. If something doesn't seem right, it's probably not. Tell me even if it's just a little niggle."

"I can do that."

I got on the computer and gave Molly the access she needed. We worked to keep the information on cases as private as possible so if anything was leaked we knew it could only have come from a select few. "I'm going to visit Jamey's wife again, then his parents.

In addition to finding out who Ramsey met with, try to get me a timeline of where he went and when. Write down everything, even if he stopped somewhere to take a piss. You never know when something will come in useful."

"Anything else?"

"See what you can find out regarding Osceola's last day. Why was he at Gas Works? Was he meeting someone? We know it wasn't Tina Burch. Maybe a different woman? Check out his phone calls and texts."

"I'm on it." She turned to the computer screen and began pounding keys.

FOUR

I'D JUST GOTTEN BACK TO THE PRECINCT AFTER talking to the most important people in Jamey's life when Chief Slight called me into her office.

"I won't take too much of your time," she said, "but I need an update on the case."

"Unfortunately, there's not a lot to tell you just yet." I sat and crossed my legs before filling her in on the investigation, including the red hair found on Jamey's couch. I'd asked Chelsea about it, but she didn't know anyone, friends or family, who were gingers.

"I'm almost afraid to ask, but is Chelsea a suspect?"

"I'm glad to say she has a rock solid alibi," I replied. "Her nieces excitedly told me how Mom and Aunt Chelsea had played *Trouble* and *Life* with them before bedtime. It certainly didn't seem like they'd been coached to lie. The same with Chelsea's brother-in-law Don, who said he'd been trying to watch the game while the women and the kids had played. He couldn't hear over the din so he went to the bedroom and watched on the smaller TV."

"That's a relief." She lifted her coffee cup, took a sip, and grimaced. "Considering Chelsea has been living at her sister's, I'm assuming they were having marital problems."

I nodded. "Jamey told me a few nights ago that he'd cheated on her several times." The chief already knew enough about Jamey's personal life that it didn't feel like I was gossiping to share the information.

"Damn, I thought they had what it took to make it." She sighed. "Cop marriages usually don't make the ten year mark. Mine sure as hell didn't."

That was one of the reasons I didn't plan on ever getting married. Even if I did have someone special in my life, I didn't see ever being able to tell my parents their only child was queer. Better for them to think I was just too focused on work than to have them disown me.

"I talked to Jamey's parents today, too," I said. "They had no idea he and Chelsea had separated or that he had cheated."

"And they don't have any idea who might've wanted him dead?" Slight asked.

"None at all. But they weren't involved in his life. He had dinner with them twice a month and didn't talk to them much more often than that." Jamey was the black sheep of the family just because he became a cop instead of getting an MBA like his father had expected.

We discussed a few other facts of the investigation before Slight paused and tapped her fingers on the desk. "I know I told you that you could use whatever resources you wanted, but are you sure you want Officer Whitmore?"

I snorted because I'd been expecting the question. Back when she was on patrol, Molly had happened on a teenage keg party and ended up using a Taser on a kid who was carrying what she thought was a gun. It turned out to be a beer bottle *and* he was the mayor's son. "Did you ever make a mistake when you were a rookie, Chief?"

She grinned. "Hell, yeah. My training officer covered my ass more than once."

"Exactly," I replied. "Is what she did any worse than what you did? Or the shit I did as a trainee? You know she's being punished because the mayor ordered you to do it. This mistake shouldn't ruin her career. And it's impressive that she's been doing the work of a receptionist for months and hasn't complained."

"I see your point."

"Besides, she's smart and has excellent instincts. I'm the lucky one to have her helping me."

"Okay, if you're sure."

"I am."

She shrugged and said, "That's all. You can go."

I rose, exited the office, and ambled to my desk. Molly was at Jamey's desk...her desk.

"How'd it go with Mrs. Nolan?" she asked.

"Her alibi's solid. She's definitely not the killer. Not that I suspected her."

"That reminds of me something I wanted to ask." Her forehead creased. "I know most serial killers are men but are we considering women?"

I chuckled. "Jamey and I disagreed on that subject. He doesn't think a woman would do this, but I think it's more than possible. The mutilation is a bit more grotesque than most women would want to even see, let alone do. But I've seen some pretty pissed-off women and believe someone with enough anger could easily be responsible for these murders. I think it's less probable a man would castrate other guys."

"Why is that?"

"My balls hurt when I even *think* about what happened to those men. I tend to imagine it being done to me. I'd think that's true for most men."

"That's not hard evidence," she said. "But I agree that it'd be stupid to completely rule a woman out as the suspect."

"There are other reasons I believe that," I said. "I'm curious what your thoughts are."

She sat up straight and examined a notepad, flipping pages back and forth. "The height of the suspect for one, according to Dr. Trencher. A woman is more likely to be that height. Plus, the killer ambushed these men. She came up to them from behind. That points to someone unable to handle themselves in a physical confrontation."

Impressed, I nodded. "You nailed it. Those were my thoughts precisely."

She blushed and glanced away. "I'm afraid I didn't get anything useful today."

"Tell me anyway."

Molly was right—nothing she had helped the investigation. She spoke to the people Ramsey met at Amazon and Microsoft but still couldn't locate Bryce Carrick, the guy Ramsey had spoken to at SeattleCarrick. She'd also managed to trace Ramsey's activity for most of the day he was killed.

"But I can't find anything after about five p.m. that day," she said. "He had some text messages from someone asking to meet him later."

"From who?"

She shrugged. "The number is disconnected now and was one of those pre-paid phones."

"Did you find out where the phone was purchased?" I asked.

She pulled her head back and eyed me warily. "Why would that matter?"

"Oh, young Padawan, I have much to teach you."

"Padawan? What are you talking about?"

"You don't know Star Wars?" I asked in shock.

"Never seen it."

"Oh. My. God." I laughed. "That's a travesty. We'll have to hang out off duty and watch the movies."

"Oh, I don't know about that." Her eyes became huge. "I like to keep my personal life separate from work."

I realized she assumed I was hitting on her, but I didn't know how to disabuse her of the thought without coming out to her. Instead, I returned to the investigation.

"Sometimes knowing where the disposable cell came from can help," I said. "Convenience stores are the worst. Their video sucks, and the clerks barely pay attention. Walmart is the absolute best. They have cameras *everywhere.*"

I contacted the cellphone provider and, thankfully, they were willing to cooperate without a warrant, which would've taken time. Luckily, the phone had been purchased at a local Walmart.

Amos, the security officer at the Renton Walmart, was more than happy to cooperate. Using the time/date stamp, we were able to pinpoint which register the phone was bought at.

"It should be any second now," I said and scrutinized the monitor.

"I bet that's our guy." Molly pointed at a person wearing a hoodie with the top on.

I was afraid he was going to keep his face covered but he lowered the hood when he pulled out a wallet. He was short, around five foot five, with dull ginger hair. Unfortunately, those were the only details we could make out. I couldn't even be sure if the person was male or female. As he—and I was going with the generic *he* until something proved otherwise—left the register, he pulled up the hood of his jacket, obscuring his face as he strode by the camera.

"Not exactly helpful, is it?" Amos asked.

I stood up straight. "Better than we had before."

Molly started to say something, but I held up a finger to stop her. I didn't want her discussing case information in front of Amos. I thanked him for his help and gave him my email address so he could send that section of footage.

On our way to the car, Molly said, "It's disappointing that we couldn't see his face. But I'd say that is definitely our man."

"Or woman."

She stopped walking and faced me. "Yes! I thought that was odd. It was almost like he purposely dressed to hide his gender."

"He was probably paranoid about the security cameras. It's good to be wary but sucks for us. Still, the tech division might be able to find something. I'll have them check out all the footage and see if they can find the guy coming in."

"Thanks for bringing me," Molly said once we were in the car. "I've been getting cabin fever being stuck at the precinct all the time."

"My pleasure."

WHEN I ENTERED THE STATION, I TURNED LEFT instead of right and headed to the tech division with Molly right behind me.

Tech was housed in the back of the building in a large, low-lit room with rows of desks. I bypassed the first several officers and went to a guy I'd worked with in the past—Azazil el Rasi. Aza and I had shared a drink or two after work a couple times. We'd discussed the joys of being American-born children of immigrants. Korean and Syrian might be vastly different, but our parents and their beliefs weren't so dissimilar. My gaydar had pinged slightly, but I figured if he was queer, he was as deeply closeted as I was.

"Hey, Aza," I said.

He peered up from his computer and grinned. "How's it going, Peter?" We bumped fists.

"I've got some video footage coming from Walmart. I'm hoping you can check it out and see if you can identify an individual. I'll forward it when it arrives and pinpoint the exact person. If at all possible, I'd love if you can get a clear facial image."

He nodded. "I'll do my best."

"I hate to pull rank, but…"

"No worries," he said. "I know anything to do with this case has top priority. I'll work on it immediately."

I clapped him on the back. "Thanks."

"I was sorry to hear about Jamey," Aza said. "I liked him. He was a fine man."

I nodded.

"I don't suppose you're free for a drink tonight? There's something I wanted to discuss with you. Just not at work."

What could he possibly want to talk with me about?

"I'm not sure how late I'll be working," I said.

"Well, I'm going to the Triangle Bar after work. Come by if you can."

"Will do."

Molly and I returned to our desks and worked on identifying more suspects, unfortunately not coming up with anything new. I forced her to go home on time but I stayed an hour late.

I was beat when I finally left the precinct and didn't feel like going to a bar but it seemed as if Aza truly wanted to talk to me. I was curious what he could possibly have to say. I hoped he didn't just want to commiserate about Jamey. I was still repressing my emotions about the death of my friend and wasn't ready to throw back alcohol and remember the good times. That would come *after* the killer was caught and not until then.

I headed to The Triangle anyway, hoping I could be in and out in less than an hour. I spotted Aza right away. Apparently, he'd been drinking fairly heavily. It was Friday night, after all. He was also dancing with an attractive brunette with long legs and a short skirt. I guessed my gaydar was wrong, judging by how close they were, and when he kissed her, I closed the door on that assumption. Figuring he had other things on his mind, I left him to his fun and went home.

I SPENT SATURDAY AT THE STATION, WORKING EVERY lead I had, but nothing panned out. It wasn't easy to focus since Jamey's funeral was the following day.

I did make a phone call to a local clean-up crew to take care of the blood and mess at Jamey's house so Chelsea and the kids didn't have to worry about it. That was one thing they definitely didn't need on their plate. I was missing my best friend, but Jamey was their husband and father. They had enough shit to deal with that making a few phone calls was nothing.

More than once I zoned off just staring at his desk. We'd been working together for so long I couldn't imagine life without him sitting across from me. Jamey was my partner and mentor, as well as best friend. I wouldn't be the man or cop I was without him.

And I had no idea how I was going to make it through his funeral without someone at my side.

FIVE

Seattle has an annual rainfall of more than three feet and is cloudy two hundred days of the year. With that information, you'd think the day of Jamey's funeral would be rain and overcast. But it wasn't. It was actually sunny and bright, which just felt wrong. As if the climate should match my dark mood.

Dozens of people stood around the casket as a minister spoke about Jamey, a man he'd never met. That was something about funerals I didn't understand. Paying a stranger to speak. A stranger who would throw in words about God and faith and all the horseshit that Jamey hadn't believed in. It was done because it had always been done. Total crap if you asked me.

I tuned out the preacher and checked out the crowd. There were lots of men and women in uniform, including Chief Slight and other members of the brass. Jamey and Chelsea's eldest son, Jim, sat next to his mother and Jamey and Chelsea's daughter, Grace, was on the other side, gripping Chelsea's hand with both of hers. Matt, the youngest, was behind them, his face buried in his hands.

Jamey's parents and brother were there, as were several family members from both Jamey and Chelsea's sides, many of whom I didn't know. Hell, there were likely kin Jamey himself had never met.

I was surveying the attendees when I spotted someone in the distance. A woman in a dark dress, hat and veil obscuring her face, leaned against a tree. She wasn't near enough to even hear the minister, but there was no doubt it was Jamey's service she was here for.

If she was a friend of Jamey's, why was she standing so far away?

Stepping out of the group of people I was bunched in, I made my way toward the woman. She spotted me and took a few steps backward. I almost called out to her, but didn't want to interrupt the service. Instead, I put a hand up, trying to signify I wasn't dangerous. She either didn't understand my intention or didn't care. Or maybe she just didn't want to talk to me.

I sped up and she turned and scurried away from me. I shifted into a jog but she began running, her hat and veil flying off as she dashed away, revealing a head of red hair. She made it to her vehicle—a light blue Honda Accord—and raced away before I could get more than the last two numbers of the license plate.

On my way back to the service, I stopped to snatch the hat the woman had dropped. I checked the inside and spotted several hairs, hopefully with the bulb still attached so we could extract DNA. I jogged to my car and deposited the hat in the back seat before returning to the service.

The preacher was finishing up, based on the proselytizing and stating that it was never too late to accept Jesus and how it should be done before "God decides it's time for you to leave this world."

Chelsea and Grace wept loudly while Jim and Matt did their best to comfort them. I envied them their ability to let their emotions loose and mourn. I wouldn't have enjoyed losing my shit in public, but I did wish I could stop repressing my feelings and get on with the grieving process. Holding it all in was beginning to make my gut ache, but it wasn't anything I couldn't handle.

With the sermon finally done, people began milling around, talking to each other and embracing Chelsea and the kids. I was waiting for my turn when Molly came over.

"I noticed you walk off," she said. "What was that all about?"

"There was a woman, a redhead, watching from a distance. I thought it was odd, so I approached her. She took off as soon as she spotted me, but she dropped her hat."

Molly cocked an eyebrow. "We keep coming back to gingers, don't we? The lady on the dock the night of the first murder was one. Plus red hairs have been found at all the scenes."

"Exactly. There are strands in the hat," I said. "I'll take it to the lab when I'm done here. I also have the last two numbers of her license plate."

"I'll see if I can run that down," she said. "Give me the info."

"Seven, three. Light blue Honda Accord. Not sure of the year but I'd say three to four years old."

She wrote it down in a notebook. "Okay. I'm heading back to the station right now." Molly weaved through the crowd and vanished.

I was finally able to greet Chelsea and the kids. Chelsea allowed me to put my arms around her but didn't touch me back. Grace gave me a huge embrace and cried on my shoulder for a moment. She had been a daddy's girl, so she had to be taking his death hard. I shook hands with Jim but Matt grabbed my arm and led me away.

"Tell me you're going to get this guy, Peter. Promise me." He wiped at his brow and clenched his hands. Matt had had anger issues when he was younger, but he'd since learned to control his rage.

I took Matt by the shoulder and stared into his eyes. "I swear I will find your father's killer. I will do *whatever* it takes. I loved him."

"I feel like I should be doing something." He kicked at the ground.

"The best thing you can do is help your mother and sister. Jim, too. Leave the cop stuff for me, okay?"

A single tear trailed down his cheek. My heart ached for the kid, and I pulled him against me. He didn't return the hug right away but eventually, he wrapped his arms around my back and the dam broke. The young man cried, and I held him until he stepped away.

"Thanks, Peter."

"Call me if you ever need to talk," I said. "I'll always be there for you."

He nodded and shuffled away. I took the opportunity to get away from the crowd and strolled back to my car. Being around emotional people made it even harder to keep my feelings in check.

I'd just unlocked my vehicle when someone called out my name. I turned and saw Aza jogging toward me.

He stopped a few feet away. "Hey, Peter."

"Sorry about the other night," I said. "By the time I got there, you were having fun with a gorgeous young woman."

He blushed and gulped visibly. "Yeah, I got rather tanked."

"Seemed like you were enjoying yourself."

Shrugging, he replied, "I don't remember much of the night, but I'm pretty sure I had a good time."

"What can I do for you?"

"I *really* need to talk to you. Do you have time right now to grab a coffee?"

I glanced at my watch. I wanted to get to work on the case but it seemed Aza had something to say. "Sure. There's a Starbucks a few blocks away. Meet there?"

He smiled and nodded. "Thanks."

I got to the coffee shop first and ordered my usual plus a blueberry muffin. I was munching on it when Aza arrived and placed his order. When he sat, I noticed the name on his cup was spelled Asia. I snickered but he didn't notice. He sipped his java and picked apart a napkin.

"What's on your mind?" I finally asked.

"I should've told you this earlier, but I did something I shouldn't have, so I was afraid of getting in trouble. I'm sorry for keeping it from you. I hope you can forgive me, but I'll take my punishment if you feel it's needed."

"Why don't you tell me what you did before we discuss reprimands?"

He sighed. "Jamey came to me the day he was killed."

"I remember that. He said it was a personal matter."

Aza's eyes darkened. "It wasn't."

"Is that right? Why then?"

"He asked me what information I had access to regarding the *Ashley Madison* hack."

"The adultery site?"

He nodded. "I'm not sure how much you know about that scandal. The group that calls themselves Anonymous got into the site's database and got information on all the members. Several well-known men were exposed, including that married Duggar kid."

I didn't say anything, hoping Aza would continue, which he did.

"There's a site up where wives can check emails to see if their husbands were members."

That was how Fiona Osceola had learned the truth about her husband.

"However, we have different access. When it happened, we set up many different ways to check on things. Sgt. Prince thought it might come in handy in case there were crimes related to it."

I took a bite of muffin and nodded.

"Anyway, Jamey asked if I would verify Tyrone Osceola was a member but also search and see if Julian Ramsey was too."

The first victim! We hadn't had any clues that he'd been a cheater, but there was a lot we didn't know about what he'd done that last day. "And was he?"

"Yes. For several years. And he was communicating with a member during his time in Seattle."

Yeah, this was information I could've used before now. It was something the two guys had in common besides business and money. That still didn't explain why Jamey had been killed or what similarity he had with the first two men. Then it hit me that Aza said he'd done something he shouldn't have.

"Keep going," I said. "There's more, isn't there?"

He avoided my gaze and wrung his hands. "I was nosy and curious about how Jamey had known, so I did another search."

"You checked to see if he was a member of *Ashley Madison*, didn't you?"

He nodded.

"And was he?"

Aza finally looked up and met my gaze. "Yes, he was."

And there it was—a connection to all three victims.

SIX

IT WAS AWESOME TO HAVE A LEAD, EVEN if it did mean focusing on the unsavory aspect of adultery. It wasn't going to be pleasant digging into the scene, but it'd be worth it if it meant catching the killer.

I filled in first Chief Slight, then Molly, regarding the new information.

"This helps our theory that the killer is a woman." Molly sat on the corner of my desk. "It's likely a wife angry about her husband cheating so she's taking it out on other adulterers."

"But how is she choosing her victims?" I asked. "Why these men?"

She toyed with a lock of her hair. "And who is she going to go after next?"

"Well, we have an entire database of potential suspects. I'm just not sure how to go about searching it." I did know someone who had the skills to find the information I needed. I'd left him at Starbucks with a hurried good-bye and a promise we'd discuss it later. I was irate he hadn't come to me earlier and wanted to chew his ass out for not doing so. I'd lost valuable time but he was also someone who could help me on the case. I sighed and dialed the desk sergeant. "Yeah, I need the contact number for Aza in Tech."

"Are you going to tear him a new one?" Molly asked.

"Unfortunately, no," I said as I dialed his number.

"Hello," he answered.

"Aza, it's Detective Tao. You ready to start earning my trust back?"

"I'll do whatever it takes."

"Excellent. Get your ass in here. Right now."

"WHAT ACCESS DO WE HAVE TO THE INFORMATION hacked from *Ashley Madison*?" I asked Aza without preamble when he arrived.

He blinked a couple times before answering, "Everything. They exposed credit card numbers, names, jobs, profiles, email addresses, and accounts that were supposed to be deleted. Literally everything." He gestured to my computer and asked. "May I?"

I pushed my chair to the side and Aza brought up an internal page labeled *Ashley Madison*.

"Like I mentioned before, the high tech division downloaded all the information to save on our servers just in case the information disappeared online."

"That's good news for us, right?" I rubbed my hands together.

"Should give us all the information we'll need," he replied. "Just tell me what I'm looking for."

Molly spoke up. "First, we need to see if any of our victims talked to the same women. The killer could've posed as someone wanting an affair."

"We also need to see if we can pinpoint who the next victim might be."

"Let me bring up the three profiles and see what information they shared. Mainly, members share things that would attract someone to sleep with them over someone else."

All three profiles had their pictures and it was odd seeing an image of Jamey, knowing that he'd been online to cheat on his wife. A flash of anger surged through me, especially now that I suspected it was his adultery that had led to his murder. If he'd simply kept his dick in his pants, he might still be alive.

"Here's something interesting," Aza said. "Ramsey, Osceola, and Jamey all listed their income as more than a hundred grand annually."

That was something I wouldn't have expected from Jamey. He hardly ever mentioned his money to anyone, but the powers of boners are strong. Apparently, Jamey wasn't above using his wealth to get with women.

"The killer could be going after wealthy members of *Ashley Madison*," I murmured. "High-profile men who cheated on their wives."

"So the next victim would be another rich guy," Molly said.

Turning to Aza, I said, "Find me everyone in Seattle and neighboring towns who were exposed. I want a list, prioritized by the most high-profile victim down to the least."

"I can do that, but I can think of one guy who had his affairs exposed and is very high profile. He's been in the paper."

"Who?" I asked.

"Bryce Carrick."

Oh shit. How could I have forgotten about him?

"I've been trying to find Mr. Carrick," Molly said. "Ramsey met with him."

Aza said, "Carrick hasn't been seen in a week, not since he was ousted as CEO and his brother took his place."

"He can't have just disappeared." I paced behind the desk. "He's off somewhere licking his wounds. I'll pay a visit to the company and see what I can find out." I grabbed my coat.

"I'll work on locating Carrick," Molly said. "I have a few ideas." She snapped her fingers, flopped back in her chair and began pounding at the keys.

I glanced at Aza. "Compare the other three profiles with Carrick's. See if they have anything in common. Who they chatted with, made plans with, etc."

"Doubtful, since Carrick was on the down low."

"I know, but I want to be sure. Also, keep working on that list of local victims of the hack. We need to contact them, either in person or by phone. They could be possible targets." I pulled on my coat. "I *do not* want any more dead bodies."

S<small>EATTLE</small>C<small>ARRICK WAS LOCKED UP TIGHT</small>. I<small>T WAS A</small> Sunday, after all, which I hadn't thought about. I did manage to get the attention of a security guard, and he informed me the new CEO, Brendan Carrick, was in the building. I insisted on talking to him, but the guard refused until I flashed my badge and said it was imperative. He left me standing outside, sauntered to a desk, and picked up a phone. A minute later, he came back to me and waved me inside.

"Mr. Carrick told me to bring you up."

Brendan Carrick resembled his brother but wasn't nearly as handsome. He had a thinner face with a sharp, pointed chin.

He shook my hand with a firm grip after I introduced myself. "How can I help you, Detective Tao?"

His office was massive with an incredible view. Obviously expensive pieces of art adorned the wall, and his marble desk appeared more sculpture than useful. I sat across from him in a wooden straight-back chair that gave a new meaning to the word uncomfortable. "I'm looking for your brother."

He screwed up his face. "Why? Is he a suspect in a crime?"

I noted the hopefulness in his voice. "He's a possible witness."

"Oh," he said disappointedly. "I'm afraid I won't be much help. I don't know where my brother is, and I couldn't care less."

Obviously, the siblings weren't close.

"I understand your brother was a victim of the *Ashley Madison* hack."

Brendan made a face as if he'd tasted something disgusting. "Victim? I wouldn't label Bryce a victim. If anyone was victimized, it was Clementine, his wife. She dedicated her life to being a good spouse to him, and he was out whoring around with perverts." He sat forward and put his elbows on his desk. "Bryce simply got what he deserved."

"Your brother's life could be in danger. Doesn't that matter to you?"

"Honestly? Not really." He smirked at my shock. "Someone who might be able to help is Thomas Grainger. He was Bryce's assistant for years. I sent him packing with my brother."

"Do you have a phone number or address?"

"He's probably still in the employee database." He sighed as if I were asking a major favor of him, tapped a few keys on his computer, and then gave me what I'd asked for.

I left and headed for Thomas Grainger's place. He answered excitedly on the first knock, as if he'd been expecting me, but his face dropped when he didn't recognize me.

"Can I help you?"

He was a somewhat odd-looking short guy with a totally shaved head—even his eyebrows were gone. Why in the world had he shaved them off? "I'm Detective Tao with Seattle Homicide. Can I ask you a few questions about Bryce Carrick?"

He furrowed his brow and asked, "Is he okay?"

"He's missing," I answered.

"Oh, wow." He stepped aside, gestured for me to come in ,and led me into a small living room decorated plainly with a leather recliner and a large screen television. There were also blank spots on the wall where pictures had once been.

"We're in the middle of re-decorating," he said to explain the lack of furniture, I supposed.

"Have you seen Mr. Carrick lately?"

He shook his head. "Not since the day we were both fired. I've called him but he hasn't answered. This scandal screwed up everything. I feel for him. He's lost so much."

"As his assistant were you aware of his…indiscretions?"

Thomas blushed, and his entire skull turned red. "Not right

away, but I figured it out. After I let him know I was aware, and didn't care, I helped him plan his meetings."

"You didn't care that he was married or that he was gay?"

"Neither. It's not my place to judge."

"Do you have any idea where Bryce might be now? Any love nests he had?"

He shook his head. "He used different motels all the time. He was paranoid about getting caught."

"For good reason," I said, "considering what happened when the truth came out."

A serious expression crossed his face, and he rubbed his eyebrow-less brow. "It's a shame." I must've been staring because he snickered. "You're wondering why I shave these."

"Actually, yeah." I didn't mean to be rude but the man was offering the information.

"I don't shave them." He waved a hand. "I have a condition called Alopecia. My body doesn't grow hair."

"None at all?"

"Absolutely none. I am entirely hairless."

"Interesting." I gave Grainger my card and left without much more than I'd started with. Thankfully, Molly had had more luck.

"I'm pretty sure Carrick's at a private beach club in Normandy Park," she said.

Normandy Park was a small city ten miles outside of Seattle that was mainly high-end residential.

"You're guessing or you know for a fact?"

"I'm not totally positive," she said. "But I scanned an interview Bryce Carrick did not too long ago. He said he pictured himself like a character from an old TV show. Blake Carrington from *Dynasty*, that nighttime soap from the eighties."

"Yeah?"

"So I searched for anyone checking in under the character's name.

I didn't have luck with that one, but I did find one under the name John Forsythe. That's the name of the actor who played the role."

"Where?"

"Tucker's Point Resort," she answered. "I spoke to the manager, but he refused to confirm it's Carrick without a warrant. You want me to check it out in person?"

"No, I got it."

THE MANAGER OF TUCKER'S POINT RESORT MAY HAVE refused Molly's request over the phone but my badge and decidedly unfriendly face changed his mind.

"Bryce Carrick's life could be in danger," I said, using my growly, bad cop voice. "I need to know if he's staying here or not."

"Yes, he's here. Room one thirteen," the manager replied. "He's been here for seven days now."

"Excellent." I tapped the counter. "I need to speak to him. Will you please call his room and tell him I'm here?"

The guy nodded, picked up the phone, dialed, and waited. Less than a minute later he hung up. "He is not answering, Detective."

"Okay, then let's go to his room."

"Very well, sir."

I followed him out of the office to a row of beachfront rooms.

"These are our suites," he explained. "Only the wealthy can afford them." He rubbed his fingers together making the money gesture.

"Gotcha," I replied.

The manager stopped at room one thirteen and knocked. When there was no response, he peered at me and shrugged.

"Do you know if Mr. Carrick has left?"

"I can't be sure but he usually checks in when he comes and goes." The manager flushed and glanced around. "He has a…guest. I saw him arrive this morning."

"Give me the key," I ordered. If Carrick's *guest* was the killer, Carrick could already be dead.

"I shouldn't."

I glared at him and held out my hand. He handed it over and I shooed him away. "I got this from here. I don't need your help."

He opened his mouth like he was going to argue, but seemed to think better of it. He turned and ambled away. I waited until he was out of sight before I knocked, then did it again when there was no answer. After the third time knocking, I slid the card in the electronic lock. No green light. I slid it again, then again 'til the lock disengaged and the door opened. I pulled my Glock, pushed the door open, and called out, "Hello, Seattle Homicide…"

Before I could continue, a wet towel wrapped around my hand, knocking my gun away and yanking me into the room. I blocked a punch but then my attacker kicked my feet out from under me. It was dark but judging by size and muscle mass my attacker was male. I spun around on my ass, knocking him to the floor. I leapt on top of him, pinning his hands to the floor and sitting on his groin. I still couldn't get a decent glimpse of him, but he was definitely a man—and naked.

"Stop resisting. I'm a cop."

He broke one hand free and connected a blow to my ribs, knocking the breath out of me. Using my weakness to his advantage, he thrust up, pushing me off of him. I rolled to the side, trying to ignore the pain, and managed to stand, but the other guy was quicker than me. He pinned me to the wall, pressing his body against mine. I wasn't sure but it felt like he had a hard-on.

He gripped one hand over my head while my other one, the one I'd been clutching my ribs with, was trapped between me and the wall.

"Who sent you?" he demanded.

I got my arm free and shoved it backward, elbowing him in the solar plexus. He sucked in a breath but didn't release me so I slammed my head backward, colliding into his forehead with an audible thwack, sending him stumbling backward, howling in pain. He clutched his head and appeared dazed. I glanced around, located my gun, and dove for it.

My attacker gained control of his senses and lunged at me, catching me around the waist and tugging me to the floor once more. He landed on top of me and tried to hold me still. Despite his sturdy grip, I twisted around and brought my gun up. He seized my hand and dug his thumb into my wrist, just below the palm, hitting a pressure point and forcing me to drop my weapon once more.

"Goddamn it!" I bellowed.

He reached for my gun, but I wrapped my fingers around his throat and held him still. He grabbed for my throat with both hands, and I managed to block one but not the other. With our hands on one another's throats and my free hand gripping his, we were at a standstill.

"Who are you?" he demanded in a thick voice.

"I'm a cop, you stupid son of a bitch."

"That doesn't mean you're not here to kill me. Someone already tried that once. I'm not taking any chances."

The light from between the curtains allowed me to identify my sparring partner—Bryce Carrick.

"I'm not here to kill you, Carrick, I'm here to save your life. I'm Detective Peter Tao with Seattle Homicide."

He lessened the grip on my neck and I did the same. Neither one of us completely released, however.

"I assume you can prove who you are?" he asked.

"Would the badge in my front pocket satisfy you?"

He nodded. "Let go of my hand so I can check."

"Don't try anything." I released his hand and he scooted back so he could have access to my front pocket. Glancing down, I confirmed his prick was indeed erect. Not that I could say anything,

I was just as hard. Adrenaline had that effect on me, just as it did with many men.

He patted one pocket but the badge was in the other one. He didn't lift his hand as he trailed across, instead, he let it run across the bulge in my pants. Carrick eyed me for a second before retrieving my shield.

He screwed up his face. "Why are you here?"

"Why don't we discuss that *after* you're satisfied I'm not here to kill you?"

He nodded. "We'll release on the count of three."

"'Kay."

"One…two…three."

We let go of one another's throats. He stood, and I rolled to the side.

"Need help up?" He offered a hand but I declined.

I got to my knees then rose. Unfortunately, I got up too quickly and ended up dizzy. He took my arm and steadied me before guiding me to a chair. I offered a mumbled thanks and was grateful we were no longer in the heat of combat or I'd be a dead man.

He flipped on the light, allowing me to get my first full glimpse of his body. Just as his picture had taken my breath away, his naked form did the same. He was in excellent shape for a man in his fifties. He had no gut at all. Instead, he possessed a tight six-pack and bulging pecs. I could see why our fight had been so even.

A light scattering of gray and silver hair dusted his upper chest and around his belly button. A small trail of hair led from his navel to a patch of pubes. There was no manscaping for him, that's for sure. Checking him out did nothing for my aching hard-on, which I could hide in my sitting position. My excitement would be obvious if I were standing so I did my best to will the erection away.

It didn't help that he didn't bother getting dressed before calling into the station. I tried to focus on his words instead of his body while getting a feel for the room. It had a desk and chair, a television, a couch and two chairs, counting the one I sat in. A kitchenette with fridge, stove, and microwave took up the other side of the big room. Behind him was an open door to what I assumed was the bedroom and ensuite bathroom.

After verifying my details, he hung up the phone. "I'm sorry about attacking you. It's been a hellish week."

"Let's just forget that and move on." I stood, grateful my problem had gone away. "I'm going to pick up my gun now, okay?"

"Yes, of course."

He remained still while I retrieved my Glock and holstered it. "Maybe you should get dressed now." I waved a hand in his direction.

"Oh, sorry about that." He put a hand over his genitals. "By the way, there's a frightened guy cowering in the bathroom right now."

I followed Bryce into the bedroom and kept an eye on him as he tugged on a pair of shorts and a black T-shirt that hugged his chest. He caught me eyeing him but I didn't glance away. I met his gaze straight on trying not to lose myself in his dazzling hazel eyes. The corners of his mouth turned up as he opened the bathroom door. "It's safe, Co Co. You can come out now."

A thin, naked, mocha-skinned guy with a towel wrapped around his waist stepped out of the shower. He eyeballed Bryce, then me, his eyes as wide as platters.

"Who's he?" Co Co asked.

"A cop," Bryce answered.

Co Co stiffened, and his Adam's apple bobbed.

"Relax," Bryce said soothingly. "I don't think he's concerned about you and me."

I eyed them both before focusing on Co Co. "How did you two meet?"

"Umm, I…he…" Co Co stammered.

"I answered an ad on Craigslist," Bryce replied. "We arranged a meeting online and through texts. It wasn't exactly on the up and up, Detective. Money changed hands."

"I don't give a shit about that," I said. "I just need to know how long he's been here."

"About two hours," Co Co said.

Bryce picked up a cell from the dresser and handed it over. "You can check my texts."

I took a quick peek at the exchanges, which backed up their story. "I'm going to forward this to my phone so I can check it out further." I sized up Co Co. "Do you advertise just on Craigslist?"

He shook his head. "A few other apps like Grindr and Growlr."

"What about *Ashley Madison*?"

"Never. Isn't that just for straight guys?"

Bryce asked, "Why are you asking about that site?"

"I'll explain in a minute," I told him. To Co Co I said, "I may need to talk to you again." I got his number and told him he could go but to be ready to answer any further questions.

After Co Co departed I gestured for Carrick to sit on the couch. He did and regarded me with an expression I couldn't read.

He pressed a hand to his cheek. "I am so sorry about the fight. Co Co and I were messing around in the shower. When I got out, I heard the key in the door and went into flight or fight mode and obviously chose fight." His shoulders drooped. "I could get in trouble for assaulting a cop couldn't I?"

I clenched my jaw. "That shouldn't be necessary, provided you cooperate."

Carrick nodded agreeably. "Of course."

I crossed my arms and regarded him, trying not to let his looks distract me. "Is it true your affairs with men were exposed in the *Ashley Madison* hack?"

"What does that have to do with what's going on?" His posture stiffened, and the cords in his neck twanged.

"It's connected," I assured him, keeping my voice low so the tension wouldn't rise. "I'll explain everything after I make sure my facts are correct."

"Okay," he sighed and sat back on the couch, lacing his fingers behind his head. "Yes, I was using *Ashley* Madison to meet guys, a fact which was revealed by that *Anonymous* group." He rubbed his temples and mumbled, "Of all the sites I could've chosen."

"There are other similar websites?" I asked.

He cocked an eyebrow. "Literally hundreds of sites and phone apps guys can use to meet each other."

Simply curious, I asked, "Then why use *Ashley Madison*?"

"I like married men."

My shock must have been evident, because he grinned.

"Or at least I like guys who consider themselves straight, guys on the *down low,* so we were all in the same position of wanting it kept quiet. You know, mutually assured destruction." He snorted and laughed. "Turns out that wasn't what I should've worried about."

"Your wife didn't react well?"

"Not even. But Clementine was more concerned about her image than my infidelity." When I didn't respond, he added, "She was furious that I made her look stupid."

"She wasn't angry you were gay or that you'd cheated on her but rather upset the truth about your affairs had been exposed."

"You got it."

"And you lost your company?"

"Yeah, the board of directors and my bastard brother voted me out. Brendan's been waiting for something like this to happen since our father passed away."

I don't know what possessed me to turn the screws, but the fact that he was a cheater annoyed me. "So let me get this straight. You lost your company and your wife just to get your rocks off?" In my mind he deserved any crap I gave him and had no room to complain. He'd made his own choices and now he was facing the consequences.

His face reddened and he ran his hands through his hair. "And my son," he replied. "That's the most important thing. Clementine won't let me see Zach. I could give a crap about anything else, but I love my son."

"How is she stopping you from seeing him?"

A tear slid down his cheek, and he quickly wiped it away. "You're not here to talk about my personal life, Detective Tao. Why don't we focus on the reason you broke into my motel room."

"I used a key. I didn't break in." I smirked when he rolled his eyes. I grabbed a chair and scooted it so I could face him with a coffee table between us. "Do the names Tyrone Osceola, Julian Ramsey, or Jamey Nolan sound familiar to you?"

"No."

"They're men, wealthy men, with profiles on *Ashley Madison*."

"Well, they're just a few out of thousands of men whose lives have blown up."

"They're also dead."

His eyes widened.

"They were murdered and had their dicks cut off." The expression on his face was priceless. He grabbed his crotch as if to check his junk was still there. I didn't feel sympathy for him, but he needed to wake up to the danger he could be in.

SEVEN

Bryce covered his mouth and gagged as if he was going to puke. I dashed to his side.

"Are you okay?"

He nodded but didn't move his hand right away.

"If you're here, you must think I could be next."

"If not next, then somewhere on the list. You said someone tried to attack you. When was that?"

"Wednesday," he said. "It was late. At least nine because it was dark out. I'd had too much to drink so I trudged back to the Warwick Hotel where I was staying. The lobby was swarming with reporters all seeking my official statement. I went around the back trying to find another way in and entered an alley."

I shot him an incredulous glance.

"Yeah, it was dumb but I wasn't thinking right. I just knew there was a door into the kitchen that way. Anyway, somebody came up behind me and wrapped his arm around my neck. If I'd been sober, he wouldn't have even got that far."

Judging by the way Carrick had fought with me, I figured that was true.

"I wasn't so wasted that he was going to get the upper hand."

"What did you do?"

"Flipped him over and tossed. Something dropped to the ground. Probably a weapon."

"Then what?"

"I got the hell out of there. I couldn't fight or I would've held my ground. Again, it was fight or flight but that time I picked flight."

"Probably for the best," I said. "Do you have any clue who it was?"

He shrugged. "I didn't see their face if that's what you're asking. I assumed it was some investor who'd lost their ass when the stock crashed."

"Can you tell me anything else about your attacker?"

"He wasn't very heavy," he answered. "Not even two hundred pounds, I'd say. Probably more like a buck fifty. When I flipped him, I stumbled afterward because I'd misjudged the weight. Being drunk didn't help, but regardless, it wasn't a large man."

If Bryce's attacker was the same person who had killed the first three victims, and I'd bet money it was, then this was new and useful information.

"Are you sure it was a man?" I asked. "Is it possible it was a woman?"

He pursed his lips then gave a half shrug. "I guess it's a possibility."

We were both quiet for a moment then he asked, "What are we doing to find the killer?"

I frowned and gave him a hard smile that I hoped made it clear this wasn't a *we* situation. "*I* am going to follow any leads my team develops. *You* are going to stay under the radar, preferably here where hardly anyone knows you are. *You* need to refrain from having any guests."

His face clouded over, and he clenched his jaw. "I can't just hang out and wait for something to happen or for someone to come after me."

I rose and towered over him. "Yes, you can and you will. I don't need you gallivanting around."

Bryce bounded to his feet and glowered at me, attempting to use his muscles to intimidate me. I almost snickered at the thought.

"I'm not the type of man who can just sit around. I'm a man of action."

I sighed and rolled my eyes. "I don't care what you are or what you *think* you are. I have too much to do to babysit you. Got it?"

"I was a marine, Detective Tao. I can take care of myself. Hell, I held off an attacker while I was drunk." He inched closer, invading my space.

I didn't back off. I just peered up into his stunning hazel eyes. "While that is so very impressive," I said, sarcasm dripping from my lips, "I'm afraid it won't change my mind. I need to know you're as safe as possible so I can focus on *everyone*."

"You do know who I am, right?" he bellowed. "I'm not—"

I'd had enough of his arrogant attitude. I poked him in the chest hard enough to shut him up. "I know who you are. You're a spoiled rich man who is so used to getting your own way you think you can bully me into allowing you to do whatever you want."

"That's not—"

"And you're the piece of shit who cheated on your wife."

"Now wait a second. You don't know the whole story."

I snorted loudly. "I don't *need* to know. It doesn't matter. I have the facts. You are married. You are having affairs. You broke your vows. I don't give a shit about your *reasons*."

Bryce's mouth opened and closed a few times but said nothing, his body sagging until he flopped back on the couch. "Fine, fine, whatever. I'll stay hidden." He waved a hand. "Now get the fuck out of here."

I dropped my card on the coffee table and took off without another word.

By the time I'd returned to the station, Aza had formed a decent list of local victims of the *Ashley Madison* hack. Most were middle and lower class men but there were a handful of men in the upper class levels. Well, not all were men, there were a couple women whose affairs had been exposed, including one wealthy lady. There was also a guy married to a man who had used the same down low section as Bryce.

I'd been at my desk an hour or so, still fuming over the argument with Bryce, when Aza called me over.

"Detective Tao, you might want to see this." Aza showed me a profile with the name *Blondstud.*

"Most of the accounts have the user's real name," he said. "But not this one. He paid with a money order and used a disposable email address."

"Smart."

"Why more men didn't do that, I don't know."

"So there's no way for us to know who he is?"

"Give me more credit than that, Detective. The fact that he did all this to keep his identity a secret just made me push harder. Disposable email addresses aren't entirely confidential. There are ways to find out who it belongs to. It took me a bit but I did finally get a name."

"Skip to the important part, Aza."

"Yes, sir." He closed that page and opened up a page from the Seattle Police Department's staff directory. I recognized the face— Dave Gomez, member of the gang task force. I'd met the guy but didn't know him very well.

"Another cop?" I asked.

"Yup."

"If Gomez's wife went on the same site as Osceola's, would she have been able to figure out her husband was a member?"

"Depends." Aza shrugged. "If she used his regular email address, no. However, if she knew about the disposable one, then yes."

I patted his back. "Thanks, man." I dashed upstairs to where the gang task force utilized a small room as their headquarters. I knocked on the door then poked my head in. Gomez and Doyle, the task force director, sat at a table having a heavy discussion but stopped as soon as they spotted me.

"Detective Tao, how can I help you?" Doyle asked.

"I'm sorry to interrupt, but I need to speak to Gomez in private."

"You need to talk to me?" He put a hand on his chest and scrunched his brow.

"Is there a place we can chat alone?"

"I have paperwork." Doyle stood. "We can finish this conversation later."

Doyle slipped past me, and I shut the door after I walked in. I sat across from Gomez, my arms on the table and fingers entwined.

"What can I do for you, Tao?"

"This is kind of a sensitive subject, Gomez, but I'm just going to get right to the point."

He swallowed hard and said, "Okay."

"Are you cheating on your wife?"

Gomez's face reddened, and he leaned forward. "What the hell business is it of yours?"

I raised a palm. "I'm not trying to pry into your personal life."

"Sure as hell feels like you are."

"I assume you heard about Detective Nolan's death."

He relaxed somewhat. "Yeah."

"He was the third victim killed in the same manner."

"Oh, damn," he uttered.

"They also had their dicks chopped off."

His mouth slackened. "What the hell?"

"We believe it has to do with their extra-marital affairs," I said. "They were all members of *Ashley Madison*."

Gomez's gaze became unfocused, and he rubbed at his eyebrow.

"I believe you've heard of the site."

"Sure, I've, uhh, heard of it. On the news, I mean."

After clearing my throat, I gave him a condescending smile.

"Gomez…Dave, you don't have to lie to me."

"What? I'm not…" His body sagged, and he rubbed his face. "Damn it. Fine, yeah, I am—was a member of *Ashley Madison*."

"Does your wife know?"

He paused, then shook his head. "I think she suspects, but I used a different email address so she hasn't found out."

"It's not my business, but you might want to tell her."

"Why would I do that now?" he asked. "I deleted my account. I learned my lesson. I don't see why she needs to know."

"There's a killer out there, and I don't know who the next victim will be. It appears he's going after wealthy men first, but he could change his MO. He already killed one cop, who's to say he won't come after you?"

Gomez rolled his eyes. "I can take care of myself, Tao."

"I'm sure you can, but what if he comes after you through your family? Wouldn't you rather she find out from you rather than from some psycho using her to get to you?"

It didn't take him long to make the right choice. "I guess you're right." He sighed.

"I'm tempted to assign you protection. If another cop is killed, I'd be spending the rest of my life in the evidence room in the basement."

He shook his head. "No, I don't need a detail."

"It may not be up to you. I have to tell Slight."

He leaned in. "You can't just *forget* to tell her?"

I set my jaw. "Not a chance in hell. If she found out I kept it from her I'd be the one with my balls chopped off."

Gomez sniggered. "Fair enough."

"Another cop?" Slight sat back in her chair and rubbed her temples.

"Is it that much of a surprise that cops have affairs?" I asked.

Slight shook her head. "Not that—just that they would use a site like *Ashley Madison*."

"At least Gomez was smarter about it than Osceola."

She glared at me. "That *does not* help at all, Detective Tao."

I folded my arms across my chest. "Gomez doesn't want a protective detail, but I told him you would make the call."

"What do you think?"

"If I were to hazard a guess, I'd say Gomez is lower on the killer's list. It seems as if our killer is targeting the upper class. If we don't bring him in, he may eventually work his way to the rest of the hack victims, but for now, there are other men the killer is more likely to go after."

"Okay, no protective detail…for now," Slight said. "Thanks for keeping me informed."

That was my dismissal so I stepped out of her office and returned to the squad room just as Gomez and a small woman with bright red hair stormed down the stairs.

"Diana," Gomez pleaded. "Please, I think we need to discuss this in private."

She held up a hand and glared at him. "Dave, this is not the time or place to discuss your…" she considered her words before lowering her voice to a whisper. "Your affairs."

He gripped her shoulders but she shook him off.

"Right now I want to talk to Detective Tao about the case," she said. "Is that okay with you?"

Gomez sighed and glanced around the room, turning red when he realized everyone was staring at them. When he spotted me, he waved me over. I didn't want to get in the middle of Gomez's mess, but her red hair had me interested.

"Tao, this is Diana, my wife. She has a few questions."

"Why don't we go someplace private," I said and led them to an interview room.

Diana sat in one seat at the table and I took the one across from her. Gomez crossed his arms and stood in the corner, appearing as if he'd rather be anywhere else. I didn't have much sympathy for him. He'd cheated on his wife, after all.

"What can you tell me about the case?" Diana asked.

"I'm afraid I can't give too many details."

She waved a hand. "I'm a cop's wife, Detective Tao. I understand all the rules. Just tell me what you can."

"I have three victims all killed the same way, all with the same wounds on their bodies. All were members of *Ashley Madison*."

"Just like my husband." She turned and shot daggers at Gomez with her eyes. If looks could kill, he'd be dead.

"Yes, that's correct," I answered. "We came across his profile while searching for local men."

"He must've hidden his tracks well." One arm hung straight down her side, and she gripped it with the other hand.

I didn't say anything—what could I?

"Your marriage is none of my business, Mrs. Gomez. But I wouldn't want you in danger. Whether you split up or not, the killer could still try to use you to get to your husband."

"What are the chances of that?"

"I'm not a psychic, but I'd say somewhat low. He seems to be targeting higher profile men. Wealthier men."

Gomez's phone rang, and he peered at it guiltily. "It's Doyle."

She sighed and waved a hand. "Go, I don't need you here. I'll see you at home."

He tried to kiss the top of her forehead, but she pulled away. He stared at her for a moment but she fixed her gaze on the floor, and eventually, he shook his head and stepped out.

"I'm sorry it had to come out like this," I said.

"I should thank you, Detective Tao."

Huh? "Thank me? Why?"

"For getting Dave to confess."

"You already knew?" I asked.

She nodded. "This isn't the first time he's strayed. He doesn't think I know about that other time, though. But I do."

"How did you figure it out this time?" He'd done an outstanding job of keeping his real name off his profile.

"I've snooped on his phone and computer. I couldn't sign into his email, but I knew about the disposable address. When the *Ashley Madison* thing happened, I plugged it into the site and got a hit."

"Why didn't you confront him?"

She shrugged. "I was pretty sure he had ended it by then. Right after the news about the hack hit, he got all sweet and lovey-dovey. Maybe he learned his lesson this time."

"So you're not leaving him?"

"When I married him, I swore it was 'til death do us part, and I meant it."

"You're in the minority, Mrs. Gomez. Most of the women have left their husbands because of *Ashley Madison*, but I respect your decision."

She stood and extended a hand. She had a weak grip. "Thanks for talking to me."

"Let me know if you need anything else."

"Oh, you've given me all the information I need."

"WAS THAT ABOUT WHAT I THINK IT WAS about?" Molly asked when I returned to my desk.

I nodded.

"Not sure if you noticed, but she fits the profile of our killer."

I had indeed noticed. She had the right hair color, the right body size, and she was a scorned woman.

"Should I consider her a person of interest?" Molly asked.

I didn't want to suspect a cop's wife but I wouldn't be a decent detective if I discredited her simply because she was married to a police officer. "Yeah, we have to," I answered.

"How are we going to approach this?" Molly asked. "Are you going to interview her?"

I shook my head and steepled my fingers in front of my lips. "I don't think that's the way to go. I'd rather see what we can find out without alerting her."

"Here's something interesting," Aza spoke up. "It seems Mrs. Gomez has a temper. She was arrested on domestic violence three years ago. The neighbors called 911 because of the yelling. Officers responded and found Mrs. Gomez hitting Dave with a broom."

"Interesting," I said. "I wonder if that was the first time she got physical."

"Or if it was something that happened more than once?"

"Exactly. If she's a violent woman, I could see her being the killer."

"How're you going to find out?" Molly questioned.

"I think I'm gonna have to talk to Dave and hope he doesn't go to Diana with our suspicions." I glanced at my watch. It was late and my brain was getting foggy, but if Diana was our killer, I didn't want to risk her doing it again. I didn't have the energy to stay awake on a stake-out, so I got permission from Slight to have her tailed.

I grabbed two patrol officers by the names of Nita Hurst and Sammy Estrada and told them I had an assignment they had to keep to themselves. "It's extremely important you don't tell anyone what you're doing. Do you understand?"

They both nodded eagerly.

"You'll need to change back into your regular clothes then go to the motor pool and get an unmarked vehicle."

"Yes, sir," Hurst said.

"You'll be watching Diana Gomez," I said in a hushed tone.

Estrada's eyes widened. "Is that the wife of—?"

"Yes," I said, cutting him off. "And that's why it has to stay between us. No one else can know what you're doing or who you're following."

They exchanged glances and both nodded.

"We won't say a word," Hurst replied.

"You better not or there will be consequences." I gave them the address and my phone number. "Call me if she leaves the house. Follow from a distance. Don't let her realize she's being followed."

"Yes, sir," Estrada said. "Thank you for the opportunity."

I DIDN'T GET HOME UNTIL AFTER EIGHT P.M., and, despite the extremely long day, I doubted I could immediately go to bed. Everything that had happened ran in a loop through my head. After stripping down to my boxer briefs, I settled down on my couch with a glass of wine and flipped through the channels, stopping on *Naked Gun*. That's what I needed—a good laugh.

Half an hour into the movie, I was relaxed and laughing when my doorbell rang. I was shocked when I peered through the peephole and saw Bryce on the other side. I tore it open. "What the hell are you doing here?"

He pushed his way inside without an invitation, and I stood there in incredulity for a moment before shutting the door and following him.

"What the hell are you doing here?" I demanded again.

He pointed at me. "Who are you to judge me? You don't know my situation."

That was why he was here, because he was mad I'd chewed his ass for being a lying, cheating bastard? "How do you know where I live? I'm not listed."

Bryce put his hands on his hips and rolled his eyes. "I'm a millionaire tech nerd. I can find out just about anything I want, Detective Peter Tao. Or should I call you Bae?"

I blanched at his use of my real first name. My parents were the only ones who ever used it. I hadn't even told Jamey. "If you have a problem with me, I suggest you speak to my boss. In the morning. At the station. *This* is my home."

"Yeah," he replied. "I just wanted to tell you that you have no right to judge me for the decisions in my life."

"Like I said before, I don't need to know the extenuating circumstances. I know the facts. You're a married man and you cheated on your wife. Nothing else matters."

His face reddened, and he came at me with a clenched fist. I didn't know if he was going to punch me, but I wasn't going to let him try. I grabbed his wrist and twisted, forcing it behind his back and upward. The move would shut a normal man down, but I'd forgotten Bryce Carrick wasn't a normal man. He lowered himself enough to ease the pressure on his arm, backed up into me, and flipped me over his sholder.

I landed on the floor with a loud whomp. Bryce's eyes widened and he gasped when he realized what he'd done.

"Oh, my God, I'm sorry. It was instinct." He held out a hand to help me up. I took it but didn't stand. Instead, I twisted and forced him to the floor. I crawled on top and grabbed for his hands, hoping to hold him down. Instead, he gripped my wrists and we fought for control.

"Feeling frisky, Bae?"

Using my name just pissed me off even more, and I bore down, forcing his arms over his head and to the floor. With me on top, holding his arms down, it appeared I was in control, but it was just an illusion. He shifted, and a second later, we were in the opposite position—him above me, holding my hands to ground.

He hovered above me, his face just an inch from mine. "You're strong, Bae. But I think I'm just a bit stronger."

"My name is Peter," I growled out.

He snickered. "Bae fits you so much better. Especially in this position." His gaze ran over my bare chest.

"Enough!" I said. "Get off me."

Bryce released my arms but continued straddling me. "You sure you don't want to stay like this?" He thrust his hips, dragging his ass across my erection.

I glared at him but didn't reply. He shrugged and stood, once again holding out a hand. I pushed it away and got up on my own.

"Why are you coming down on me for being gay when you're just as queer as I am?"

"I'm not coming down on you for that, and I am not gay." I regretted the statement as soon as it was out of my mouth.

He chuckled and gestured to my hard-on. "Your body says otherwise."

I could blame it on the adrenaline, but it didn't matter. "My sexual preference isn't any concern of yours."

After marching into my bedroom, I threw on a pair of sweats and a white T-shirt. Bryce was sitting on my couch drinking my wine when I returned to the living room.

"I take it you're in the closet," he said.

I considered denying it but didn't see the point. "I'd appreciate it if you didn't say anything."

He waved a hand. "Your secret is safe. But I'm still confused about why you're so pissed at *me* for being gay."

I retrieved a second wine glass from the kitchen and poured myself a fresh drink. "It's not you being queer that pisses me off, it's the fact that you're married."

Bryce leaned back and sipped. "I've known I was gay since I was a kid, but I grew up in a conservative family. My father would've blown a gasket if I had come out. I decided it wasn't worth the hassle. Then I joined the Marines. Even with d*on't ask, don't tell* being repealed, it still isn't the most welcoming environment. After ten years, I got out so I could be free to date who I wanted."

Apparently, he felt the need to tell me his story, and I had to admit I was somewhat curious. "But you didn't." I sat on the couch sideways so I could face him.

"No. I didn't. You see, I started working at Dad's company. Not only was he grooming me to succeed him at SC, I'd found my niche, and that was all I wanted to do. I realized coming out would put that in danger so I decided to put that off until I was in a better position. It was better than the Marines. At least it was easier to find men to spend a night or two with."

His motives made more sense to me, but I still couldn't condone what he'd done.

"I met a guy named Emmett, a hot young African-American guy who enjoyed sex as often as possible. We spent the weekend at his motel room. I thought Emmett didn't want anything serious. Turns out he did want something. Pay day."

"He blackmailed you?"

He nodded. "Had pictures and everything. I paid him a hundred grand, and I thought that was the end of it."

"But it wasn't?" I asked.

Bryce shook his head and tugged on his ear. "His sister ended up with the pictures."

"Sister?"

"Yeah, Clementine."

"Your wife?" I gasped.

He sighed. "Yeah, she wanted more than a one-time pay day. I didn't see a way out of it."

"So you married her?"

"It wasn't the perfect situation by any shot. However, she said she didn't care who I slept with as long as it remained private. It was a marriage in name only. And it's worked out okay for almost twenty years. Clementine isn't pissed because I cheated on her. She's embarrassed because *everybody* knows her husband is a fag."

The word made me cringe.

"Her word, not mine."

I finished off the wine with a big swig. "Sorry, that sucks."

"Does it make you look at me a little less harshly?"

I had to admit it did. I gave him a slight nod.

"I didn't mean to dump on you like this," he said. "It's just been a stressful couple of weeks after some crazy years. I don't have any friends, not real ones, anyway."

I'd always figured being rich would take care of all my problems, but for Bryce, it seemed the money just made things worse.

He stood. "I'm sorry for everything. Coming here and fighting." He stumbled and put a hand to his face.

"Are you okay?"

"Just tired," he replied. "I haven't slept much, and it's all hitting me at once." He reached for the door and I noticed his hand shaking.

"How long has it been since you ate anything?"

"Ummm…I don't remember."

I put my hand on his back and led him back to the couch. "Sit. I'll make you a couple sandwiches. Peanut butter and jelly okay?"

He flopped down and nodded. "Thanks."

I slapped together a couple sandwiches and returned to Bryce, handing them to him. He scarfed them down and licked his fingers clean. "Thanks." He stood. "I guess I'll go now."

Pressing on his shoulders, I made him sit back down. "You're too exhausted to drive anywhere. You can sleep here."

He waggled his eyebrows and shot me a mischievous grin.

"On the couch," I amended.

"Are you sure you don't want me in bed with you?"

Actually, yes, I did. I'd love to sleep with him. Not that there'd be much sleep if we shared a bed. "I'll grab you a blanket."

"Your loss," he muttered as I strolled away.

I believed that one hundred percent.

He was sound asleep when I came back. He'd taken off his shirt so I took a moment to admire his chest before covering him with the blanket.

It was incredibly hard getting to sleep knowing one of the sexiest men I'd ever met was in the other room. Add in the fact it seemed he was more than willing to have some fun, and it took every ounce of strength not to drag the man into my room.

EIGHT

THE SMELL OF BACON WOKE ME IN THE morning. Dressed only in a pair of sweats, I shuffled into the kitchen. Bryce stood at the stove, frying bacon and scrambling eggs. He was shirtless and his pants hung low on his hips, exposing the top of his ass. Man, I wanted to reach in and squeeze those gorgeous butt cheeks.

"Good morning, Bae."

"Peter," I growled.

He chuckled. "We're both half-naked, and I'm making you breakfast. I don't get to be a tiny bit more personal?"

"Even the men I sleep with don't get to use that name." I leaned against the counter and crossed my arms.

"I think it's a beautiful name and fits you perfectly." He scooped some eggs and bacon onto a plate, and I took it. I shook some pepper on the eggs and sat at the kitchen table. He joined me a moment later.

"Thanks," I mumbled between bites. "I don't usually eat breakfast. I'm not much of a cook."

"Judging by what's in your kitchen, I can see that. Not that I can say much. I've had cooks my entire life. This"—he waved over the food—"is about the best I can do."

I finished the meal in silence, waited for him to be done, and then rinsed the plates and put them in the dishwasher.

"What are your plans for the day?" he asked.

I cocked an eyebrow. "Why're you asking?"

"I'm hoping you might change your mind and allow me to come along. It's not like I can't take care of myself in a bad situation."

"You're a possible victim. I can't be taking you with me and putting you in danger. I need you to stay out of sight."

"I'm not used to sitting on my ass not doing anything," he said. "Right now, I have nothing in my life. No business, no son. Before this happened, I was going stir crazy. Now I can't concentrate on anything but this."

"I'm sorry, but you are not coming with me. Maybe you should figure out what you're going to do with your life without the business. I assume your money is still yours?"

"Yeah. Until Clementine gets her hooks in me during the divorce."

"So you have plenty of cash to do whatever you want. I suggest using your free time to decide what comes next in the life of Bryce Carrick." I wiped down the counter. "I'm going to take a shower and get ready for work. Lock the front door behind you."

A few minutes later, I tried not to think about Bryce as hot water pounded against my back and I ran a bar of soap over my body. My place was empty after the shower. I should've been relieved he had left like I asked, but I was actually rather sad. The man was intriguing, and I wanted to know more about him, but he was too close to the case. Even if I was interested in pursuing something, he was forbidden, at least until after the case was over. At that point, well, I'd figure things out then.

BY THE TIME I ARRIVED AT THE STATION, I'd managed to push thoughts of Bryce to the back of my mind so I could focus on the case.

I checked my email and saw a message from Jill.

Hair found at Jamey's has DNA and is in the system. No matches yet.

The red hair in the hat you found at the funeral didn't have DNA but there was glue on it. That means it came from a wig.

A wig? I could understand the killer wearing a wig to disguise herself but why make it the same color as her natural hair? It would make more sense to use a different shade.

Just one more question to find an answer to.

Molly, Aza, and I took a few minutes to fill each other in on our plans for the day.

"I'm contacting as many of the hack victims as possible," Molly said. "I'm organizing a meeting with them later this afternoon so you can do a mass briefing."

"Sounds good," I said.

"I'll continue compiling our list of victims of the hack who live in Seattle." Aza tapped a pencil on the desk. "I'm dealing with profiles like Gomez's, ones that are a little harder to track down. But don't worry, I'll find them."

Molly and I chuckled. "I have no doubt about that, man," I replied. "I also want you to dig into Diana Gomez's online activity."

"What are you working on, Detective?" Molly asked.

"I going to speak to Dave, then I'm heading over to the alley behind the Warwick Hotel where Bryce Carrick was attacked. I doubt I'll find anything useful since it's been so long, but it couldn't hurt."

I headed over to the gang task force area and caught Dave changing his shirt.

"You got a minute to talk?" I asked.

He glanced at his watch. "I'm off. Can it wait 'til later?"

"I'm afraid not. It's rather important."

"Okay. What's up?"

I chewed on my lip, unsure how he would take my line of questioning.

"I don't like poking into your personal life, but I'm afraid I don't have a choice."

He furrowed his brow and glowered at me.

"Is your wife a violent person?"

Dave's face reddened angrily. "What the hell kind of question is that?"

I held up a hand. "I'm sorry about this, man. I truly am. But it's important or I wouldn't be asking."

He scrubbed at his face but didn't speak.

"I've seen Diana's arrest report. She beat you with a broom."

"We had a fight. You're not married or you'd know what it's like. It can get pretty heated."

"Had it happened before? Or since?" I asked.

Dave paced a few steps. "Why are you asking this?"

"It pertains to my case."

"Your serial killer investigation?"

I nodded. "Like I said, it's important."

Dave took a deep breath and exhaled. "Yeah. It has."

"A lot?"

"Nothing that major. It's not like I'm an abused husband or anything."

If she had beaten him more than once, he was indeed a victim but it was hard for anyone to admit that. I imagined it was even harder for a cop to acknowledge it, even to himself.

"How many times?"

"Maybe a dozen times over the space of ten years. I've managed to avoid the cops. She gets angry. Most of the time rightfully so."

"She uses her fists?"

He nodded. "The broom a couple times. A bat once or twice. Broke my arm. I made up a story to explain the injury."

"Would you say her anger has been getting worse over the years?"

Dave pursed his lips and ran a hand down his chest. "Yeah, I hadn't thought of it until you asked just now. The first few times, it was just her fists or she threw things."

The more he talked, the more Diana fit the profile.

"Do you know her whereabouts for Tuesday, Wednesday, or Thursday?"

"'Fraid not," he answered. "I've been working graveyard for months. The past two weeks, I haven't had a day off."

I wanted to ask where he found the time to cheat on his wife if he was working so much, but I knew it didn't matter how busy a man was. If he wanted to cheat, he would find a way.

"Can you tell me what this is all about?" he asked. "Diana's not a suspect, is she?"

My silence supplied the answer, and his eyes bulged.

"You think my wife is a murderer?"

"I'm afraid so." I provided him with the profile, pointing out where his wife fit the different aspects.

"I know she has a temper, but I don't think she's a killer."

"I have my crew checking out her activities. If we can prove she was somewhere other than the murder scenes, then I'll gladly admit she isn't our serial killer. Until that happens, I have to consider her. I'm not discounting other ideas, though. I have other lines of investigation I'm following."

"Damn, I just can't believe this."

"You can't tell her, Dave. I know that's going to be tough, but she cannot know we're looking at her. She could run."

"Fine, I understand. I don't like it, but I won't say anything to her. You have to know I don't think she's the one, but I'll see what I can find where she was on the nights of the murder without alerting her."

Before I left to check out the Warwick, I assigned another set of officers to take over the stakeout from Hurst and Estrada, who reported the suspect hadn't left the house all night.

I WASN'T EXPECTING TO FIND ANYTHING IN THE alley, considering it had been four days since Bryce had been attacked. However, I had to exhaust every possible lead. After putting on rubber gloves, I threw aside bags of trash that had been tossed on the ground and pushed around the heavy green dumpsters. I was about to climb into a bin when the back door to the Warwick opened and a guy in all white, complete with chef's hat, stepped out. He lit up a cigarette and took a puff before he noticed me.

"Hey," he said. "Looking for something?"

"You could say that," I replied. "There was an incident a few nights ago. Someone was attacked."

"Is that right?" He sniffed, covered one nostril, and blew a snot rocket.

"Yeah. There's a chance a weapon was dropped. I'm hoping it's still around here somewhere."

"Hmm." He was trying to sound disinterested but the flutter of his eyes and the way his left hand started shaking told me it was an act.

I removed my gloves, offered my hand to him, and he took it. "Detective Peter Tao. Seattle Homicide."

"Marty Hines."

"You the chef here at the Warwick?"

He nodded.

"Don't suppose you've seen anything that might be useful to me?"

"Huh?"

I repeated my question even though I knew he'd heard me perfectly fine.

"Well, I wouldn't want to be accused of hiding evidence or anything like that," he said. "I mean, hypothetically, if I did find something and kept it, it wouldn't be a crime, would it?"

"Not if you hand it over right now," I said in my deepest, best scary cop voice.

He opened the door and cocked his head for me to follow him. Just inside was a small break room with half a dozen lockers. Marty opened the second one and retrieved a steak knife.

"I found it Thursday morning," he said. "It was partially hidden under the dumpster. I don't normally pick things up off the ground but this is a Victorinox Rosewood Straight Edge. Spendy motherfuckers, ya know what I mean?" He held the blade in his hand, flipping it over again and again. "Only professional chefs can afford this type of knife."

"What did you do with it after you picked it up?" I had a feeling I wasn't going to like the answer.

"Washed it."

I sighed and rubbed my temples. There went any chance of finding fingerprints on the knife, if it was even the murder weapon. "I'm afraid I'm going to need to take that from you, Marty."

He sighed and handed it over. "I was afraid of that. I kind of figured I wouldn't get to hold onto it anyway."

"Why is that?"

"Thursday afternoon there was a lady in the alley searching for it, too."

"What did she look like?"

"Short, petite redhead."

"Did you talk to her?"

He shook his head and replied, "She took off like the Flash the minute I came out."

"Call me if you think of anything else." I handed him my card.

Still eyeing the knife, he said, "Any chance I can get that back?"

"I'll tell you what, Marty. If this turns out not to be the weapon I'm after, then I'll bring it back."

"Fair enough."

I headed back to the station, calling Jill enroute. "I may have found the first murder weapon. I'm on the way to log it into evidence right now."

"I'll have one of my techs get it so we can start running tests on it ASAP."

Chief Slight was stepping out of an interview room when I ambled into the squad room.

"Seems like you were right to put your faith in Officer Whitmore."

"What happened?"

"She found a witness to the Ramsey murder."

I rubbed my hands together. "I knew she had it in her. How'd she do it?"

Molly exited the room right then and Slight said, "I'll let her fill you in."

Turning to Molly, I put my hands on my hips and regarded her. "Fill me in."

She tried—and failed—to contain her excitement. "Aza provided me with a list of local women Ramsey had chatted with. Six in total. Five were easy to contact. The sixth one was not. I didn't even have her name at first. She'd used a fake one on her account and paid with bitcoin. It wasn't easy but I figured it out."

"How?" I asked.

"I tried to use facial recognition with the pictures on her account but most of them weren't full face shots so that didn't help. Instead, I enhanced the pictures and checked out the landmarks in the background. Once I had those identified, I ran a comparison through Instagram and grabbed all pictures that were taken at the same spot at roughly the same time of the year. Then I narrowed parameters to women and then age groups. Turned out this woman took pictures she shared on Instagram and cropped them for use on *Ashley Madison*."

Damn impressive.

"Her name is Eloise Nash. She's been staying with her younger brother."

"Is she the woman we saw on the Walmart footage?"

"No. Height, weight, and hair color are all different. Plus, this woman didn't text with Ramsey. They communicated purely through private messages on the site."

"What did your witness see?" I asked.

"I was just about to get her official statement," she answered.

"Join me?"

I stretched out my arm toward the room where Eloise Nash was waiting. "After you."

Eloise Nash was pacing the room when Molly and I entered. She was rather tall and on the heavy side with light brown skin and short, curly gray hair. She wore a pink and purple dress with a poofy skirt and loose waist.

"Eloise Nash, I'm Detective Peter Tao. I'm here to record your official statement."

"Yeah, yeah, okay," she said nervously.

"Why don't you have a seat and we can begin?"

She pulled out the metal chair, sat, tugged down her skirt and crossed her legs. The way she held one hand near her mouth told me she was a smoker.

"How do you know Julian Ramsey?" Molly asked.

"We met online through *Ashley Madison* and have been chatting for a week. We were supposed to meet Monday night down at the docks." She paused and examined her long nails for a moment.

"Did something happen?" Molly kept her voice soft and low.

Eloise sniffled and wiped at her eyes. "Yeah. You could say something happened."

"I'm sorry, but I need you to tell me precisely what happened. I know it's tough."

"I was running late and didn't see Julian at first. It was dark and hard to see anything. I was looking around when I heard an odd noise. That's when I saw Julian and the other person."

"What did you see?"

She uncrossed and recrossed her legs and rubbed a hand down her skirt. "I saw them—the other person—yanking a knife out of Julian's neck. I don't know why I didn't scream or why I didn't run away. I was literally frozen in fear." Tears began streaming down her face. "Julian went down to the ground like that." She snapped her fingers.

"And then what happened?" Molly questioned.

"The person straightened Julian's body then tugged down his pants. I was so scared. Terrified. But I couldn't move. I tried to tell my legs to move but it didn't work. Not until after what the killer did next. That kicked in my flight response and I got the hell out of there."

"And what was it the killer did?"

Eloise covered her mouth and closed her eyes for a moment like she was re-living the situation. "They grabbed Julian's...penis. I thought they were just gonna fondle it or something. That would've been bad enough. But that's not what they did. No, they took their knife and sliced off his dick." She burst into tears. "God damn it, they chopped his prick off right in front of me, and I didn't do a thing. I ran and hid."

Molly stood and dragged her chair next to Eloise and patted her leg. "There was nothing you could've done. Julian was dead the moment that knife cut his spinal cord. You did what was best for you. There's no shame in that. None at all."

Impressed, I watched Molly calm her witness so we could continue the interview.

"What can you tell us about the killer?" Molly asked. "Height. Weight. Gender."

"I'm not sure if it was a man or woman. I didn't get a good look at their face. They were on the short side. Small body. Red hair."

That matched what we already knew about the killer.

"Oh, there was something on their left wrist. I think it was a tattoo. It was dark and I only saw it when the light hit it just right."

Molly took Eloise's hand and patted it. "Can you describe the ink?"

Eloise shook her head. "Only that it was about an inch long."

Molly was going back over Eloise's statement with her when a voice came over the intercom.

"Detective Tao, you have a visitor."

I allowed Molly to continue and stepped out, immediately spotting Matt Nolan sitting at my desk. What was Jamey's son doing there? Had something happened to his mother? I strode over and Matt stood when he spotted me.

"Hey, Peter," he said.

"What's up? Is something wrong?" I asked.

"What?" He appeared confused for a moment. "Oh, no, that's not why I'm here. I know you're busy, but I kind of need to talk to someone. Well, to you specifically."

I pursed my lips and regarded him for a moment. Jamey had been like family, and if one of his kids needed help, I would do whatever I could. "Okay, is here okay or..."

"No," he said quickly. "Some place private. Maybe we can grab a coffee."

"Sure, there's a place just around the corner." I grabbed my coat and slid it on.

Matt didn't say a word until we had our java and sat in a booth in the back of the small shop.

"So what's going on?" I asked.

He had both hands on the mug as if he were freezing.

I'd just taken a sip when he finally spoke, and I damn near choked on the warm liquid.

"Are you gay?"

I had a split-second decision to make. Honesty or denial? The truth or self-protection?

"Sorry, didn't mean to shock you." He chuckled. "I overheard Mom and Dad talking a couple years ago."

I shrugged. "It's not something I share with many people. Your dad was one of the few."

"I won't out you, if that's that you're worried about. I just wanted to know for personal reasons."

Personal reasons? Why would he possibly need to know such a thing? He wouldn't unless...

Unless he was questioning his own sexuality.

"When did you know you were gay?" Matt asked.

"From a very young age," I replied. "I had a crush on my best friend Mateo when I was nine. I didn't know what it meant. I just knew when you liked someone you were supposed to kiss them. So I did."

"Oh, shit."

"Yeah, Mateo called me a fag and pushed me away. That was my first sign that I shouldn't tell anyone the truth. My parents certainly wouldn't have handled it well then. Or now, for that matter."

"Is that why you're in the closet?"

I nodded. "I'd likely be disowned. As far as I'm concerned, what they don't know won't hurt them."

"But my dad," Matt murmured. "He was okay with you? Didn't care you liked guys?"

I snickered at all the times Jamey had teased me about my personal life, including my sexuality. "Your dad was fantastic. He didn't care one bit. Hell, I didn't even tell him. He figured it out on his own."

"Really?" Matt glanced up and made eye contact.

"He told me he knew a few months after we became partners. I tried to deny it but he said he didn't give a shit."

Staring at his coffee cup again, Matt asked, "So he wouldn't have cared if...if I was gay?"

I'd called that one right.

I reached across the table and put a hand on one of Matt's. "Your dad loved you, and nothing would've changed that. Certainly not being gay."

"I wish I would've told him before he died. I thought I had time to figure things out."

"It's not too late for your mom or your siblings," I said.

His eyes bugged out. "You think I should tell them?"

"I'd give anything to be able to share the truth with my family. To be open and honest with them. You have the family I wish I had. Your mom won't care, and I doubt your brother or sister will either. They might be surprised, but they'll come around."

Finally, he nodded. "You're right."

"Of course I am." I sniggered.

"Smartass." He tried to appear gruff but the corners of his lips turned up. He stood, and, after I did the same, he wrapped his arms around me and hugged me.

I patted him, giving him the fatherly hug he seemed to be craving. "I'm here for you, kid. Don't hesitate to call if you ever need me."

I made it back to the station just in time for the meeting of hack victims who were also possible future targets of the killer. Molly had finished with Eloise Nash and was in the conference room with Aza, and I allowed her to brief the people while I read over their files.

Among the people whose affairs were exposed was Lowell McClure, a bisexual man who cheated on his husband with Johanna Armstrong, the sole wealthy woman Aza had tagged as a possible target, and Seth Duffy, a gay man who cheated on his husband using the same down low section of *Ashley Madison* as Bryce.

There were ten files but a quick headcount told me there were only nine people present. I matched faces to photos until there was one image left. Tanev Singh—a middle-aged Indian man and bank vice-president.

Aza took over for Molly and I pulled her aside. "Did everyone say they were going to be here?"

"Yes. Probably because I told them their lives were in danger."

I pointed at Singh's picture. "This guy isn't here."

"That's odd," she replied. "He assured me he'd be here. He was scared shitless when I mentioned a serial killer."

"Did you reach him at his home?"

She shook her head. "No, his wife kicked him out. He's staying at the Alexis, room three twenty."

"I'm gonna go find him," I said.

"You think he's in danger? Should I come with you?"

"It's possible he had something else come up."

As I exited the room, Aza was telling the men, and woman, that their membership on *Ashley Madison* had made them targets.

I didn't mess around when I arrived at the Alexis. I told the concierge I needed a key to room three twenty in order to save a man's life. I wasn't convinced that was the case, but I didn't want to take any chances. Thankfully, the guy scared easily and eagerly gave me the card I demanded.

At the room, I knocked twice before I slid in the key and pushed open the door. "Seattle Homicide," I called out. "Anyone here?" I put my hand on the handle of my Glock and undid the clasp.

One step into the room, I saw the body of Tanev Singh on his back, blood oozing from his neck. I took two more steps in, realizing too late what *hadn't* been done to the body. Specifically, that his pants were still up and his cock hadn't been cut off.

And that could mean the killer was still in the room.

The floor squeaked behind me and I dodged to the left. The move saved my life but didn't save me from pain. Something stabbed into my shoulder. It hurt like a bitch but wasn't disabling. I fell forward, putting out my arms to catch myself, then rolled over, pulling my pistol as I did so. My eyesight was blurry from pain. I could see my attacker, just couldn't make out details. She was coming toward me with the knife extended when someone tackled her from behind.

They both tumbled forward into the room, and the knife flew out of her hand. I swiveled and kept my gun trained on both of them.

"Police. Freeze," I ordered but neither one did. I recognized Bryce as my would-be rescuer, not that I needed saving. He had the killer face down on the floor, and, for a moment, I thought he would be able to hold her. Bryce lowered his head and the killer reared back with her own and slammed into his nose. Bryce fell over, clutching at his face and moaning.

The killer bounded to her feet but I was right behind her. "Stop," I screamed and pulled the trigger a moment later. The bullet hit the door frame as she dashed out of the room with me on her trail. Unfortunately, the gunshot caught everybody's attention and every guest nearby opened their doors and stepped out.

Before I had a chance to identify myself, the killer called out, "Help, my ex-boyfriend wants to kill me!"

Smart lady.

Normally, I'd be pleased by so many people coming to the aid of a woman in need, but in this case, it didn't work to my advantage. A couple of the guests were large men and two of them tackled me to the ground and wrestled my gun away before I could inform them I was a cop. By the time they let me up, the killer was long gone.

I returned to the hotel room as Bryce put his cell away.

"I called 911 and asked for immediate backup. Said you were already here."

"What the fuck are you doing here?" I demanded.

"I just saved your life, you ungrateful asshole." His nose had stopped bleeding but not before covering his face and more. His dark gray and black double-breasted suit was now sporting red.

"I didn't *need* you to save me." My nostrils flared, and I barged into his personal space, bumping chests with him before stepping back. "I had my gun. If you hadn't interfered, I could've shot her. And she wouldn't be free." I accentuated each word with a poke in the chest. "Free. To. Kill. Again."

That deflated his sails. "Damn." He grimaced and pinched the bridge of his nose. "I didn't think about it. I saw him standing over you with the knife and I acted on instinct."

"You may have this innate need to protect people, but I am not some helpless victim. I can take care of myself."

He raised his arms in surrender. "I'm sorry. I should've stayed out of it."

"Yes, you should have." I tugged at my ear and strode over to Singh's body. "Exactly how did you end up here at the same time as me and the killer?" I asked.

"I've been following you," he admitted.

I glared at him and demanded, "Why?"

"I wanted to help. Thought you might need backup."

I appreciated the thought. Other than Jamey, I'd never had anyone put his life on the line for mine. Even if what he'd done was monumentally stupid, I couldn't help being grateful.

"When I take your statement, come up with a different story," I said. "Otherwise, I'll have to arrest you for interfering with an official investigation."

"Got it."

Moments later, the room and the hotel became a zoo with a dozen cops, including Chief Slight, Molly, Aza, and several paramedics. I immediately had Molly bag and tag the knife and get it taken to evidence so Jill could check it out as soon as possible.

I gave an abbreviated statement of what had happened, and the chief insisted both Bryce and I go to the hospital to get checked out.

"You're a lucky man," the nurse stitching me up said. "Closer to the neck and the blade could've severed your spinal cord."

"That's what the person wanted," I said. Instead, all I got was minimal bleeding, a few stitches, and some strong pain meds.

Bryce was fortunate as well. His nose wasn't broken. His only loss was his expensive suit. He was released first but waited outside the hospital for me.

"You ready to come in and make your official statement?" I asked.

"Sure. Whatever you need." His voice was sugar sweet and, for a moment, what I wanted was to feel his arms around me, as if that would make everything better.

And why I thought that, I had no clue.

CHIEF SLIGHT AND MOLLY TOOK MY STATEMENT FIRST, followed by Bryce's. I nervously waited for him to come out of the interrogation room. Would he be able to lie convincingly? Considering he'd managed to hide his sexuality for years, I shouldn't have doubted his abilities, but I just couldn't relax until the interview was finished.

While I waited, I checked in with the officers assigned to watch Diana Gomez. If they'd kept an eye on her the entire time, then she couldn't be the killer. However, if they'd followed her to the Alexis then we had her.

I'd be disappointed if Diana wasn't the killer because that left us with no suspect, but I wasn't thrilled about proving a cop's wife was a serial murderer. I called Officer Whitehead, confident he'd know something, one way or the other.

"Have you kept eyes on Diana Gomez all day?"

"Oh, umm, yeah, that was going to be in the report."

I did *not* like the sound of that.

"What the fuck happened?"

"Well, Mrs. Gomez visited the gym. I waited outside in the car while Officer Morse went inside. Mrs. Gomez slipped out the back and neither one of us realized it for at least thirty minutes. We eventually tracked her down at home, but I'd say she knew she was being followed and lost us on purpose."

"What time was she out of your surveillance?"

"Between two and three thirty p.m., approximately."

Damn it! The same time I'd had my encounter with the killer in the hotel room. I still couldn't prove or disprove Diana Gomez as the killer.

"I am so sorry, sir," Whitehead said, but I wasn't in the mood to hear his excuses. I ended the call and slammed my phone to my desk. A powerful headache came out of nowhere, and I cradled my head in my hands.

The stress of the day came crashing down on me, and I was suddenly exhausted. My skull pounded, and all I could hear was throb-throb-throb. Nothing else. Not even the usual loud din of the police station.

I felt a hand on my back, and I supposed they were saying something, but I heard nothing. Finally, I lifted my head and saw Bryce and Molly gawking at me. I pressed at my temples until the pulsing lessened and I could make out what they were saying.

"Are you okay?" That was Molly, though Bryce was asking the same thing.

"Just have a little headache," I said.

"That's it?" Bryce scoffed. "I doubt it."

Chief Slight strode over. "What's going on?"

I tried to wave her off but another thud ran through my head.

"I think he's got a stress migraine," Bryce said. "I get them from time to time."

"What does he need?"

"I lay down in a dark, quiet room."

"I'm fine," I lied. "I'll be fine in a couple minutes."

"Bullshit," Slight spat. "You're going home."

I was about to argue but my head thumped again and I couldn't deny I needed to leave. I wouldn't be able to do anything even if I did stay. "Okay," I acquiesced. "I'll go."

"He shouldn't drive," Bryce said. "It's not safe. I can take him."

Slight furrowed her brow and stared at him. "We're done with you, Mr. Carrick. You're free to go. I'll arrange for an officer to take Detective Tao home."

Bryce nodded and quickly exited.

Molly volunteered to take me home and was kind enough to escort me all the way into my bedroom.

"Thanks," I said. "I can take care of myself from here."

"You sure you're gonna be okay?"

"Absolutely. Get back to the station and work the case like I wish I could."

She waved and left. I didn't bother locking the front door behind her. Instead, I stripped, closed the curtains in my bedroom and lay down in the dark. Minutes later I was asleep.

AT SOME POINT I HEARD A NOISE IN my kitchen or *thought* I heard something. I wasn't sure thanks to the pounding in my skull. I sat up and thought about checking out the source of the sound but the pain intensified so I lay back down and prayed to fall asleep again. At least it didn't hurt as much then.

"Bae." I heard his voice over the pulsing and groaned. Only one person would be referring to me by that name. I should've been grateful it was Bryce and not someone out to hurt me, but I didn't want to see anyone.

"My name is Peter," I snarled.

He chuckled. "You need to eat. I made grilled cheese."

"Go away. Not hungry." I said without opening my eyes. However, the scent of the sandwiches, one of my favorites, hit my nostrils and my stomach growled.

"You sure about that?" He put an arm under my shoulder and helped me up. "Just eat one and you can lie down again."

I begrudgingly lifted my eyelids and took the plate he offered. He sat on the bed next to me, our legs brushing against each other.

"How're you feeling?" he asked.

I rolled my eyes. "What do you think, smart guy?"

"Wow, the headache didn't hurt your sarcastic attitude, did it?"

The grilled cheese tasted great. Fabulous, even. I mumbled a thanks when I finished the sandwich and handed him the plate,

"You're welcome."

He handed me a water bottle. I cracked open the lid and took a swig as he exited the room. I expected him to leave and was slightly disappointed at the thought.

When Bryce returned to the room, he had a small bag. "Take your clothes off."

"Excuse me?" I snapped.

He smirked and raised a hand. "I'm going to give you a massage. It'll help the migraine."

"That's not necessary. I'll be fine," I said.

He sighed and shook his head. "I get migraines every so often. I know a few tricks. I'm just trying to help." He retrieved a couple plastic containers, dumped out a couple pills from each, and held them out to me.

"What are these?"

"Migraine meds for the pain and nausea."

I took the pills, popped them into my mouth, and washed them down with water.

"Lie face down," he instructed.

I eyed him for a second did as he instructed. It didn't seem like he was going to leave. Plus, if I was going to be honest, a massage sounded good, especially if it relieved the ache.

After I rolled to my stomach, Bryce straddled me and poured something cool and liquid on my back. The sweet smell of lavender hit me a moment later. He rubbed his hands together then began stroking them over my lower back. His hands were damn magic. The way he rubbed my sore muscles elicited a slight moan from my lips.

"Feels amazing, doesn't it?"

I nodded then grunted again when he ran his palms up to my shoulders, being careful not to put too much pressure on my wound. He ran his hands up and down my back, rubbing each muscle with just the right amount of compression. The touch made my body react and my cock hardened. Bryce had the same response. His erection rubbed against my ass, but not in a sexual way. He wasn't trying to hide it, but he wasn't going out of his way to make sure I knew about it, either.

When he climbed off, I immediately missed his hands on my flesh. It had felt nice and not just because it was helping my migraine. I enjoyed the feel of him on top of me and of him touching me.

"Scoot over," he said, and I did without questioning why. He rearranged a couple pillows and sat on the bed, his back against the wall. He spread his legs and patted the space between them.

"Huh?"

"Lie down on your back," he replied. "I'm going to rub your temples."

"You don't have to do all this."

He furrowed his brow. "I'm here because I want to be."

"Why?"

"I'm not totally sure," he admitted, shrugging. "I like you."

I situated myself between his legs, resting my head on his firm stomach. "Don't think this means I'm going to sleep with you just because you're helping me."

"That is certainly not my intention. I'm just trying to help."

He began with a scalp massage that relaxed me immediately. Firm, but still gentle. Perfect pressure. The drums in my head lessened somewhat and I relaxed into the marvelous sensations. By the time he got to my temples, I was so calm and comfortable I didn't resist the allure of sleep. Couldn't have even if I'd wanted to.

I was in the same position when I woke sometime later. Bryce was too. His hands rested on my chest and his head reclined back. I shifted so I could check him out for a second. He was an amazingly handsome man. If we'd met under different circumstances, I might've already thrown my rule against hookups out the door. If he wasn't married. If he wasn't part of my case. Too many obstacles.

He opened his eyes and peered down at me. "Hey, Sleeping Beauty. How're you feeling?"

I took a second to consider the question. The pain was mostly gone. It was simply a dull ache now. "Much better," I replied. "How long have I been out?"

"Couple hours."

"And you just sat there the entire time?"

He shrugged. "Not like I have anywhere I need to be."

Still, sitting there had to have been boring. Not sure I would've done it for somebody I barely knew. Hell, I wouldn't have done it for someone I cared about.

I moved to sit up, but he slowed me down. "Be careful. Don't move too fast."

After I was vertical, Bryce rubbed my shoulders. "There's a lot less tension in there now."

His touch caused goosebumps to ripple over my skin. It also did nothing to alleviate my achingly hard dick. Damn, I liked him touching me. Liked it far too much. It was like smelling a steak but not being able to take a bite.

"You hungry?" he asked.

I nodded. "Starving."

"Why don't you take a cool shower, and I'll order some food?"

I swung my feet to the floor and waited to see if I was ready to stand. Bryce bounded off the bed and put a hand on my arm, helping me up.

"You don't have to…"

"You'll want to keep the water a little cold," he said before disappearing from the room.

It didn't appear he was leaving anytime soon, and I couldn't deny I was rather glad. I showered, keeping the water on the chilly side. In addition to helping the remains of the headache, the cold aided in making my cock soften. I didn't want Bryce knowing how much he turned me on. It was better if we kept this as professional as possible. Of course, him being at my place massaging me wasn't professional at all. But it hadn't crossed the lines into a sexual or romantic relationship. We were just…friends. Barely more than acquaintances. Not entirely kosher but not unforgiveable either. As long as that was where it stayed we'd be okay.

After my shower, I pulled on a pair of sweats and a T-shirt and found Bryce in the living room watching an episode of *Strikeback*. The character Damian Scott, played by Sullivan Stapleton, was having sex yet again. The guy was always getting lucky, but at least it meant decent shots of his ass.

"I ordered baked chicken and Caesar salad," he said. "You don't want any fried foods right now."

I shrugged. "Sounds good."

"You're not allergic to healthy food?"

"Why? Because I'm a cop? We're not all stereotypical coffee-swilling donut eaters."

He chuckled and blushed. "Sorry."

"Don't get me wrong, though. I love my java and my donuts, but I eat other stuff as well. The only reason I don't eat better is because I'm single, and I don't like cooking."

He patted the seat next to him. "Sit."

I chose the other side of the couch and stretched my feet out so they pushed against his thigh. He grabbed a foot and rubbed it.

"Do you know anything about reflexology?" he asked.

"Isn't that the belief that certain points on the foot connect to other points of the body"

He nodded.

"Sounds like a bunch of mumbo jumbo to me."

"You'd be surprised how well it works."

I snorted. "If you say so."

"How's your shoulder wound?"

"Aches a bit," I answered.

He pressed hard just below the base of my toes. It hurt a bit for a moment, then he released.

"How about now?"

I rubbed the spot where the knife went into my trapezius muscle. "Huh? It doesn't hurt."

Giving me a shit-eating grin, he said, "Told ya."

"That was luck."

He cocked an eyebrow and pressed two fingers to the base on top of my right foot near the ankle bones. He squeezed hard for half a minute, and I closed my eyes as my cock hardened again. His sweet touch was driving me crazy. When he released the pressure, he grinned at me.

"What part of the body is *that* supposed to affect?" I asked.

"The groin."

Damn it.

"Did it work?" he asked. I ignored him but he persisted. "You have an erection, don't you?"

I yanked my feet away from him. "I'm not telling you that."

He chuckled and crossed his legs. "That means yes."

Focusing on the TV, I did my best to will my erection away, but the more I thought about it the more my groin refused to respond. I didn't look directly at Bryce, but every so often, I could see him in my peripheral vision watching me and smirking. Damn him, he certainly knew how to get to me. Way too easily.

The food finally arrived and we ate in silence. I took care of the trash and was in the kitchen when a sharp stab of pain pulsed in my head. I dropped the plate in my hand and it shattered as it hit the floor.

I leaned on the counter and grabbed my head. Bryce was there a second later, gripping my shoulders.

"What's wrong?"

I breathed through the pain until I could talk. "Felt like someone stabbed my temples."

"Aftereffects of the migraine," he said. "You were probably doing too much." He guided me into the living room, and I lied down on the couch. "I'll take care of the mess."

I nodded because that was about all I could do. Five minutes later, Bryce returned, lifted my head and scooted under so I was resting on his lap. After putting a wet rag on my forehead, he began rubbing my temples again.

"Why are you here?" I asked. "Why are you doing this for me?"

"Because you needed it. I take it you don't have many friends."

"Why me though? I'm basically a stranger. We've known each other a couple days and most of our interactions have involved either a physical fight or a verbal one."

He pursed his lips and paused before answering. "I can't really say, because I'm not sure. There's just something about you that intrigues me. You're feisty."

"Feisty? You make me sound like a cat."

He chuffed a laugh. "Nah, you are definitely not a pussy cat. There aren't a lot of people who can challenge me in a fight. You didn't back down when I tried to push you around."

"Well, I am a cop."

"Do you have any idea how many times I've talked my way out of getting a ticket simply by throwing my name out?"

"Really?"

He nodded. "It's not like I can't afford a speeding ticket, either. But I've always been able to use either my size or my name to get what I want. I fully expected you to back off too."

"Yeah, that's not my style at all."

"I know. That impressed me. Even with my lovers, I've never found anyone who truly challenges me. In the bedroom or out. I haven't been able to get you off my mind since meeting you. I've imagined what you'd be like in bed. Neither one of us wanting to give an inch."

I craned my head back so I could look him in the eye. "You need to get that idea out of your head right now."

"What, like you haven't fantasized about fucking me?"

I had but that didn't mean it was going to happen. "That's not the point."

"I suspect you want me as much as I want you. What would be wrong with going for it and having fun?"

Holding up a finger, I said, "First of all, I have a rule against hookups and one-night stands."

"It doesn't *have* to be a one-off. I'd have no problem with getting together again."

I lifted a second digit. "Secondly, you're a witness in my current investigation. We shouldn't even be spending time together like this, but…"

"You're drawn to me." He leaned down and put his lips to mine. I should've pushed him away immediately, but it felt so outstanding I lost my train of thought for a moment. I came back to my senses when his tongue traced my lips.

I put a hand on his shoulder and he moved back.

"Third, and this is the most important argument," I said, "I do not sleep with married men."

"Really? Never?"

That brought back memories I'd rather forget. Goddamn Darren Finney. "Never *again*."

"What's the problem? If you've done it once, you can do it again."

He lowered for another kiss, but I put a hand on his forehead and stopped him.

"I mean it, Bryce. It's not going to happen. Not if you're married."

He sat up and regarded me with half-lidded eyes. "Something bad happened to you, didn't it?"

I nodded.

"Want to talk about it?"

"Not even a little bit."

He shrugged. "Okay. I can wait. But as soon as I'm divorced, I'm going to seduce you. I want you in my bed, Bae Peter Tao."

"And you always get what you want?"

His eyes gleamed and a playful grin formed on his lips. "Usually."

Cocky bastard. "I'm not going to hold my breath on that divorce. I have a feeling your wife is going to take you for everything she can."

He huffed. "You're right there. Clementine was always in it for the money. I'll get my divorce, but it may take a while."

"Don't expect me to wait. Just because I'm attracted to you doesn't mean it'll last."

"The lure can't fade if I don't let you forget me."

"And how do you plan on doing that?"

"Right now, I'm not sure, but I'll find a way. I always do."

Damn, he was arrogant and, God help me, I liked it. He was a man who knew what he wanted and wasn't afraid to go after it.

We were quiet for a few minutes before he asked, "If you don't do hookups, does that mean you only have sex in a committed relationship?"

"For the most part," I replied. "I do have a friends-with-benefits relationship with a buddy named Haro. We've known each other since we were kids. Neither one of us can come out to our parents so relationships are difficult. But between us, it's strictly no strings.

Haro has the occasional one-nighter but I generally don't enjoy it. Sex with someone I care about is much more enjoyable."

"But you're not in love with Haro?"

I shook my head. "But I care about him enough that I can have fun in bed with him. He's not my usual type, but the sex is fantastic. If he met someone, I'd be happy for him."

"If Haro isn't your type, then what is?" he asked.

I blushed. "Older. Larger. Stronger."

Bryce chuckled but didn't point out he fit every one of those aspects. He didn't need to mention it because we both knew. Mercifully, he let me off the hook by going silent.

I slipped in and out of sleep but he didn't move until after nine p.m. He rustled me awake. "Why don't you go to bed? I'm sure it's more comfortable."

After sitting up, I stretched and slowly stood. The pain in my head was mostly gone, thank God. He followed me into the bedroom and watched as I pulled off my sweats and shirt. I should've cared I was wearing nothing but my boxer briefs, but I didn't. I liked the way he checked me out, his eyes taking me in and the gulp that told me how much he desired me. It made me a cock tease, but I didn't care.

I took his hand and tugged him toward me. "Stay the night, please."

He cocked an eyebrow.

"No, I'm still not going to have sex with you, but I do like being with you. So you can stay if you promise not to try anything."

He screwed up his face as if he was contemplating the offer. "Can I hold you?"

That sounded nice. Haro wasn't a snuggler and I missed it. Darren had liked to spoon. It was one of my best memories with him. One of the few. "Can you keep it at that and not more?"

He held up his hand in the Boy Scout salute. "I have *excellent* self-control."

I chose not to point out his self-control wasn't so strong that he couldn't keep his dick in his pants. I felt for him and how he'd ended up in a loveless marriage. It wasn't something I would've done, but I understood why he had. As much as I despised cheaters, I didn't hate him. That didn't mean I was going to break my rule about sleeping with married men. I'd done it before but never again, no matter how much I liked Bryce. I'd drawn my line in the sand, and I wasn't going to cross it. I may toe the line but that was as far as I was going to go.

He stripped down to his underwear, pulled back the sheets, and climbed in. I followed and lay facing him. I stared into his gorgeous hazel eyes for a moment then leaned forward and kissed him. I felt his surprise but he soon gave in and returned the liplock. I opened my lips and allowed our tongues to press for a moment before pulling away.

"Goodnight, Bryce."

"Goodnight, Bae."

I scowled then rolled over on my side. He wrapped an arm around me and tugged me against his warm body. His crotch rested against my ass. He was hard, but he didn't grind against me or do anything sexual. Bryce kissed the back of my neck, sending shivers throughout my body.

And that was how I fell asleep, spooning with a half-naked Bryce Carrick. Lord help me, what was I getting into?

NINE

THE INSISTENT RINGING OF MY CELL STIRRED ME from one of the best nights of sleep I'd ever had.

Whoever was calling me at five a.m. better have a damn fine reason.

"Yeah?" I answered.

"Detective Tao, this is Officer Hurst." The recognition of her name made me sit up straight, now fully awake. She was one of the officers assigned to follow Diana Gomez.

"What's going on?"

"Shots fired at the Gomez residence. Estrada and I are about to enter."

"I'm on my way." I dropped the phone on the bed as I leaped out, grabbed fresh clothes from the closet, and pulled them on.

"What's going on?" A disheveled Bryce sat up and rubbed at his eyes.

"Work shit," I replied. "Gotta go." Without thinking, I leaned over and kissed him as if we were long-time lovers. I froze when I realized what I had done, but he grinned and waved me off.

I sped all the way to the Gomez residence. As much as I wished I could take the time to ponder what was going on with Bryce Carrick, such as what the hell was I thinking, I couldn't. Work was the one thing I could think about. What I *had* to concentrate on. I had my game face on when I arrived and entered the modest home.

In addition to Officer Hurst, a couple other patrol officers were also there. Dave Gomez sat in the living room on a tan, flowery couch, hunched over with a blanket covering him. I caught the sight of a bare hip when the quilt slipped down for an instant. Hurst was speaking to Gomez but stopped when she saw me and strode over.

"You'll want to check out the master bedroom." She pointed down a hallway. "Last door on the left."

She returned to Gomez, and I headed for the bedroom. The door was open, and I stepped in. It was empty except for Officer Estrada. Well, him and the dead body on the king size bed.

The corpse of Diana Gomez was splayed out on her back—several bullet holes in her chest. Her mouth and eyes were open in an odd expression of surprise and terror. Just to the side of her right hand was a wood-handled kitchen knife. I leaned close so I could read the brand of the knife without touching it—Victorinox.

Without glancing at Estrada I asked, "What happened?"

"Hurst and I entered the residence after hearing three gunshots. We identified ourselves and heard someone in here. When we entered, Officer Gomez still had the gun in his hand, but I retrieved it from him and secured it."

I stood and faced Estrada. "Did he tell you what happened?"

He nodded. "He said that she came after him with a knife and he had to shoot her to save his own life."

"When CSU arrives, make sure they get pictures of where Dave was when he fired."

"Yes, sir."

I checked out the rest of the room before returning to the living room. Dave was still on the couch but Hurst was speaking to Doyle, Gomez's boss on the gang task force. I approached Gomez and sat on the coffee table in front of him.

"What the hell happened?" I asked.

He wiped tears from his face. "My fucking wife was going to kill me, Tao. That's what happened."

I held up a hand. "Take a breath and tell me exactly how it occurred."

He inhaled a deep breath and slowly let it out. "I woke up from a deep sleep and Diana was straddling me, my dick in one hand and a knife in the other. I kicked her and she fell back, giving me enough time to grab my gun from under my pillow. She sat up and came at me with the knife again. I didn't have a choice. I had to shoot." Tears welled up in his eyes. "Damn it. I shot my wife." He buried his face in his hands and wept loudly.

I patted his back and left him to his grief.

Chief Slight arrived a moment later, and I filled her in on what I knew, which so far wasn't much. What I did suspect was that there was far more to the story we needed to uncover.

Slight pulled me aside so no one else could hear us. "This certainly points to Diana Gomez being our serial killer, doesn't it?"

I shrugged. "I'm trying not to make any assumptions. I'd rather wait until I have all the evidence."

"Of course." She brushed her palms together. "But it would be nice to put this case to bed."

Dave stood. "Would it be possible for me to get dressed?" The blanket slipped, momentarily revealing his nudity.

"I can't let you take anything from the scene," I said.

"I have clothes in the extra room. Would that be okay?"

I glanced at the chief and she nodded her approval. "Go with him."

Dave shuffled to the room and I followed, shutting the door behind me. He dropped the blanket, allowing me a quick glance at his ass before I lowered my gaze to the floor.

"This is unbelievable," Dave said. "She was going to kill me. She was gonna hack off my cock, for Christ's sake." He opened a dresser drawer and pulled on a pair of tighty-whiteys, a pair of black jeans, a gray T-shirt, and finally socks and shoes.

Fully dressed, he faced me and said, "Looks like you were right about Diana being the killer."

I folded my arms across my chest. "I'd rather wait and see if that's where the evidence leads."

"I'd say the evidence is rather clear. She was going to chop my cock off. Just like what happened to those other guys." He narrowed his eyes and glared at me.

"I'm not saying she *isn't* the killer. I just prefer not to make assumptions before I've checked out everything."

He stared at me for a minute with narrowed eyes. His posture was rigid, the cords in his neck twanging. Then he relaxed almost forcibly and smiled. "You're a good cop. I'm sure you'll figure it all out." He patted my back on his way out. There was something about the guy that made me not like him all that much. I preferred not to think it was my natural predisposition to dislike cheaters. There had to be more to it than that, I just didn't know what it was.

AN HOUR LATER, MOLLY, AZA, AND I WERE poring over the evidence in the shooting of Diana Gomez. Her laptop had been password protected, and Dave had claimed not to know it. It hadn't taken long for Aza to hack the code and get access to all her files. It was damning almost immediately.

She had been writing in an electronic diary for years but we focused on the most recent entries. One dated a few days before the first murder seemed to detail the beginning of a break down.

Dave is cheating on me. Again. Why do men do this? When will they learn? More importantly, who will show them that adultery has consequences? I want to be the one who teaches them a very important lesson.

There weren't many details in her diary, but she did write about creating an account on *Ashley Madison* to get proof of her husband's cheating and how she could use that account to put her plan into action.

"Aza, you need to find her account and see who she contacted through it."

"Already working on it," he said. "I should have it within the hour."

Turning to Molly, I asked, "Were you ever able to establish where Diana was on the nights of the murders?"

She shook her head. "I can't find anything. She's not a big user of social media so there's no online trail to follow. There's no odd emails or phone numbers either."

I tapped my chin as I paced around my desk. "It's not proof she was the killer, but it doesn't clear her either."

"There's more evidence pointing to her being guilty, though," Molly said. "Cases have been prosecuted and won with less concrete evidence than this."

"I know. I just want more. I want to be absolutely sure I found Jamey's killer." Unlike in television and movies, there wasn't always a smoking gun, or in this case, a bloody knife, that proved a person was guilty. There wasn't always eyewitness testimony that led to absolute proof. But that's what I wanted in this case. It's what I needed before I could rest. But as they say, you don't always get what you want, and I had a feeling that was what was going to happen with this case.

Molly continued reading Diana's journal but, while it was rather incriminatory, it wasn't solid confirmation either. She referred to arranging meetings with men so she could "show other cheaters the consequences of breaking their marriage vows." I would've preferred that she come right out and state she met with Julian Ramsey or Tyrone Osceola or Jamey and exactly how she planned to accomplish her plan. Instead, her entries were frustratingly vague. I wasn't sure it would've been strong enough to use to prosecute Diana had she been alive. With her being dead, I didn't have to worry about a trial, but I still wanted the evidence to be just as strong.

My eyes were beginning to cross from reading the journal when Jill called.

"I have some stuff you'll want to hear," she said. "I'd rather show you in person."

"I'll be over in a few."

JILL STOOD NEAR THE BODY OF DIANA GOMEZ when I arrived.

"What do you got for me?" I asked.

"First of all, the red hair found at Jamey's place is a positive match to Diana Gomez."

"No doubt?" She glared at me, and I chuckled. "Sorry, I had to ask."

"One hundred percent match. She was definitely at Jamey's place at some point. Obviously, I have no way of knowing when."

"Got it."

"Secondly, the knife found at the scene today matches the brand, make, and style of the other two we have in evidence."

"Is there a way to tell if they came from the exact same set?" I asked.

She shook her head. "However, when I was at the Gomez scene I did snoop around the kitchen. There was a Victorinox set, and it was missing two fillet knives."

"Which would make sense if she'd lost two of them. One when she attacked Bryce Carrick and another when she killed Tanev Singh."

"She went after her husband with a meat cleaver, which is bigger than she's been using."

Change of MO this late in the game was unusual, but considering she'd lost her favorite toys, it wasn't unlikely. Plus, she probably wanted to make her husband hurt the worst, which also explained why she hadn't killed him first. She hadn't needed the other victims to suffer, but Dave was a different story. She would've wanted him to hurt big time.

It was beginning to seem like Diana Gomez truly had been

the killer. The evidence was stacking up against her, and there was nothing to disprove it.

Both Molly and Aza had information for me when I returned to the station.

"Her diary never goes into specifics," Molly said, "but in it she does say choosing high profile and wealthy men would ensure better news coverage. She also writes that cheaters should lose what they value most—their genitals."

"Wow."

She held up a finger. "There's more. She googled a search for quick and painless deaths and found a page explaining how to stab someone in the back of the neck."

The wonders of the internet.

"I found her *Ashley Madison* account," Aza said. "She must've been rather confident because she didn't try to hide her trail."

"Makes sense," I pointed out. "Who would've even suspected her of doing something like that?"

"She contacted her husband and every one of our victims, even Bryce Carrick and Seth Duffy, who both used *Ashley Madison* down low. Neither one of them responded, however, but her husband did, though he never agreed to a meeting."

"Who did?"

Aza gazed at me and pursed his lips. "Julian Ramsey, Tyrone Osceola, Detective Nolan, and Tanev Singh."

"The only men who arranged meetings are the ones who are dead?"

He nodded.

"Holy shit." It still wasn't a smoking gun, but it was sure damn close. As close as I figured it was going to get. "Time to talk to the chief."

"So we have physical evidence Diana Gomez was at Jamey's place?" Chief Slight said, repeating what I'd just told her. "The weapon she was going to use on her husband matches the other two used by the killer. Her journal talks about making men pay for cheating. And she contacted every single one of our victims online to set up a meeting."

"Yes," I confirmed. "And she researched the death method our killer used."

"Of course, I can't forget that." Slight snapped her fingers. She was quiet for a minute then asked. "What do you think, Detective? This is your case."

"If she were alive, it wouldn't be a slam dunk prosecution, but there is a ton of evidence against her. And nothing to say she was innocent. She certainly appears pretty damn guilty."

"It's your call. If you want to close the case, you can. If you're not sure and want to keep investigating, I can allow that for a bit longer. However, if there are no more murders, I'd have a hard time justifying it, considering what we do have against Diana Gomez."

"Can I have to the end of this day to let you know?"

"Absolutely."

I thanked the chief and returned to my desk. I stared at my computer screen and the picture of Diana Gomez. Was she truly my killer? It felt sort of…anti-climactic. I wasn't sure what I'd expected to happen when I caught the murderer, but something more than this. For one, I'd hoped I'd be the person to bring her in. I would've preferred she come in alive so justice could be served, but I wouldn't have hesitated to kill her if needed. But I'd wanted to be the hero of the story. I felt robbed of that opportunity, but that wasn't a reason not to close the case.

I examined every single shred of evidence we had in the case. I didn't like that I couldn't link the car from the funeral to Diana, but that wasn't enough of a niggle. When five p.m. hit, I'd made up my mind. Diana Gomez was our killer. The case was over.

TEN

AFTER NOTIFYING CHIEF SLIGHT OF MY DECISION TO close the case, I left the station and paid a visit to Chelsea, who was still staying at her sister's. Everyone hugged each other—and me—when I told them the killer had been found. They invited me to stay for a celebration, but I begged off and headed home.

I'd just poured myself a vodka and cranberry juice and taken a sip when there was a knock on the door. I wasn't in the mood for company, so I'd decided not to answer when Bryce's voice came from the other side.

"I know you're in there, Peter. I'm not going away so don't even try ignoring me."

Realizing he was indeed a persistent bastard, I opened the door and stepped away without greeting him.

"What're you doing here?" I growled.

"Hello to you, too."

I stomped into the living room and flopped down on the couch with Bryce right on my heels.

"So the case is closed?"

"Yup."

"Why didn't you tell me yourself?"

Without looking at him I answered, "Not my responsibility."

"I thought we were…"

"What?" I demanded with a glower. "You thought we were what?"

He shrugged and peered at the floor. "I don't know. Friends at least."

"Not sure why you thought that," I said coldly.

He stared at me incredulously for a moment. "Damn, you run hot and cold, don't you? Excuse me if I thought there was an attraction between us. Especially after last night."

I chuffed and rolled my eyes. "I was out of it last night. Call it a case of temporary insanity."

"You kissed me, Peter. I didn't imagine that."

Meeting his gaze, I shot him an exasperated expression. "Christ, Carrick, what do you want me to say? You're attractive. I admit that. That doesn't mean anything."

"Doesn't mean anything?" He threw his hands in the air. "I can't stop thinking about you. You fascinate me. You're strong and one helluva cop. But there's pain and hurt deep inside that you don't want to let go of."

I bounded to my feet and got in his face. Our chests bumped, and I could smell his woodsy cologne and minty mouthwash. "Don't act like you fucking know me! Because you don't. Not at all."

His face reddened, but then he took a deep breath and said in a low voice, "No, I don't. But I want too. If you'd just give me a chance."

Part of me wanted to let go of the anger I was feeling, but I just wasn't ready to let down some of those walls. They were there to protect me, after all. I tore them down when I was with Darren and had ended up regretting it. The one other person I'd let get close to me was Jamey. And he was dead.

"You're nothing but an arrogant, entitled, rich son of a bitch," I snarled. "I'm just another of your conquests. You want me because you can't have me."

His eyebrows knitted together in a furious scowl. "That's not true. Not even close."

I turned away from him and shrugged a single shoulder.

"Whatever. Go find someone else to screw over."

"God, you're a stubborn asshole," he snapped. "Why am I wasting my time?"

"That's a good question." I faced him again with a daring expression.

"Fuck off, Peter." He spun and stormed toward the door.

"Bye. See ya never."

He turned back to face me.

"I thought you were leaving," I said with a smirk.

"I have just one more thing to say." He took slow, measured steps back to me. His eyes bored into my skull, but I refused to be the one who looked away first, even if it did make me extremely uncomfortable.

Bryce didn't stop until he was less than inch away. For a moment, he said nothing, just peered at me with those enthralling hazel eyes. Then he put his hands on either side of my face and pulled me into a kiss. It took me a second to react, to realize what was happening. Once more, I was torn about how to respond. My body and mind warred with each other. The kiss was amazing, and my cock responded, but my brain told me this wasn't what I had wanted, not consciously anyway.

I put my hands on his chest and shoved him away. "What the fuck are you doing?"

"Trying to get you to drop your defenses. You need to see I'm not here to hurt you."

"I'm not going to sleep with you. If that's what you're after, you might as well give up now."

He sighed dejectedly. "I don't care about that. You are not some conquest I'm out to seduce. Do I want you? Hell, yeah. You're sexy as fuck and turn me on so much. But it's not just a physical thing. I've had plenty of guys in my bed over the years but it's always been lacking something. Would I love to take you to bed right now? Hell, yeah. But if that's not in the cards, I can accept whatever you can give me."

"I don't know if I can give you anything." I spoke softly. So low even I almost couldn't hear it. "There might not be anything *to* give."

He took my hand and rubbed it. "That's not true. I know it isn't. You need something right now. Your emotions are just under the surface. I can be whoever or whatever you need right now. A friend. Someone to talk to. Someone to lean on. I can be *that* person, Peter. Just let me."

Damn it, he was right. I'd been holding my emotions in since Jamey died. I'd sworn I wouldn't grieve until the killer was caught, and it seemed that had happened. Tears welled up in my eyes, and one escaped, rolling down my cheek. Bryce reached out and wiped away the single drop.

"I'm not going anywhere," he said. "Might as well accept that." He wrapped his strong arms around me, and I breathed in his intoxicating scent. I didn't return the embrace, but I didn't push him away, either. I felt safe and secure in his arms. Comfortable. Home.

The dam broke, and I began to weep. Large tears poured out as I sobbed. He patted my back and guided me to the couch where we sat with me resting against his chest. Bryce caressed my back in a soothing motion. "Yeah, that's it. Let it all out."

"He was my best friend," I murmured between sniffles. "Jamey was like a brother to me. I can't believe he's gone."

Whispering calming words into my ear, he held me until I could breathe normally again. He left me for a minute to get me a bottle of water, and then we were back in the same position on the couch. He didn't care that I cried like a baby and slobbered onto his expensive silk shirt. There was no judgment, just comfort. I dozed for half an hour or so and woke with a start, momentarily forgetting where I was or who I was with.

"You're okay," he murmured. "I'm here."

Why did that make me feel better? He was a virtual stranger, yet it felt as if I'd known him almost forever. It made no sense at all, but being around him made me feel better. His words and his touch soothed me in a way no other man's ever had. I wanted to feel more of him and even considered violating my rule of no sex with married men. A good fuck would make me feel even better. Make the pain go away at least for a short time. But I'd made my line in the sand, and I wasn't going to cross it. Even if the sex was marvelous, I would regret it afterward. I'd felt used and degraded before, and it wasn't going to happen again.

I was glad when he didn't try to get me to change my mind. There was no pressure from him whatsoever, but he didn't leave me. He ordered pizza and we ate while watching *Avengers*. Afterward, we snuggled and watched *Age of Ultron*, arguing over whether that version of Quicksilver was better than the one in *X-Men: Days of Future Past*. I thought the X-Men one was far cooler, but Bryce said the one in *Avengers* seemed more realistic. We argued about it for at least twenty minutes, and it was enjoyable to have a discussion not about a life or death matter.

I fell asleep in his arms watching—what else?—*X-Men: Days of Future Past*. At some point I woke up and Bryce had also dozed off. I sat up and jostled him. "C'mon, let's go to bed."

He opened his eyes and shot me a questioning glance. "You sure?"

"It's not an invitation for sex, but I'd like it if you stayed. Can we share a bed like we did last night without you wanting to have your way with me?"

"I can't control my desires," he said with a smile. "But I can control my actions. I promise no unwanted touches. I assume spooning is allowed."

I nodded. "Yeah, I'd like that."

We both stood, and he took my hand as we shuffled to the bedroom where we both stripped down to our underwear and climbed under the covers. He pulled me close and I felt his hard-on pressed against my ass.

"Sorry," he murmured embarrassedly. "But like I said, I can't control what I want."

"It's okay," I replied. Knowing that he wanted me made me feel warm inside. I also realized that he was going to respect my wishes and not ask for more than I was willing to give, and that made me like the man even more.

BRYCE WAS SOUND ASLEEP AND SNORING QUIETLY IN my ear when I opened my eyes Wednesday morning. I couldn't believe it was barely over a week since Jamey and I had taken the case. And now Jamey was dead and I was in bed with one of the wealthiest and sexiest men in Seattle.

I glanced at the clock—six a.m. I didn't have to report to the station until eight, but I didn't want to go in at all. I wondered if the chief would care if I took a mental health day. After all, the case was closed, and I didn't have any other cases as of yet.

Careful to not disturb Bryce, I slipped out of bed and padded out of the room with my cellphone in hand. In the kitchen, I started the coffee maker and dialed the chief's number.

"What's up, Peter?"

"I was hoping I could convince you to give me the day off. I need to…"

"Absolutely," she said quickly.

I was expecting at least a small argument.

"You've been hyper-focused on the case and you did an excellent job. Feel free to take the day and enjoy yourself. I have plenty of detectives here to handle what comes up."

"Thanks, Chief."

"Don't mention it." She ended the call without another word, and I chuckled as I set the phone down.

"Something funny?" Bryce padded into the room. His hair was mussed and standing in awkward directions. Even with bedhead, the man was sexy. He stirred desires in me I hadn't felt in a long time. Not since…Darren. Fuck, it always came back to Darren. Bryce and Darren didn't have much in common. Their bodies were different. Hair and eye color different. But they had one thing in common— they were both married. At least with Bryce I knew he had a wife. Whereas with Darren I hadn't known right away. Hadn't known for far too long, and by the time I did, I was in love with the man.

"Hello, McFly?" Bryce snapped his fingers in front of my face. I blushed and chuckled. "Where'd you go?"

"Just thinking about someone from a long time ago. But I don't want to talk about it." I poured two cups of coffee and handed one to Bryce. "You have any plans today?"

He pursed his lips and tapped the edge of the mug. "Let's see. I have no real home and no job. Yup, I think I'm free today. Why do you ask?"

"Because I took the day off," I replied. "And I'd like to spend it with you."

"Moi?" He palmed his chest in mock surprise. "Oh my, I feel so special."

"You should." I pinched his cheek. "Most days off I spend alone watching reruns of *Different Strokes.*"

Bryce made a pitying face. "My God, that is so fucking sad."

"Bite me." I snorted and chucked his chin.

He grabbed my hand and tugged me against him then pretended to chew on my neck. It tickled, but also sent erotic shivers down my spine and to my crotch. I shoved him away and he stared at me like I'd taken away his last meal.

"What?" he acted hurt. "You told me to bite you. I was just doing as instructed."

"I'm going to take a shower."

"Can I join you?" He waggled his eyebrows, and I laughed at his goofiness.

I *almost* said yes. I kind of wanted to let him join me. To be naked with him. Touching and washing. It didn't have to end in sex, but even if it didn't it would be toeing that line in the sand. "Thanks, but I can clean myself."

"Are you sure? I can wash your back."

I ignored him and strode to the bathroom, shutting and locking the door behind me. My willpower wasn't at maximum capacity. If Bryce were to come in and strip, I doubted I'd be able to turn him away.

The hot water felt extraordinary on my body, and I let it beat down on my back and the shoulder without the wound. My life was at a crossroads, and pretty soon, I was going to have some decisions to make. My partner was gone, and in all likelihood, I was going to get a new one. Would it be one of the current homicide detectives or a newly promoted one? Would Slight let me choose? Probably not, considering I didn't have the most seniority. I'd worked with Jamey for as long as I had because he was top man on the totem pole. I was somewhere in the middle, so I would be assigned someone new unless someone above me wanted to work with me.

But I needed to make personal changes as well as professional. I wasn't about to come out to my parents, but that didn't mean I couldn't look for a little happiness. I could manage a relationship, provided they accepted that fact that they most likely wouldn't meet my parents and be introduced as my boyfriend.

However, that would mean dating, which was never something I actually liked doing. I didn't want random hookups and many gay men wanted to have sex first. I wanted feelings first and wasn't about to send cock pics to various men before they even decided to go out with me.

If only Bryce wasn't married. The case was over so that was no longer an obstacle. But he had a wife. And I couldn't get over that. Even if it was a loveless marriage that he had been trapped in. No matter how much I liked him—and I did, a lot—I couldn't just ignore the ring on his finger. I supposed I could wait until he was divorced, which I was sure was imminent. But if she wanted to make him pay, she could stretch out the divorce for a year or more. And even if I did wait, Bryce wouldn't necessarily want to jump into a committed relationship with me.

Fuck! I was getting ahead of myself. Way, way, way ahead of myself. Take it one day at a time. And today we were going to have fun.

I finished washing myself and strolled from the bathroom to the bedroom in nothing but a towel. Bryce's eyes bugged out, and I chuckled at his exaggerated expression.

"Drop the towel. Show me some of that *boo-tay*."

"Ha! Keep dreaming."

"Oh, I do, Bae. Every night."

I searched through my closet, trying to find the perfect outfit, as if I were going on a date. In a way I was, just not necessarily a romantic one. Yeah, I wanted to make Bryce drool. I supposed that made me a cock tease, but he could deal with it. I'd been honest with him, and he knew where I stood. He could either choose to spend time with me as a friend or not.

Choosing what to wear wasn't usually a big deal. At work, I wore the same basic things. Dark or khaki trousers with a white shirt and a tie. The most accessorizing I did was to switch up my tie. I tried on a couple pairs of jeans and settled on a pair of faded black ones. They were several years old and tighter than I usually preferred, but I loved how they hugged my ass like a second skin. For a top, I chose a short-sleeve midnight blue button-up with red accents.

Examining the completed outfit in a full-length mirror, I had to admit I looked damn fine. I hadn't dressed to impress in far too long.

Darren had taken away the desire to date, and I'd become complacent having Haro as a fuck buddy. There was something heady about going out and hoping men turned their eyes on me. Even if they weren't my type, I liked being noticed.

Bryce was just stepping out of the steamy bathroom when I exited the bedroom. He took one glance at me, smiled ear to ear, and whistled a catcall. "You are looking hot, Detective Tao."

I did a model pose, jutted out my hip and put my hand on it.

Bryce held up a finger and rotated it. "Give me a twirl. Let me see the whole package."

Despite feeling rather awkward, I spun around slowly so he could get a decent glimpse of my ass. The rotation ended with a flourish of jazz hands and a cheeky grin. Bryce busted out laughing and slapped his knees.

"That was terrific. I've never seen you like this. Considering how we met, that isn't surprising."

"We're not discussing that today. No negative talk. We're going to do something fun. I just haven't decided what yet."

"Well, I need to go to my hotel room and change into some fresh clothes." He patted his shirt. "Do you want to join me or should I come back here and pick you up?"

"You going to try to seduce me in your room?"

He cocked an eyebrow. "Bae, if I was going to do that, I would've done it when we were half-naked in bed together."

As much as I'd originally hated it when he used my first name, I'd grown to enjoy it. It was something no one else called me, except for my parents. "True enough," I said. "Okay. I'll go with you. We can discuss plans on the way."

I don't know what kind of car I'd expected Bryce to drive but it wasn't a Hyundai Sonata.

"A hybrid?"

He scowled. "Don't be dissing my baby. It's the newest model."

"I just expected something sportier. Or a muscle car."

Bryce shrugged. "I may have one or two of those sitting in my garage. But for driving around town I prefer this." He hit the unlock button, I opened the door and sat down. I had to admit the car was damn nice inside. Plenty of leg and head room and luxurious leather seats.

He started up the car and we took off. It definitely gave a smooth ride even in the pothole filled parking lot of my apartment complex.

"What's the plan for the day?" he asked.

"We could do the touristy shit," I replied. "Space Needle. Zoo. Pike's Market."

Bryce responded with a scowl. "I've done all that so many times."

I pulled up my phone and googled *things to do in Seattle*. "What about the Museum of Flight?"

His eyes bugged out. "I've been meaning to see the new exhibit. I took Zach there when he was younger but it's been years."

"There's also the Asian Art Museum in Capitol Hill and the Museum of History and Industry."

He glanced over at me with questioning eyes. "Those things are interesting to you?"

"Definitely." I nodded enthusiastically. "What about you?"

"Well, yeah."

"Then what's the problem?"

"I'm just used to guys who want to do so called cooler things like fancy restaurants or exclusive parties."

I shrugged. "You know I'm not spending time with you because of your money, don't you?"

"Yeah, I know it." He kept his eyes on the road as he made the turn toward his hotel. "Just not what I'm used to."

I patted his leg. "You've been hanging out with the wrong type of people."

His honest grin was heartwarming. "I guess so."

Inside his motel room he changed quickly, not bothering to shut the bedroom door. Hell, I'd already seen him naked, and I didn't mind getting another glimpse of his body. Yeah, I stood where I could get a perfect view of his ass, and I don't think he minded. He shot me a shit-eating grin when he peered into the mirror in front of him and didn't try to hide his nudity at all. Bryce was definitely going to test my resolve, that was for sure.

We were headed out the door when both our phones rang at the same time. We both chuckled at the coincidence before answering it.

"Hello."

"Hey, Peter, it's Chelsea."

"How are you? How are the kids?"

"We're doing as well as can be expected," she answered without any emotion. "I'm moving back to the house today. Thank you for arranging to have it cleaned up, by the way."

"You're welcome. Let me know if there's anything I can do."

"Thanks for the offer, but I don't need your help. Jim and Grace are leaving soon but Matt's staying. He's taking a break from school. Normally, I would've insisted he go back, but I could use him around, and I think he needs family."

She didn't mention Matt's homosexuality so I guessed he hadn't come out yet. He'd do it when he was ready, though I hoped he chose sooner rather than later for his own sake. Holding the secret in created an ache that never disappeared.

"Anyway, I called for a reason," Chelsea said. "The reading of Jamey's will is today at four p.m."

"Okay." I wasn't sure why she was telling me this.

"Can you make it?"

My mouth dried up and I choked out a response. "Me? Why do I need to be there?"

"Oh, I assumed you knew," she said. "Jamey named you in his will. He left you something."

"He didn't have to do that."

"Well, he did."

"You should be getting everything," I said. "I don't need anything."

She sighed. "I'm sure he left us well taken care of. He didn't take things like this lightly. If he gave you something, that means he wanted you to have it."

I rubbed my forehead. "Of course I'll be there. Where?"

"Our house."

"See you then."

Bryce had migrated into the other room to take his call so I waited patiently for him to finish. Judging by the tone of his voice it wasn't a pleasant call. He didn't seem happy when it finally ended.

"Who was that?" I asked.

"My lawyer. Clementine wants to meet tomorrow to iron out the divorce."

"Aren't you ready to get it over with?" What if he wanted to stay married? It was his choice, of course, but any chance of a future relationship flew out the window if he was going to stay with her.

"Hell, yeah," he replied. "I just wanted more time to figure out what I was going to give her to get her out of my life. Not that it matters."

"What do you mean?"

"I simply want one thing. At least partial custody of Zach. I'll give her half of everything if she gives me that."

"And if she doesn't?"

"Then I'd have to take her to court and the divorce would be stalled until everything was worked out."

"Do you think she'll fight you on custody?"

He shrugged. "Honestly, I'm not sure." He ran a hand through his hair. "Enough talk about that. What was your call about?"

"The reading of Jamey's will is at four today," I said. "I guess he left me something."

"Interesting. Any idea what it is?"

"Not a clue." I squeezed his shoulder. "What do you say we forget all this crap and enjoy ourselves?"

"Hell, yeah."

THE MUSEUM OF FLIGHT WAS INCREDIBLE. CHECKING OUT all the exhibits with Bryce and watching him get excited about things was a thrill. I especially loved the IMAX movie *Journey to Space* narrated by Patrick Stewart. It felt like Captain Jean Luc Picard was giving me a tour of the future.

The Asian Art Museum had collections from all over the world and through the centuries. My favorite was a Korean collection from the 1800s.

"My dad's a Korean history buff," I said. "This was his favorite time period."

The art pieces consisted of a ten panel folding screen with birds and flowers from the Joseon Dynasty, a porcelain jar with red peonies, and a porcelain water dropper in the shape of a fish.

"What's a water dropper?" Bryce asked.

"They were part of the Joseon writing tools," I said. "Usually in the shape of fish, animals, or fruits."

"Interesting," he said. I examined his face for signs of boredom or duplicity but there was neither.

"The nineteenth century was significant for Korea because it was the start of them entering the modern era. There was a lot of political maneuvering, which weakened the leadership, but culturally things improved greatly. However, a succession of weak kings and a lack of visionary leadership meant Korea eventually signed a treaty with Japan and came under Japanese rule in 1910."

I rattled on for a good half hour before I caught myself. "Sorry, I was rambling there, wasn't I?"

"No worries. It was interesting. I liked seeing you talk about something you find captivating. Your face lights up."

I blushed and changed the subject. "I'm hungry. How about you?"

"Yeah, I could eat."

We found a nearby diner, and I ordered a burger while Bryce ordered a Caesar Chicken Salad.

"I assume homosexuality is frowned on in Korea," Bryce said. "Even nowadays."

I nodded and stuffed a French fry in my mouth before replying. "It's seen as a perversion. Even in modern Korean society, homosexuality is looked at as a disease and a sin. Gay men are seen as something to be frightened of because they prey on *normal* people. It's still common for them—for us—to be misunderstood as feminine or crossdressers or transgender."

"That's sad." He shook his head slightly before stabbing a piece of chicken with his fork and popping it into his mouth.

"Sex is seen as only legitimate within monogamous heterosexual marriage. However, people who have sex before marriage or have affairs are not as despised as gay people." I tugged on my ear and chuckled. "The thing is there are clubs all over Korea where men go to fool around with other men."

"Prostitution?"

I nodded. "But it happens in the shadows, and no one officially acknowledges it so it continues. It would take a miracle for Korea to enter modern thinking when it comes to homosexuality."

"And your parents are old school that way?"

"Oh, yeah. They follow all the rules of the church."

"Even though they came to America?"

"They did that for me, as they tell me *all the time*. They wanted me to have a better life."

"Are they okay with you being a cop?"

I shrugged. "Mom worries about me being safe but they let me choose my own career."

"Just not your sexuality."

"Nope. That would be a major leap for them."

"And you're okay keeping that part from them?"

"No, I hate it," I replied. "But what's my other option? If I tell them, they'd likely disown me, and I'd never see them again. I'd rather have a relationship with them and keep a secret than lose them altogether."

"Makes sense."

We made small talk for the rest of lunch before heading to the Museum of History and Industry, which was interesting. My favorite exhibit was toys from the fifties, sixties, and seventies but the Legacy of Seattle Hip-Hop was fascinating even if it wasn't the type of music I usually listened to.

The closer it got to four, the less I was able to concentrate, and Bryce must've noticed my distraction.

"You okay?" he asked.

"Yeah, I'm sorry. I'm just thinking about Jamey's will and what he could possibly have left me."

"It's three now," he said. "Do you want to head over? You'd be there early but I'm sure the family wouldn't mind."

"Yeah, I think I'd like that."

"Okay, well, let's get going. I'll drop you off at your place."

"What? Oh…okay." I tried and failed to hide my disappointment.

"Is that not what you want to do?" he asked.

"Well, I was kind of hoping you'd come with me. I could use a friend there and maybe afterward, depending on what happens, we can go somewhere. I've been having a great time, and I don't want it to end."

He grinned and took my hand. "I'd love to be there for you. I've had an excellent time today too. The best I've had for as long as I can remember. You have a way of making me forget all the shit that's going on around me. I appreciate that."

I leaned forward and kissed him gently on the lips. "So do I."

WE ARRIVED AT JAMEY AND CHELSEA'S PLACE TWENTY-FIVE minutes early. It was a small group, made up of his parents, his brother, and Chelsea, and the kids. I introduced Bryce to everyone as my friend. Jamey's parents and brother were indifferent to me as always, Chelsea was standoffish again but the kids gave me a warm welcome. Matt pulled me aside.

"I haven't told anyone yet," he said. "About me being gay, I mean."

"I figured. Don't worry, I'm not going to say anything until you're ready. But Jim and Grace are going to be leaving soon. You should do it before they go."

He rubbed his forehead. "I know. I'm just trying to gather the guts."

"I'm sure it's not going to be anywhere near as bad as you're imagining it."

"Yeah. It's just terrifying."

"I heard you're staying with your mother for a while. That's sweet of you."

"Thanks. I don't feel like being alone. I'm not sure college is what's for me anyway. At least not Business like I was studying."

"No plans to go into the family business?"

"Oh, hell no. Jim can handle that. I might follow in Dad's footsteps."

My eyes bugged out. "You're considering being a cop?"

"Yeah. What do you think?"

"Well, of all the kids, I'd say you're the one most suited for it. That doesn't mean your mom's going to love the idea. She'll likely be more freaked out over you joining the force than the fact you like men."

He chuckled. "I think you're right on that score."

Shortly, the family lawyer called everyone into the kitchen, where a couple rows of chairs were set up. Jamey left his parents and brother specific mementos since they didn't need his money. He bequeathed each kid a personal bank account of six million dollars each with the provision they couldn't spend more than a hundred thousand at a time or one million in a year without Chelsea signing off on it.

Chelsea got an estate worth over ten million to do with as she pleased, whenever she pleased. Knowing Chelsea, I doubted she'd touch more than she needed to live. She'd never lived off of Jamey's wealth, and I didn't see her doing it now.

I was the final person listed in the will.

"To Peter Tao, my longtime partner and friend," the lawyer said, "I leave two million dollars."

ELEVEN

DID I HEAR THAT RIGHT? EVERYONE STARED AT me with wide eyes and dumbfounded expressions. No one had been expecting this.

I was still processing it all when the lawyer said he was done and packed up his briefcase. On his way out, he stopped by my chair and handed me an envelope.

"What's this?" I stared up at him blankly.

"A letter from Mr. Nolan. He gave it to me when he changed his will a year ago. He said to read it in private."

I took it and nodded. Everyone stood from their chairs, but I remained sitting. Bryce nudged me with his shoulder and asked, "Are you all right?"

I shook my head. "Yeah. No. I'm fine."

He chuckled. "Which one is it? Yes or no?"

Even glaring straight at him I couldn't seem to focus. "Um… I'm not sure. It's rather overwhelming."

"Do you want to read the letter?"

The envelope sat crumpled in my lap, so I shoved it in my pocket. "No. I'm not ready."

"Should we get out of here?"

I nodded enthusiastically. "Yes, please, yes."

Bryce took my hand, and I stood then followed him to Chelsea.

"Jamey really did like you," she said without an ounce of emotion in her voice.

"Are you sure?" I asked. "I'm not. I think you and the kids should've gotten everything. I can give you the money."

She pursed her lips and scowled. "I didn't need his money, and I sure as hell don't need yours. Just accept it."

Her coldness was like a slap across the face. "I need to go," I said. "We'll talk soon."

A moment later, we were out the door and driving away. I rolled down the window and let the cool air blast me in the face.

"You want to go home?"

I peered at Bryce for a moment before answering. "Hell no. Take me somewhere with overpriced drinks and loud music."

"You sure?"

"Absolutely."

We ended up in Capitol Hill at R Place, one of the busiest gay bars in Seattle. It had three floors with a bar on each one as well as different types of music. It attracted all sorts of crowds, not just twinks like other clubs.

Once inside, I pulled myself close to Bryce and whispered in his ear, "Buy me a drink?"

"What would you like?"

"Dirty Martini."

"You got it."

I snagged a corner table and waved Bryce over after he had our drinks. I gulped down a large swig of the martini.

"Take it easy," he warned.

"Why?"

"Well, unless you take another day off you have to go to work tomorrow."

"Do I? I have two million dollars for fuck's sake. I could quit my job and do whatever the hell I want."

He shot me a surprised glance. "Did you become a cop for the paycheck?"

"Of course not."

"Exactly. You did it, I assume, because you wanted to make a difference."

Damn it, he was making too much sense. I waved a hand dismissively. "Never mind all that. I just want to have fun. Forget everything for a couple hours."

"Well, let's do it. Care to dance?"

I took another mouthful of the drink, took Bryce's hand, and pulled him onto the dance floor. For an older man, Bryce still had excellent rhythm and moves. We swayed to the music both apart and touching. At times, my back was to his front, and his erection pressed against my ass. It was never anything lewd or demanding, but I certainly knew how he felt. And fuck if I didn't feel the attraction just as much as he did.

And that scared me.

When we took a break, I slammed back a couple of shots before getting another martini for each of us.

"Having fun?" Bryce yelled over the din.

I nodded and continued moving to the music even in my seat. I had an itch I wanted scratched but it would entail breaking one of my self-imposed rules. I wanted to get laid something fierce, and that would mean either having a random hookup with a stranger or going after the man I really wanted—Bryce—despite the fact he was a married man.

As if it was a sign from above, a hot young guy in his mid-twenties wearing nothing above the waist sauntered over and asked if I'd like to dance. I glanced at Bryce, hoping he wouldn't mind, and he gave me the nod to go for it. The guy grinned when I took his hand and hit the dance floor.

"Is that your boyfriend?" he asked after a minute, having to lean in so I could hear him.

"No. Just a friend," I replied.

Apparently, that made him extremely happy, and his face lit up. "Excellent. I'd hate to hit on you if you were taken."

Brash! I liked that.

He spun me around so my ass was pressed against his groin. "My name's Freeman."

"Peter," I replied.

"You are one sexy motherfucker, Peter." He gripped my hips and ground his hard-on into my butt. Substantially different from how Bryce had signaled his feelings, and I suddenly lost all my inhibitions.

I spun around and pulled Freeman into a passionate, mouth-devouring kiss. He was breathing heavily when I finally pulled away.

"Damn, that was hot."

"I needed to know how well you kissed."

"Why?"

"To judge how well you suck cock." I wasn't sure what had come over me. I had never been so forward.

He gulped and, for a moment, I thought I'd pushed too far too fast. Then he smiled. "I'll blow your mind if you give me a chance."

"Are the bathrooms monitored here?"

"Only on the weekends. There isn't as much traffic during the week."

"Perfect."

I tugged him into the restroom and then into a handicap stall before kissing him again. I swept my tongue into his mouth, tasting him and reveling in the way he moaned at the intimate touch.

Freeman pulled away, then licked down my neck, stopping to nuzzle in the crook of it. He slowly unbuttoned my shirt before lowering his lips to my right nipple, taking it between his lips and sucking gently.

"Oh, damn, that's nice," I groaned.

"I've been told I have magic lips."

Okay, that line was rather corny but it didn't make my hard-on go away whatsoever.

Freeman had just turned his attention to my left nipple when the door to the stall flew open and Bryce stood there, staring at us. I tried to ignore the expression of hurt on his face.

"What the hell?" Freeman demanded. "We're kind of busy in here."

"You disappeared," Bryce replied. "I was worried about you."

"He's fine, as you can see," Freeman snapped.

Bryce ignored the guy and stared at me. "Peter, are you sure you want to do this?"

"I'm a big boy. I don't need you taking care of me."

"You've been through a lot lately. Today especially. I just want to make sure you're not going to do something you'll regret later."

Freeman kissed my neck and cupped my groin. "He won't regret *anything* I do to him."

Bryce shrugged. "Okay. If you're sure."

I looked from Freeman to Bryce and said, "Yeah, I'm sure." I wasn't. Not really. But I tried to make it sound like I was. I was horny, but the man I really wanted wasn't available. I wouldn't break my rule about married men, not that having a random one-off was a much better choice. I wasn't sure which one would make me feel sleazier.

Bryce stepped out of the stall, and Freeman locked it.

"Now, where were we? Oh, yeah. Right here." He kissed my nipple and bit it gently before trailing his tongue down my stomach. He was about to undo the button on my jeans when I stopped him with a hand on his.

"Wait, I'm not sure about this."

"What? Don't let your buddy cock block you. He's just a jealous old queen who can't get his own piece of ass."

That did it. If I hadn't been positive letting Freeman blow me was a mistake, I certainly was now. I pushed him away and he pouted.

"I'm sorry. I really am. This was a mistake. I can't do this."

"Your loss." Freeman shrugged, unlocked the stall door, and slammed it behind him.

I secured it again and sat on the toilet, burying my face in my hands. Bryce was right. I would've regretted it afterward and hated myself for allowing it to happen. I shifted and heard the sound of paper crinkling. I retrieved the envelope, opened it, and unfolded Jamey's letter.

Peter, I bet you're shocked as hell at my gift. I wish I could see your face right now.

First of all, I want to say how much I've enjoyed being your partner and friend all these years. It has honestly been my pleasure to get to know you. I couldn't have asked for a better man to have at my side. You've always had my back just as I've had yours.

You're a true friend. You never cared that I came from money. You never treated me differently, and you never once asked for a dime even when you had to give your savings to your parents because they were losing their house. That was an honorable thing to do. You allowed your parents to keep their beloved home while you kept living in a shitty apartment.

I'm giving you this money so you can take care of yourself. I can't imagine you not being a cop, but if that's what you choose to do, that's fine. Whatever you do with your life, just be happy doing it. That's all I ask.

I don't see the money changing you, and I hope I'm right. I never let my wealth affect how I lived, but I used it to make my life easier when I needed to. I hope you do the same.

I've always tried to stay out of your personal life and never gave unsolicited advice so forgive me for doing so now.

You need to let down those walls that keep people out. You need love in your life but you won't find it hiding. I know why you think you have to protect yourself from being hurt, but you'll never find happiness that way. I wish I could've stayed around to see you find Mr. Right but don't let that stop you from searching. Please.

Your friend and brother, Jamey Nolan

I didn't think I had any more tears after my sobfest the previous night, but holy hell, was I wrong. Sitting there on that toilet, I had one of the strongest and most cathartic cries ever. It wasn't long, and it wasn't loud, but it did the trick. I never imagined I'd have an epiphany in a men's restroom, but that's exactly what happened.

Eventually, I cleaned myself up and found Bryce. "I'm ready to go if you are."

"You okay?" he asked. "I saw your friend leave but then you didn't come out. I was getting worried."

"Never been better," I said, and it was the truth.

We both remained silent on the drive to my place and when we got there Bryce didn't make a move to get out of the car.

"You want to spend the night again?" I asked.

He smiled ruefully. "More than anything, but I'd better not."

"Why?"

"It's no secret how much I want to be with you, but I haven't pushed you or tried to get you to change your mind."

"And I appreciate that. You have no idea how much."

He ran a hand through his hair. "I was jealous tonight when I saw you with that other guy. So fucking jealous I saw red."

"I stopped him. We didn't do anything."

"That doesn't matter." He paused and furrowed his brow. "Okay, it does matter. I'm glad for you, but that doesn't change how amped up I am. Sexually amped up, I mean. I'm not sure I would be able to stop myself from mauling you tonight. I think it's best if I go back to my hotel. We can talk tomorrow."

"Okay," I said sadly. "I understand. I'll miss you."

"Me too."

Before getting out of the car, I leaned over, put my hand on the back of Bryce's neck, and kissed him. It was sweet and sensuous and erotic. His tongue prodded at my lips, and I allowed him entrance. I melted at his touch and wanted more. So much more. And I was so close to giving in when he broke away.

"Damn!" He wiped sweat from his forehead. "You better go."

"Good night, Bryce."

TWELVE

WHEN I GOT TO WORK THURSDAY MORNING, BOTH desks that had been occupied most recently by Aza and Molly were empty. No signs of life whatsoever. It made sense that Aza was back in the tech room since the case was over, but for some reason, I'd expected him still to be there. Molly, however, was still assigned to the homicide division on desk duty, I thought.

I walked over to Detective Shep Adley's desk and asked, "Have you seen Whitmore?"

He didn't bother glancing away from the report he was writing to answer. "Her punishment's been lifted. Chief Slight was so impressed with her work on the case with you that she put her back on patrol."

"Oh, good for her." I wandered back to my desk and took a seat. I was happy for Molly. She certainly deserved to be taken off desk duty, but that didn't mean I wouldn't miss her. I'd grown accustomed to having her around. In fact, I'd liked working with her a lot. Just more changes in my life I had to deal with.

I stared at my computer for a minute, unsure what to do next. Jamey and I hadn't been working any major cases before Diana Gomez had started hacking up cheaters, though we did have a couple of cold cases I could try working on. I'd just opened a report on the death of an elderly man named Hassan Barr when Shep came up to my desk.

"There's been a shooting on Capitol Hill near Melrose and Pine. I don't have a partner at the moment. Would you like to work this one with me?"

I was taken aback because Shep and I didn't usually get along. He could quote every single rule and regulation and insisted on following everything to the letter whereas I believed that to be a decent cop one had to cut corners every once in a while. But Shep, a tall, skinny, freckle-faced ginger, was a cop with a strong clearance rate. And most of all, I didn't feel like sitting around with my thumb up my ass until another case came along. Besides, it wasn't like I was going to be partnered with Shep forever.

"Sure, I'll join ya. Thanks." I stood, grabbed my coat and gun, and we headed to the scene of the crime.

According to several witnesses, the victim, 30-year-old African American Roosevelt Robinson, had been sitting in his car outside The Baltic Room, a popular nightclub, when he was approached by three men. A verbal confrontation ensued and Robinson was shot multiple times. The shooters then took off in different directions. The victim was transported to the nearest hospital, Harborview Medical Center, where he was still undergoing surgery.

Despite the number of witnesses, I didn't get one solid description of the shooters other than they were black and wore hoodies. Not much help there. Our best hope was that Robinson could name the guys.

Shep and I spent the day talking to Robinson's girlfriend and family and then finally to the victim himself. He said he knew all the guys but only by their gang nicknames: Dice, Gig, and Weasel Boy. Gig was Robinson's girlfriend's ex-boyfriend and not happy that Robinson, who appeared not to be gang-affiliated, had stolen his girl. With Gig, at least, we were able to get a name, Omar Hewitt.

At the end of the day, we didn't have any solid leads but had places to check out on Friday. I invited Shep for a drink at The Blarney Stone.

"I don't drink alcohol, but I'll still join you."

I ordered a mug of whatever was on tap and Shep had a Coke, then we sat in a booth.

"Thanks for inviting me today," I said.

"No problem. I figured you would want to stay busy."

"Yeah, that's the truth."

"I wanted to say I'm sorry about Nolan. He was a good man."

"I was lucky to have worked with him," I said.

"So I know we've had our differences in the past…"

I waved a hand. "Why don't we forget about that and focus on the future?"

He grinned, showing pearly white teeth. "I'd like that."

We lifted our glasses and clinked them together. The idea of working with Shep, or anyone else, no longer bothered me. I'd learned a lot from Jamey, and I could probably do the same with Shep, even if he did annoy me a lot of the time. And maybe I could teach him a thing or two.

I was exhausted when I got home but stayed awake to have a short phone-call with Bryce, who had good news and bad news.

"Clementine isn't fighting me on custody of Zach. We'll have joint custody. I'm giving her the house, which is fine, because she decorated it and it isn't my style at all. I'll work on finding a new place soon. We agreed on almost everything. I had to fight to keep a cabin at Vale that my father built but she accepted a couple pieces of art in trade."

"Excellent. What's the bad news?"

"Because of everything the divorce entails, such as the splitting of assets, the money and all that, it could take up to six months for the divorce to be finalized."

Six months? I'd have to wait half a year before I could be with Bryce, if that was even what he wanted.

"How do you feel about that?" he asked.

Honestly, I wasn't sure. Should I tell him I had hoped we could have a relationship? Was that what he wanted?

"Let me think about it," I said. "Let's have dinner tomorrow night and talk."

"Perfect. I'll pick you up at seven?"

"It's a date."

"A date, huh? I like the sound of that."

THIRTEEN

SHEP AND I WERE BACK ON THE JOB first thing in the morning. Gig had seemingly vanished. None of his friends or family claimed to know where he was. Even if they had known, I doubted they would have shared the information with me. They weren't lovers of law enforcement, thanks in part to years of piss poor treatment of African Americans by racist members of the force. Most of them had been weeded out but they had done the damage, and the rest of us had to deal with the shit they left behind.

Around two p.m. we got a call that a patrol car had pulled over a drunk driver by the name of Myron Bean, who had initially given his name as Dice. The officer, Molly as it turned out, had recognized the name from the BOLO we'd put out and called it in.

While Shep spoke to Myron, I talked to Molly.

"I'm so glad your restriction was lifted."

"It's amazing being back on the streets," she said. "I owe it all to you."

"Not at all. You earned it. I couldn't have closed the case without you."

"I was thinking about that and remembered something we never discussed."

"What's that?"

She scratched at her neck for a moment. "When Eloise Nash described the person who attacked Julian Ramsey, she said the killer had a tattoo on their wrist."

"And Diana Gomez *doesn't* have a tattoo?"

"That's right. I don't mean to question your decision to close the case, but—"

I waved a hand. "Don't worry about it. If I remember right, Nash wasn't detailed about what she saw. It could've been a bracelet or even a trick of the light."

"So I shouldn't worry about it?"

"It's great that you brought it up, but there's no need to stress about it."

Shep ambled up. "He's our guy. He admitted he was there when Gig shot Robinson but claims he didn't have a gun. We'll have to wait 'til he sobers up to get an official statement."

Shep and I took Myron in, and he didn't puke until he was out of the car. We threw him in with the other recent arrests and told the guard to let us know when he was sober.

While Shep wrote up the report on the arrest, I sat at my desk, unable to get what Molly had told me out of my head. I'd told her not to stress about the closed case, but now I was doing that very thing. It wasn't *just* the fact that Diana Gomez didn't have a tattoo that bothered me. There were other things that didn't feel right even if I couldn't pinpoint them. My gut told me something was wrong. The question was, should I listen to my instincts or not?

My instincts had been wrong before. Especially with Darren. But most of the time they served me well. The case was closed and the killer dead. Part of me wanted to let it go and move on. However, if Diana Gomez *wasn't* the killer, then I wanted the real one caught. Damn it, I was frozen with indecision. Definitely not something I was used to.

I didn't have time to focus on it because Shep told me he'd found a lead on Gig and off we went. The lead didn't pan out, but we spent the day searching homeless shelters and other places a young guy might hide. There was simply no way to check every single homeless encampment in Seattle. We did our best but still came up with nothing.

We ended the day at six, and it gave me enough time to get home and clean up before Bryce arrived for our date. Yeah, I liked the sound of that too.

Ironically, he took me to Palisade, an elevated seafood restaurant overlooking Elliot Bay, not too far from where we'd found the body of Julian Ramsey. Though it didn't help me forget about the case, Bryce was stunning in a navy blue suit. The top few buttons of his white shirt were open, allowing me a glimpse of his hairy chest.

We were halfway through the meal when Bryce finally brought up the subject we'd been avoiding—his divorce.

"I think it's time you tell me how you feel about it being six months until my marriage is over."

I stalled for time by stabbing a piece of lobster with a fork, dipping it in the warm drawn butter, and popping it into my mouth. I decided honesty was the best way to go, even if it did end up with me getting hurt.

"Okay, I'm going to put all my cards on the table." I took a deep breath. "I like you a lot, Bryce. Certainly more than I'd expected. But you're married and will be for a bit longer."

He reached over the table and took my hands. "I like you too, Peter. More than any man for a long, long time."

For a moment, I was stunned by the public display of affection, but if he wasn't worried about other people, then neither was I. I entwined my fingers with his. "If you were single right now, I'm sure we would have already slept together."

He chuckled.

"However, I don't like sex outside of a committed relationship."

"And if I wasn't married that is precisely what I'd want too."

God, it was a relief to hear that. I'd suspected but hadn't been one hundred percent sure. "If you want me to, I'll wait for you. Six months or even longer, I suppose. I want to be with you, Bryce. No one else. And if I have to wait for that to happen, then I will."

His face lit up and he grinned widely. "I would absolutely love that. I was afraid to ask."

"I was fearful you wouldn't want to go from a marriage into a commitment with anyone."

"You're not just anyone, though. You very well might be the guy I've been waiting for all these years."

My entire body warmed at that statement. No one had ever said anything so sweet to me.

"Can you go six months without sex?" I asked.

"It's going to be hard," he said. "Pun intended. But I'll manage, if you can."

"It'll be worth it. I'm sure of it."

"I don't doubt that at all."

We finished our meal and took a stroll along the dock. We held hands and even made out like teenagers with Bryce pressing me against the wall. Our hands wandered, and I slipped one under his shirt to play with a nipple. He caressed my crotch and traced the outline of my cock. However, when he made a move to reach into my pants I stopped him.

"That's far enough, mister."

He groaned and dropped his head on my shoulder. "Damn, I want to touch you so badly. Feel your cock in my hand. Stroke it. Pull it. Kiss it." He kissed my neck, and my entire body shivered, but I found the strength to push him away.

"We're waiting, remember?"

He sighed. "You must've been a monk in another life. I don't know how else you can be so turned on and still push me away."

"I have my reasons," I said and continued walking.

"Are you ready to tell me about your reasons?"

I paused. "Yeah, I am."

He pulled me to a small outdoor table and we sat.

I took a deep breath and focused on things I'd been trying to forget. "It was about five years ago," I began. "His name was Darren Finney, a pilot. I met him when Jamey and I investigated the murder of one his coworkers. There was an instant spark between the two of us, and he called me a few days after we'd closed the case. He asked me out, and I said yes. We had an incredible dinner and a nightcap at his hotel room and then we had wild, fuck-me-through-the-mattress sex."

Bryce cocked an eyebrow and shot me a scowl.

"I was younger and quicker to jump into bed with someone, though even back then, I didn't have many one-night stands. Darren was intoxicating and passionate. He was older than me by ten years, and he seemed so mature and worldly. He told me all about the places he'd visited and the famous people he'd met. I fell in love with him almost right away. Definitely too quickly. He mainly split his time between Seattle and New York and usually slept at a cheap apartment he and other pilots and flight attendants shared. I thought that was unnecessary and told him he could stay with me when he was in town.

"He basically lived with me for six months, though he was gone most of the time. I missed him when he was gone and loved every minute of being with him. We discussed the future. Talked about getting married and even having kids."

"Sounds like a fairytale romance," Bryce said.

"Yeah. But you know the saying 'If it seems too good to be true...'"

"It probably is."

"About seven months into the relationship, I began to feel like something was wrong, but I just couldn't put my finger on it. He acted odd when I began to push the idea of making it permanent. He claimed I was moving too fast but I thought it was more than that. One time, I greeted him at the airport and he freaked out. Pushed me away like he didn't know me."

"What an ass."

"Later he claimed he didn't like his coworkers knowing anything about his relationships. He claimed he was out of the closet, but it all seemed so strange. I told Jamey about it and he was convinced Darren was hiding something. He even encouraged me to look him up in the system."

"I'm surprised you already hadn't done that," Bryce said.

"I was young and trusting," I said. "Not anymore."

"You checked me right away, didn't you?"

"I already knew all about you before we met." I chuckled. "Anyway, finally I took Jamey's advice. Turned out Darren was married. Had a wife of ten years and a couple kids."

"Damn," Bryce murmured. "Total asshat."

"I confronted him and he admitted it. Claimed he loved me and didn't know what to do."

"Is that when you dumped him?"

"Ha! I wish. I was in love with him and believed him when he said he would leave her for me. At first, anyway. It didn't take me long to realize he was full of shit."

"And that's when you dumped him?"

"Yes. He was furious and begged me for another chance. When I refused, he told me I'd never been anything more than a piece of ass. One of many he had along the way."

"One in every port, as they say."

"Exactly. From then on I swore off random hookups and married men."

"You haven't had any relationships since him?"

"A couple." I answered. "Never lasted more than a few months. I can see now I wasn't open with them. We never had a chance. For the past two years, it's been only Haro in my bed."

"Thank you for telling me," he said. "I appreciate you opening up."

"Well, it's something new I'm trying. Being accessible to the men I'm dating. Not that we're dating."

He mock gasped. "We're not?"

I shook my head. "I don't know what to call it, but I don't want to think that I'm dating a married man. How about we just be friends?"

"Friends who kiss?"

I tapped my chin like I was pondering a deep question. "Sure. Friends who kiss."

He laughed loudly, stood, and pulled me against him. "Cool. Because I love kissing you."

FOURTEEN

Saturday was officially my day off, but I went in to see if Shep had any new leads or needed my help.

"I'm just doing Internet searches," he said. "I can handle it, but I'll call you if I need you."

"Thanks, man." I said and patted his shoulder.

On my desk was a message from a guy named Mason Patel requesting I call him back. The name rang a bell but it took a minute for me to remember who he was. Jamey and I had interviewed him at the docks on Elliot Bay. He'd been near where the body of Julian Ramsay had been found. I checked out my notes to refresh my memories, and it came back to me.

Patel had been partying the night of the murder but he had seen a redheaded woman on the docks. I had no idea why he'd be calling me but I returned the phone-call. I'd been just about to hang up when he answered.

"Hello, Mr. Patel, this is Detective Tao returning your call."

"Oh, hey, Detective. You told me to call if I had more information for you."

I considered telling him the case was closed, but wanted to hear what he had to say.

"I saw that woman again. The one I told you about."

"The woman on the docks? You saw her again?"

"Yeah. She's a drag queen. I saw her sing at Le Faux, the cabaret bar on Broadway. She, or he, performed as Lavish Gloss."

"You're sure it was her?"

"Well, not a hundred percent, but I'm pretty positive it was her."

"Okay, thanks."

After ending the call with Patel I visited Le Faux's website and learned Lavish Gloss was performing again that night.

"Wonder if Bryce likes drag shows?" I whispered to no one in particular.

I closed down my computer and was heading to the restroom when I bumped into Aza. *Literally* bumped into him because neither of us was looking where we were going.

"Peter! How are you?"

We shook hands. "I'm good. How about you?"

"The same. I've missed working with you. I enjoyed getting out of the cave." He nodded toward the dark tech room.

"I liked it as well. I hope we can work together again sometime."

He paused and had a concerned expression on his face. "There was something I wanted to talk to you about but I wasn't sure if I should." He glanced around like he was searching for eavesdroppers.

"You want to grab a bite at the diner across the street?" I asked.

"Yes, I would like that very much."

We crossed the street and took a booth, waiting until we ordered to start talking.

"What's on your mind, Aza?"

He chewed on his lip for a moment. "I know the case is closed, but there are things that bug me. It doesn't feel right."

I chuckled and he shot me an inquisitive stare. "Molly just talked to me yesterday and said the same thing. I'd be lying if I said I didn't have the same concerns."

Aza relaxed and took a sip of water. "I can't tell you exactly what bothers me and that's the problem. I have nothing concrete. Just a gut feeling."

"Ditto," I said. "I wouldn't even know where to start."

"I have a few ideas but wasn't sure if I should do anything."

"It can't be anything official. I don't want it getting out that we have doubts. If we were wrong we'd all be screwed."

"I can do it in between other cases," Aza said. "It won't alert anyone. We have free rein back there as long as we get results. I just wanted to get your thoughts beforehand."

"I say, go for it. Report to me as soon as you find anything."

He grinned. "Working together again. I love it."

TURNED OUT BRYCE WAS A BIG FAN OF drag shows and was ecstatic about going to Le Faux. I didn't tell him the entire truth about the visit, just that a friend had recommended I see Miss Lavish Gloss.

Turned out Gloss, with enormous fake boobs, caked on makeup, and gigantic red wig, was indeed fabulous. She performed more than any of the queens that night and rightfully so. She had the best voice and was funny as all get-out.

When the show was over I pushed through the crowd, hoping to speak to Miss Gloss. She spotted me from across the room, and her eyes bulged immediately. She didn't just turn and walk in the opposite direction. She ran away from me and bolted into the dressing-rooms. I was close behind her but a huge, burly bodyguard blocked my way. He stepped aside when I pulled out my badge, but by the time I got there, Gloss was gone. She'd dashed out the back door and vanished.

The proprietor of Le Faux was no help. He refused to give me Lavish Gloss's real name unless I had a warrant. And I couldn't get a warrant without alerting others I was working on a closed case.

"What was that all about?" Bryce asked when I found him an hour later. "Were you here on official duty?"

"Not really."

"Either you were or you weren't. Which one?"

"I don't feel like talking about it, okay? Just fucking drop it," I snapped.

He held up his hands and stepped back. "You ready to go?"

"Hell, yeah."

The rest of the evening was a bust. I couldn't concentrate on anything but the case. Who was Lavish Gloss, and why did she run? Did she know me or just peg me as a cop? I hated questions without answers.

I apologized to Bryce and asked if we could end the night early. "Let's hang out tomorrow," I said. "I promise I'll be in a better mood."

He kissed me goodnight at my door and drove off. I missed him the second he was gone and realized I was closing myself off to him again. I just wasn't sure I should involve him in my secret activities. If Diana Gomez *wasn't* the killer, that meant the person who attacked Bryce was still out there. I didn't want to worry him but I also would hate myself if he ended up hurt because I hadn't been forthcoming.

Fuck my life.

FIFTEEN

I DRAGGED MYSELF OUT OF BED AROUND NINE Sunday morning, started the coffee maker, and took a shower. While eating a bowl of cereal, I pondered how to handle the argument I'd had with Bryce. Normally, I wouldn't be able to involve him in an official police investigation. Then again, this wasn't an *official* investigation. This was off the books, and in addition to being involved, he might just be able to help me.

I was reaching for my cell to call Bryce when it rang, making me jump. Caller ID said it was Aza.

"Hey Aza, what's up?" I asked.

"Is it okay for me to be calling you on your day off?"

"Don't worry about it."

"Excellent, because I have something I am sure you will want to know."

"Involving our little secret?" I asked.

He chuckled and said, "Yes. I went back to the Walmart footage. I hadn't been able to do much with it so I'd set it aside."

"I assume it was Diana Gomez buying the go phone," I said.

"That's what I assumed as well, until I started to question everything."

"And you found something?"

"Footage like this doesn't always work to prove an identity. That is, I couldn't take it and present a profile. However, it *disproves* an identity."

I shook my head and rubbed my neck. "You lost me there, Aza."

"For example, I can put in your characteristics: height, weight, etc. And it would prove it wasn't you based on those factors. So I did the same with Diana Gomez."

"And?"

"And it wasn't her. There are aspects of the person's face that don't match Diana's. The height is even off by a quarter of an inch. It's not something I could use in court because it's not precise enough, but it adds to what our suspicions are already telling us."

"Good job, Aza. Though it's not quite enough to go on."

"Yeah, I know. I'm just starting. I have other leads to follow as well. I'll let you know when I find anything more." He ended the call without another word.

I set the phone down and finished my coffee before calling Bryce.

"Hey there," I said.

"Morning."

"I'm sorry for being an ass last night. I'm ready to talk about it if you're ready to listen. Can you come over?"

"Of course. See you soon."

I GREETED BRYCE AT THE DOOR WITH A hug that turned into a hot kiss before he even got inside.

"Now that is a greeting I could get used to."

"Me, too." I took his hand and led him into the living room. We sat on the couch facing each other.

"What's going on, Bae?"

I took a deep breath and told him about what Molly had said about the tattoo, what Aza had discovered about the Walmart footage, and how the three of us all had our guts telling us something wasn't right with the case.

"So you're not convinced Diana Gomez was the killer? You think whoever hacked up all these guys, and who attacked me, is still out there?"

"Yeah, but it's not enough to go to the chief with. If I did, and I was wrong, it wouldn't look good and could harm my career."

"What are you going to do?"

"Investigate it on the sly, I guess."

"How does the drag show fit into this?"

I told him about Mason Patel and the woman he'd seen on the docks that night and his recent call. "I'm not sure that woman was the killer, but I'd sure like to talk to her. If it was Lavish Gloss, it seems she might have something to hide, considering how fast she ran from me last night. The club owner won't give me any information about her without a warrant."

"Which you can't get because this is an unofficial investigation."

"Correct, so I don't know how to proceed."

He pulled me close, and we snuggled. "You'll figure it out. You're smart."

I pressed up against him, taking in his exquisite smell. We stayed like that for several hours watching movies and talking.

Around two p.m., we decided to go out for a late lunch and decided on Changes, a gay-friendly pub with a homey décor and chill atmosphere. There was music playing and a small dance floor where several guys danced, but it wasn't so loud we had to yell to have a conversation.

"Their menu is small," Bryce said, "but their burgers are fabulous."

We'd just ordered when one of the couples dancing broke apart and headed our way, holding hands intimately. I'd just taken a drink of my beer and nearly snorted it out my nose when I recognized one of the men. He wore cargo shorts, sandals, and a salmon-colored T-shirt, but it was still the man I worked with.

"Shep?"

His eyes damn near bugged out of his head. "Peter. What are you doing here?" He eyed Bryce warily.

"Grabbing a bite to eat. And you?"

Shep's dance partner wrapped his arm around Shep and pressed close against him. "Shepherd, who is this?" He had to be several years younger than Shep. I put him at around twenty one or twenty. Definite twink, complete with lilting voice.

"Oh, this is Peter. We work together."

"Detective Peter Tao." I extended my hand, and he took it. His grip was firmer then I'd expected.

"Ryan Watkins."

"And I'm Bryce Carrick."

After the introduction, Ryan and Shep just stood there like deer in the headlights. Finally, Ryan said, "I'm gonna grab a table. Join me when you can, babe." He then placed a kiss on Shep's cheek and strode off.

"And I…need to use the restroom," Bryce said and made a hasty exit.

"Have a seat," I said. "I think we need to talk."

Shep flopped down in the chair and leaned forward, tugging nervously at a large leather bracelet on his left wrist. "I didn't know you were gay."

I shrugged. "I don't hide it but don't advertise it either. Jamey knew and others might too. I don't know for sure. I had no clue you were gay either."

"Bi, and in the closet, at least at work. My family knows."

I snorted. "That's funny. I'm the opposite. I'll likely never tell my parents, but I don't care if people at work know."

"I have my reasons." His face reddened as if I'd insulted him.

"No worries here, man. I'm not going to tell anyone. Your secrets are yours."

He relaxed. "Thanks. I appreciate it."

I gestured across the room to where Ryan was sipping what appeared to be an appletini. "Your boyfriend's cute."

His grin was warm and wide. Shep obviously cared for the young man a great deal. "Yeah, he's special. We've only been dating a few weeks but I like him a lot." He faced me. "You and Bryce Carrick? He's married, isn't he?"

"Yeah. It's a long and complicated story." I took a swig of the beer. "But he's an awesome guy. One of the best I've ever met."

Shep shrugged. "You'd never catch me with a married man, but what you do with your life is your business."

Bryce returned. As soon as he sat, Shep stood. "Well, I better get going. It was nice seeing you, Peter."

"We'll talk tomorrow."

"It was a pleasure meeting you, Shep," Bryce said warmly. Shep replied with a curt nod and marched to join his boyfriend.

"Was it something I said?" Bryce asked.

I waved a hand. "Don't worry about it. He's an odd duck."

"I take it neither one of you knew the other liked guys?"

"Nope, it was a total surprise," I admitted. "My gaydar never once went off with him."

"Is it going to be a problem working with him now?"

"Nah, I don't think so." If anything, it might be easier knowing we actually had something in common.

SIXTEEN

Shep and I hit the ground running on Monday morning thanks to a lead on the location of Weasel Boy, one of the three guys who shot at our victim. We ended up in one of the worst neighborhoods in Seattle, affectionately known as Sinner's Row. It was a large homeless encampment where a lot of drug dealing and using took place. No matter how many times it was raided and emptied out, it wasn't long before people migrated back in.

A confidential informant for the gang task force had told them Weasel Boy was living at Sinner's Row with a few other homeboys. All we had to go on was that the guys lived at the far east corner in a large black and red tent they'd tagged with their gang sign.

We were halfway down the row when I heard my name called out. I turned to the voice and a raggedy looking man stumbled in my direction.

"You are Tao, right?" he said. "I thought I recognized you."

"I'm sorry, sir," I said. "Do I know you?"

"We meet a few weeks ago near Elliot Bay. My name's Manny."

Oh, yeah. He'd seen Julian Ramsey before he was killed. "How are you doing?"

He eyed Shep. "Where's your other partner? The one that bought us the sandwiches?"

"Detective Nolan passed away," I replied, not wanting to say more.

"Oh, I'm sorry to hear that. I liked him."

"Thank you. Now if you'll excuse us…"

"Ya'll want Weasel Boy, don't ya?"

I cocked an eyebrow and peered at him. "Yes, how did you know?"

"Word gets around here pretty quickly. Them boys in that tent heard you was coming and hightailed it out of here. They got scouts everywhere. Spotted you the moment you came in."

"You wouldn't know where Weasel Boy went, would you?"

He paused and chewed on his bottom lip. "I mighta heard him. But I got a shitty memory, ya know?"

I reached for my wallet and chuckled. "Would a couple twenties refresh your memory?" I handed him two bills. He reached for them but I pulled back. "Information first."

"He was going to that Japanese park. Kabooki or Toyota."

"Kubota Gardens?" Shep asked.

Manny snapped his fingers. "That's the one." I handed him the money as well as another business card.

"I don't need the card. I got a photographical memory." He tapped his temple.

"Well, I owe you one. Call me if you need anything."

He nodded and gave me a wink. "Will do."

"You had a good rapport with him," Shep said as we drove away.

"One of the best pieces of advice Jamey ever gave me was not to discount anyone as possibly helpful, even the homeless. They watch people all day long and no one pays attention to them."

"That is excellent advice."

We were quiet for a couple minutes until Shep spoke again. "So about yesterday."

"I already told you I won't spread your secret around the station. That's not my style. I'd appreciate the same."

"I thought you said you didn't care."

I threaded a hand through my hair. "It's not so much that I'm gay

I don't want getting out, as much as…

"As who you're seeing?"

"Yeah."

"I have to say, you being gay didn't surprise me as much as the fact you're dating Bryce Carrick."

"You have something against the man personally?"

He shook his head. "It's just the fact that he's a cheater."

"You don't know all the facts. His marriage isn't exactly a fairytale."

"Obviously not, if he's cheating. But it doesn't matter to me why he sleeps around. The fact that he does makes him a douche bag in my book."

He sounded a lot like me when I'd first met Bryce. I'd been determined not to like the man either, but he'd wormed his way into my life and my heart.

"I don't mean to be a dick," Shep said. "It's your life and I'm not here to judge you. It's just that my dad screwed around on my mom. All the time. He barely tried to hide it. Even when my brothers and I were young we knew Dad had a girlfriend. He'd come home stinking of booze and her perfume. Hickeys on his neck. It was disgusting."

"What did your mom do?"

"Nothing." He clenched the steering wheel hard and the veins in his neck throbbed. "Not a damn thing. She never said a word about. But it hurt her. She killed herself when I was sixteen. I blame my father because he drove her to it."

His attitude toward Bryce made sense even if Bryce was absolutely nothing like Shep's old man. I didn't know Shep well, though I was getting to know him better. He could be an infuriating idiot at times but knowing more about his past and his life made me like the guy.

He wiped tears from his face with his left hand, and I spotted the same bracelet he'd been wearing at the bar. I hadn't noticed it before because he always wore long-sleeve shirts and never rolled them up, even in warm weather.

"Sorry," he said. "You didn't know my life story."

I patted his shoulder. "I don't mind. It makes you seem more human. I was beginning to wonder."

He flipped me the bird but smiled. "Fuck off, Tao."

WEASEL BOY WAS EASY TO FIND AT KUBOTA Gardens. He was lying in the grass enjoying the sun when Shep and I happened on him. He tried to run but Shep tackled him to the ground and arrested him while I read him his rights.

Weasel Boy's real name was Nestor Cotton, which explained why he went by Weasel Boy. What the hell kind of name is Nestor? He sang like a canary as soon as we promised to go easy on him if he talked. He admitted to firing at Robinson a few times, but swore that Gig was the one who shot the most. He even told us where we could find his gun.

Shep continued interviewing him while I went to grab a uniformed officer to take with me to where Weasel had hidden his gun. The first cop I saw was Molly.

"You busy?" I asked.

"Nope. My partner's taking off early to go to his kid's play. I was just about to head out solo."

"Excellent. I need you. Let's go."

"I hope that you mean you need me for *official* business and not anything else?"

I froze, wondering if she thought I was coming on to her. I blanched and said, "Of course it's police work. I would never..." I stopped when I saw her crack a smile.

"Gotcha," she said and made her hand into a gun.

"Smartass. Let's go."

In the car, she said, "The look on your face was priceless, Detective."

"Yeah, that wasn't cool. I thought I had to worry about a harassment claim."

"You know, there was one time I thought you were coming on to me. When you invited me over to your place."

"I remember. I was freaked out then too."

"But then I got to know you and realized you weren't *that* type of guy. By the time I learned you were gay I was convinced I had overreacted."

I choked on my spit and nearly swerved onto a sidewalk. "Excuse me? When you learned I was…gay?"

She regarded me with narrowed eyes. "Yeah?"

"When was this?"

"When I got back on patrol. The first guy I worked with mentioned you were gay. It's not a big deal, is it?"

I shrugged. "Guess not. I haven't hidden it at work, but I didn't know other people knew."

"Yeah, it's out there, Detective. No one cares though."

"Good to know."

We got to the spot Weasel had mentioned. It was an abandoned and boarded-up house with an exterior access to a dirt floor basement. He'd dug a hole and buried it before stacking a couple pallets on top. We found it easily and put it into a paper evidence bag.

After we left the gun in the evidence room we were returning to the squad room when Molly grabbed my arm.

"Oh my God, I almost forgot to tell you. Not sure if it matters or not, but I thought it was interesting."

"Go for it."

"I was at a club last night having fun with my friends when I saw Dave Gomez. But he wasn't alone. He was with a younger, *very* pregnant woman. At first I thought it might be a family member or something, but she was all over him. Kissing his neck, holding his hand, all that. And he definitely wasn't resisting."

"Fascinating."

"I thought so too. In fact, I was curious so I waited until she was alone and struck up a conversation. Her name is Marnie and she has an annoying, high-pitched voice. Like Alvin and the Chipmunks. Anyway, she told me that she and Dave have been together for a year and have plans to get married. I wanted to know if she knew about his dead wife and asked if either one of them had been previously married."

"And?"

"And…." She said with dramatic pause. "Marnie said no. As in no dead, homicidal serial killer wife."

"Holy shit."

"I don't know if any of it matters to you but I found it noteworthy."

I didn't have time to focus on it because I had to get back on the case I was actually working. I did file away the information in my head in a folder I liked to call 'What the Fuck?'

I DIDN'T GET HOME UNTIL AFTER SEVEN AND was exhausted. I just wanted some food and my bed. Then Bryce called and my plans changed.

"Hey, what are you up too?"

"About to crash. I'm drained."

"You can't do that. We're going out."

"Bryce, I have no energy at all."

"I think you'll change your mind when I tell you where we're going."

I sighed. "Fine. Where do you want to take me?"

"Tuck."

"What the hell is Tuck?"

"A drag queen bar where Miss Lavish Gloss is doing a surprise performance."

That got my attention. "How did you find that out?"

He chuckled. "I have my connections. So, you up for another show?"

"Absolutely. Get your ass over here."

NOT WANTING TO HAVE A REPEAT PERFORMANCE OF when I first tried to talk to Lavish, Bryce and I came up with a plan. After the show I would try to talk to her, and if she ran Bryce would be waiting outside the back door. He couldn't put hands on her but hopefully he could delay her long enough for me to get there.

Sure enough, as soon as Gloss spotted me heading her way she took off like her wig was on fire. Thankfully, our plan worked, and by the time I was out the back door Bryce was standing staring at Miss Lavish Gloss. His eyes were bugged out like he'd just seen his mother having sex with an elephant.

As soon as Gloss turned around and removed her wig, I understood why Bryce was freaked out. I was feeling the exact same way.

"Shep?"

SEVENTEEN

"Hello, Peter." His voice was nonchalant like I wasn't supposed to be shocked that he was Miss Lavish Gloss.

"Shep?" I asked again. Things weren't clicking in my head. This didn't make sense.

"Are you going to say anything?" Shep asked.

"I'm not sure what to ask?" I rubbed my face. "You're Lavish Gloss?"

He nodded. "That's correct."

"Why?"

"Why what? Why do I do drag?"

"No. I don't give a shit that you do drag. Why did you run from me the other day? Why didn't you tell me after we came out to each other?"

He scratched his face, smudging some of his makeup. "When I saw you the other night I just freaked the fuck out. I was afraid if you talked to me you'd figure out who I was."

"That's why you ran? Because you didn't want me to know your real identity? No *other* reasons?"

His forehead creased. "No, that was it. What else would there be?"

Bryce put a hand on my arm. "This might be a long conversation. Why don't we get a table at Denny's across the street instead of standing out in the cold?"

"You okay with that?" I asked Shep.

"Sure."

After we all had our coffee mugs and our waitress put in an order of chili cheese fries, I focused on Shep, who was tugging at the leather bracelet.

"I'm sorry about dashing out on you the other night and for not coming clean. I'm more terrified about people at work finding out I'm Lavish than I am about them learning I'm bi. I'd never hear the end of it, and other cops might think less of me."

"I understand your fears, and I can forgive you for that. But I have a few questions for you that I need answering."

He gulped loudly, and his Adam's apple bobbed quickly.

"Where were you two weeks ago from tonight?"

He flinched back slightly, and his posture tightened. "Why would you want to know that?"

I tapped the table and stared at him. "Could you please just answer the question?" My voice became taut.

His blinking increased. "I just don't know why you would possibly need to know where I was on that exact date. Does this have to do with a case? You aren't assigned any except the one with me."

"Please, just tell me where you were," I said through gritted teeth.

"I just…" He bit at his finger nails and shifted in his seat. Finally, he put his hands on the table palms down. "Okay, fine. You want to know what I was doing? Fine!" His voice began to get louder, but he took a deep breath and the tension in his body eased. "I was meeting a guy. Someone I met through Adult Friend Finder."

Bryce spoke up for the first time since we'd sat down. "You were going to cheat on Ryan?"

It was a question I'd been about to ask. I didn't take Shep for the cheating kind of guy, especially after what he'd gone through with his parents.

Shep glared back. "You're judging me, considering your life right now?"

Bryce raised his hands and leaned back in the seat. "No judging."

"For your information, Ryan and I have an open relationship. He gets off on hearing about what I do with other guys. In fact, he set this up."

"Like Bryce said, there's no judging here. I just need the facts."

The waitress came with our fries, and we each took a couple bites.

"Where did you meet this guy?" I asked.

"Elliot Bay."

Shit! I'd been hoping this had all been a coincidence. Now I had Shep at the scene of the crime. He didn't seem the killer type, but neither had Ted Bundy. Appearances were most definitely deceiving most of the time.

"Dressed as Lavish?"

"Partially," he admitted. "Not as much make-up and no wig. I don't have to do too much to pull off the look."

"Were you at the dock around eleven?"

Shep nodded. "I was supposed to meet him there at eleven, but he was late and didn't show up until a quarter to twelve."

"What's his name?"

"Uh, I don't know it." Shep's face turned bright red.

"You had sex with the dude, right?"

He nodded.

"But you didn't get his name?" I didn't understand how anyone could do that.

Bryce squeezed my leg. "They're called anonymous encounters for a reason, Peter."

"Exactly," Shep replied and shot Bryce a grateful expression. "It was one of those don't ask, don't tell situations. That's what Ryan and I like. We ask if they're married and if they are drug and disease free. And I always use condoms."

"What can you tell us about the guy?"

"His screenname was AlphaDog55. The numbers probably refer to his age or close to it. He was African American. Tall, maybe six foot two. A lot taller than me."

"Where did you guys...um...hook up?"

"A motel a few blocks away. Total flea bag called The Gettaroom."

"You can pay for the room with cash and use whatever name you want," Bryce said.

"You've been there?" I asked.

He shrugged with a hint of embarrassment on his face. "There was a time I had to be as secretive as possible."

"We signed in as Mickey Mouse and Donald Duck," Shep said. "We weren't the only Disney characters there. An Ariel was in a room with Pocahontas. Tom Cruise was signed in as well."

"That wouldn't help at all."

"Help with what?" Shep demanded.

"Proving you weren't at the docks at midnight?"

Shep crossed his arms and scowled. "What *exactly* is going on here? Why are you asking me…?" He paused. "Two weeks ago is when the first body was found in the case you and Nolan stole from me."

"Yeah," I admitted. "And you were at the scene of the crime and didn't say anything."

Shep's head snapped back as if he'd been slapped. "I couldn't tell you or the chief that I'd been there to have a one-night stand with a man I'd never met. Besides, I didn't see anything. Some young dude having a party invited me to join him, and I turned him down. I left as soon as my date arrived."

"But you can't prove your alibi, can you?"

He slapped the table. "Why would I have to? The case is closed. The killer is dead, right?"

"Officially, it's closed," I said.

Shep sat back and regarded me carefully. "But you're not sure are you? Why else would you be asking these questions?"

"Let's just say I'm making sure I did the right thing by closing it."

He fiddled with the bracelet again, and for the first time I got a decent view of it. Dark leather with three letters. Seen in the dark someone could've mistaken it for a tattoo. A tattoo just like Eloise

Nash had seen on the killer.

"What do the letters on your bracelet stand for?" I asked.

Rubbing his fingers over the stitching, he examined in for a moment. "My mother's initials. RGA. Rosalie Guinevere Adley."

"That's a beautiful name," Bryce murmured.

Shep smiled. "Thanks. She was a beautiful woman."

"Do you ever take the bracelet off?" I asked.

"Only when I shower," he replied. "Otherwise it's on all the time."

"Even when you're having sex?"

"Yes, even then." He paused. "You don't think I could be a murderer do you?"

"Sorry, Shep, but I can't ignore the facts. I certainly don't want to consider the idea. My gut tells me it's not you. But my instincts have been thrown amuck lately." I met his gaze. "I'd like to prove beyond a reasonable doubt that it was you."

He breathed deeply a couple times. "It's fine. I'd do the same thing in your situation. I messed up by not coming forward sooner. I was embarrassed."

"Will you work with me then to find a way to prove your alibi?"

"Sure. I'll do whatever it takes."

"You understand this is all covert at the moment. Besides the three of us here, only two other people know I'm not convinced Diana Gomez was the killer. I can't share too much with you right now. But if I can eliminate you as a suspect then I'll bring you in."

"Fair enough. What can I do?"

"Give me access to your Adult Friend Finder account as well as Ryan's. That will allow me to see what's been going on. Hopefully, I can track down this AlphaDog person."

"You can talk to Ryan as well. He can at least verify the plans I had that night."

"I'd have to go talk to him right now," I said. "If I waited, that'd give you time to fill him in on what was going on. Again, sorry for any accusations but you know what I'm talking about."

He waved a hand. "No worries. You're doing everything I'd be doing. Only you're being nicer about it than I would be."

"Yeah, you can be a bit of a douche at times."

Shep glared at me, then smiled. "I'd deny it if I could."

SHEP TOOK ME TO RYAN'S PLACE THAT NIGHT. Unfortunately, we had to wake the poor kid up. Talk about confused. Jostled out of bed at midnight and asked to tell a virtual stranger about your boyfriend's clandestine meet-up with a guy.

Ryan managed to confirm Shep's story without any inconsistencies, which was excellent. However, he had no clue about AlphaDog's real identity and claimed the account had since been shut down.

Before I left, Shep gave me the username and passwords for both their accounts and said he'd see me in the morning.

I yawned and stretched in the car as Bryce drove me home. If I'd been beat after work, I was a total wreck now.

"What does your gut tell you about Shep?" Bryce asked.

"Well, he was at the first scene, but we have no idea about the rest. I'll dig into that tomorrow. He hates men who cheat, which was part of the profile for the killer."

"But…?"

"But I don't think he did it. He's cooperating too easily, even to the point of his own embarrassment. If he was the killer, he would've worked harder to block me. He didn't have to give me his passwords or let me talk to Ryan. The fact that he did tells me he doesn't have anything to hide."

"I'm not a cop, but I'm inclined to agree with you. It'd be a shame to have to put him away."

"Why's that?"

"I'd hate to lose Miss Lavish Gloss. She's a fabulous singer."

EIGHTEEN

Tuesday morning I paid a visit to Aza.

"I was going to find you in a bit here," he said. "I have some interesting information."

"Awesome. I have something I need you to check out." I handed him the Adult Friend Finder account info. "I need you to check out these two profiles especially in regard to a user name AlphaDog55."

He immediately went to the website and typed in Shep's user info.

"This has to remain strictly confidential."

He gave me a side-eye. "I *am* a professional." A moment later he pulled up the profile and his eyes widened. "Holy shit, this is…"

I put a finger to my lips to quiet him. Aza read further and whispered, "He likes to do *what* with a fist?"

"Just concentrate on locating this AlphaDog for now."

"Yeah, okay."

"What did you have for me?"

"I was searching through the accounts on *Ashley Madison* and found *another* one owned by Diana Gomez."

"So she had two? Why?"

"No reason I can think of," he replied. "And, before you ask, there is no doubt it was Diana's. It was tied to her personal bank account and has enough of her private information I'm positive the account belonged to her."

"Anything interesting in the second profile?"

"For sure. On this account, the one I just found, she only messaged two guys—her husband and Detective Nolan."

"Not our other victims."

Shaking his head, he replied, "No one else at all."

"But she did on the other account, right?"

"That's correct. It's almost too convenient."

I didn't have time to ruminate on the subject for much longer because, right then, Shep screamed my name from the squad room, and I dashed out.

"We have a visitor in the interview room. Omar Hewitt and his attorney."

"Gig's here?"

"Yup, just turned himself in."

GIG HAD RETAINED A SHARK OF AN ATTORNEY, one by the name of Alastair Warlock of Wreath, Kravitz, and Warlock. Gig admitted to being there but claimed he hadn't done any of the shooting. He said it was the other two guys, despite the fact neither one of them had reason to dislike Robinson and Gig did. Neither Shep nor I believed his story but he held tight to his claims. It'd be up to Shep and me to disprove his claims.

We officially arrested the young man, and Shep left to book him into jail. I was about to return to my desk when Warlock touched my arm. "Could I have a word with you in private, Detective Tao?"

"Sure," I said, and we returned to the interview room.

"You already wanting to make a deal for your client?"

"No, this has nothing to do with Mr. Hewitt." He set his briefcase on the table and leaned on the chair.

"Okay, I'll bite, what does this have to do with?"

"I'm not one to normally go *to* the police with information on a client, but I think the facts justify it this one time."

I leaned against the wall and crossed my arms.

"You were the lead detective in the case involving Diana Gomez, correct?"

I nodded. "Do you have information regarding that investigation?"

"Not per se. That is, if she was a serial killer she never confessed it to me. If she had, I wouldn't be telling you that, despite her death. But I do have information you might find noteworthy."

"I'm listening."

"Diana Gomez is a long-time friend of the family. She came to see me last Monday regarding divorce proceedings."

That was the same day the officers following Diana had lost her for a few hours. At the same time I'd had an encounter with the killer after finding Tanev Singh's body. If she was at Warlock's then she couldn't have been killing Singh and fighting me. "She was leaving her husband?"

"Yes. And she wasn't going to be gentle with the man. She wanted to take him for *everything* she could. I was prepared to get her half of everything, including his retirement, as well as hefty alimony payments. The law was on her side. He was the one who cheated, after all. Numerous times in fact."

"Do you know when Diana was going to tell Dave her plans?"

"I urged her to wait but she insisted she was going to tell him that night. I can't be sure. As you know, she was dead the following morning."

"I don't suppose there's any way you can prove to me that Diana did meet with you that day?"

"Easily. We have sign-in logs and security cameras everywhere. I'll have my assistant send you what you need."

I handed him my card. "Have it sent to my email but please don't mention this to anyone else."

"If there's one thing you don't have to worry about with lawyers, it's their discretion." He tapped his temple. "What I keep in this brain could topple empires."

I thanked Warlock for his time and returned to my desk. The new information was definitely curious. If Diana had indeed been at Warlock's when Singh was killed, that obviously meant she wasn't the killer. That, added to the things regarding the case, that didn't feel right. But I didn't know what to do with the evidence against her, including the journal. I also didn't know where it fit in with the other information I had, such as the fact that Dave had a pregnant girlfriend.

Once more, I didn't have time to focus on that case because the demands of my official assignment pulled me away. Shep and I spent the rest of the day playing round robin with our three suspects. As much as we wanted to nail Gig, we simply didn't have the physical evidence against him. Weasel Boy had admitted to the shooting and unless we could prove Gig had a gun, he might be the one going down for the crime.

Each guy stuck to his story no matter how hard we tried to trip them up. By the end of the day Shep and I were both frustrated. Shep even lost his temper and screamed at Dice. I'd never seen Shep lose his cool before. That was my cue that we were done for the night. Shep wasn't ready to go home, but I convinced him we weren't going to accomplish anything else.

Before I left the office, I grabbed the file on Diana Gomez and took it home with me so I could continue to pore over it. I had to be missing something that would help the clues fall into place, and I was determined to find it.

I was halfway home when my cell rang. I didn't recognize the number and almost ignored it, but chose to answer it.

"Yeah," I said, using my vehicle's Bluetooth.

"Detective Tao?" A low voice asked.

"Yeah. Who is this?"

"This is Manny. You remember me?"

The homeless guy I'd talked to the other day. "I remember. What's up?"

"You said you owed me a favor. Does the offer still stand?"

"Of course."

"I'm in the ER so I ain't doing so good at the moment. I got beat up pretty bad by some thug friends of Weasel Boy. They was pissed I ratted on him."

"Fuck, how bad are you hurt?"

"I'm in pain but nothing serious. But they took everything I own. Not that I had much, but now I got nuthin'. They even stole the clothes off my back. I'm buck ass naked except for this hospital gown they got me in. I was lucky I was near a hospital and didn't have to walk far. They let me use the phone, and like I said, I had your number member-ized. I didn't know who else to call."

"Where are you?"

"University of Washington Medical Center."

"I'll be there in ten minutes."

"Oh, God bless you."

I spun around and drove to UW, grateful I'd worked late enough to miss rush hour traffic. I dashed inside the ER and found Manny in the waiting room. He grinned and stood when he spotted me, then walked over holding the gown closed behind him.

"Thanks for coming. They wouldn't let me go unless someone signed for me. If you didn't come I'd probably be taken in for public indecency."

I went to the front desk, signed Manny out, covered him with my coat, and helped him back to my vehicle.

"Thanks for the ride," he said. "You taking me to a shelter?"

"No, you're coming home with me. You can have a shower and sleep on my couch. In the morning I'll arrange for you to get some clothes."

"I wasn't expecting you to do that," he replied. "I just didn't want to be walking around with my wiener hanging out."

"It's no problem. Just don't make me regret it. I'd hate wake up and find my place robbed."

"I ain't no thief, Detective. A drunk, yes, but not a thief."

WHILE MANNY SHOWERED, I HEATED UP SOME CHICKEN noodle soup and made a couple roast beef sandwiches. When he emerged forty-five minutes later, I almost didn't recognize him. He'd taken advantage of my offer to use my razor and had shaved off his ratty beard. With his hair combed, he looked like a totally different person. I'd also given him a pair of flannel pajamas I hadn't worn for years.

"Woohoo," he exclaimed. "I haven't felt this good in years." He spotted the food on the table, and his face lit up. "Are those for me?"

"Help yourself."

He sat down and began scarfing the food down. I wondered how long it'd been since he ate anything substantial. There were plenty of shelters in Seattle where the homeless could get free meals, but I heard some were pretty dangerous thanks to the surrounding neighborhood. While Manny ate, I glanced over the file I'd brought home. A picture of Diana Gomez slipped out and floated to the ground. I went to pick it up but Manny grabbed it first.

"I know her," he said as he handed the image to me.

"How do you know Diana Gomez?"

"We call her the Saint of Sinner's Row. She visits the camp several times a week, usually at night. She brings us homemade food. Sometimes it's soups or casseroles. But she's also made salads, cookies and lots of stuff. She also provides blankets or coats or sleeping bags when it gets cold out."

"When was the last time you saw her?"

He scrunched his face as he thought about it. "It's been a couple weeks at least."

"Think hard, Manny. Can you tell me exactly when?"

"Oh, I remember." He snapped his fingers. "It was the day I first met you and your partner. That night I was in Sinner's Row. She came around with spaghetti. It was damn fine stuff. She said she was a professional chef and I completely believed it."

"Did you used to have a watch? Is it possible you know what time she got there?"

"That old clock tower right there still works. She was hanging out when I got there about 11:45."

Damn, she still would've had time to kill Tyrone Osceola at Gas Works Park.

"But she stayed late. First she was chatting with me, then she talked to Mrs. Garfunkel."

"When did she leave?"

"It was after midnight for sure."

If he was right, then Diana wouldn't have had time to get across town to kill Osceola. I couldn't use Manny's statement in court, but it added to what I already knew. And to what I suspected—that Diana Gomez was *not* the killer.

IN THE MORNING, I GAVE MANNY SOME CLOTHES of mine and also took him to a shelter where he could get more of what he needed.

"Thanks a lot," Manny said as he shook my hand.

"Anytime," I replied. "Keep in touch."

When I got to work, I finally had the chance to read the email from Alastair Warlock's assistant. Diana Gomez had indeed signed in that day, but that could've been faked. The security footage was another matter. It was time/date stamped and showed that Diana Gomez had been there during the same time Singh was killed and my encounter with the murderer took place.

If Diana Gomez wasn't the killer, who was and what should I do with the evidence against her?

The sole conclusion I could draw was that the evidence had been faked to frame Diana. But when I asked myself who would do such a thing, I could only come up with one answer, and I didn't like it. Dave had reasons to want to get rid of his wife. He wouldn't want to give his wife half of everything, especially not half of his retirement. That loss would mean he had to put in even more years as a cop or get a different job when he retired from the force. Plus, he had a pregnant girlfriend who had no idea he had been married.

I despised suspecting that a cop would do such a thing, but lord knew rotten apples got past the screening process. Officers breaking laws had been in the news a lot lately, I was just grateful there were far more good cops than bad ones. I never thought one would be in my station. The question was, what did I do now?

Knowing I needed help, I called Aza and Molly and arranged to meet in an interview room. We filled each other in so we were all up to date before I told them what I suspected.

"Are we ready to go to the chief yet?" Molly asked.

"No," I answered. "We don't have anything solid yet."

Aza scratched his chin. "So how do we get something that is solid?"

"First of all, we need to find out more about the morning Dave shot his wife."

"Such as?" Molly took out her notebook.

"How long was it between when Hurst and Estrada heard the shots and when they entered the bedroom? Was there enough time for him to have planted the knife?"

"Estrada is working today," Molly said. "I'll ask to ride with him and see if I can find out."

"You can't make him suspicious."

"Don't worry, I'll play it cool."

Aza said, "I'll examine the journal. If it was faked, I'll be able to see it somewhere. There weren't any obvious signs, but if whoever did it was skilled, there wouldn't be. But you can't hide the *entire* trail. If it's there, I'll find it."

"I'll probably be busy working my current case with Shep," I said. "But I'll let you know if I think of anything else."

SHEP AND I SEARCHED GIG'S PLACE, BUT OF course, he'd gotten rid of anything incriminating. Our sole hope was that he was dumb enough to leave something we could use against him. The only thing we found was a go phone hidden in a vent. There were a couple texts on it, but they were written in some kind of gang code.

"We might have what we need if we can break the code," I said.

"Do you think one of our techs can do it?"

"Maybe eventually, but don't forget we have two gang bangers in custody desperate to save their own skin."

"They're ripe for deal making, I bet."

"Exactly."

SURE ENOUGH, BOTH DICE AND WEASEL BOY WROTE down the code we needed to scramble a message to Gig from someone he called Etc. It read:

Nine in the drink.

Gig had replied:

Good looking.

The first message, Weasel Boy explained, meant that a gun, a nine mm, had been tossed in the water. The second message wasn't Gig replying that he thought Etc was attractive. He meant thanks for looking out for him. Gig had given the gun to Etc to dispose of. It was a gang trick so one gun couldn't be traced back to someone.

The chances of us finding the gun were slim to none. However, we could use the message against Gig, especially if we located this Etc. Our two snitches were helpful on that account too. Etc was Elayna Teresa Carlotti, one of the female members of the gang. She was barely eighteen and terrified when we arrested her. Though not as scared of us as she was of her mother. Etc confirmed not only that Gig had told her he'd shot Robinson but had also given her the gun to throw away.

We had Gig brought into an interview room and showed him the cellphone we'd located.

"Damn, I had to hide that when my Moms came in and musta forgot it." He shrugged. "Oh, well. Not like you know what was said."

"You mean because of your *secret gang language*," I sneered. "Too bad your former buddies are watching out for themselves. They gave it up."

"And we located your lady friend, Etc," Shep added. "She talked too."

Gig frowned and crossed his arms. "I ain't saying nothing else until my lawyer gets here."

"Smart choice."

Shep and I left him to sweat it out until Warlock made it. While waiting, I got a call from Molly.

"I only have a minute but I wanted to let you know what I found out."

"You got what we were looking for?"

"Of course I did. I am *that* good."

I chuckled. "Enough with the cocky attitude, Officer Whitmore. Spill it."

"Three minutes," she said, "from the time they heard the gunshots and got to the bedroom."

"More than enough time."

"Especially if he was prepared, which I think he was."

"Great job."

I ended the call and leaned back in my chair.

"What was that about?" Shep asked.

"Just a personal matter."

He examined me like he didn't believe me but I wasn't going to explain. If Diana Gomez wasn't the killer, then that meant the real one was still out there. And Shep, unfortunately, was a suspect. I hadn't had time to check his alibis for the other nights.

I excused myself to use the bathroom and after taking a piss headed to the Tech Room to speak to Aza.

"You must be psychic," he said. "I just found something."

"What is it?"

"Diana's journal was tampered with. Whoever did it, did an admirable job trying to hide their cookies. They're good, but I'm better. Significant parts of her diary were deleted. I haven't recovered everything yet, but by the end of the day, I should be able to tell precisely what was added and what was removed."

I patted his back as I left. I was getting more and more clues. I just needed that one thing for it all to fall into place.

Warlock had arrived as I entered the squad room, and Shep was escorting him to the interview room where Gig was being held. As we got there, Dave exited the room. His face was flushed like he had been yelling.

"Detectives," Warlock said, "I know you weren't interviewing my client without me present."

"He's not on the case," Shep remarked.

"Then what was he doing with my client?"

"Good question." I strode up to Dave. "Why were you in there?"

"Why was I in there?"

"Yeah?" Shep demanded.

"I was not doing anything wrong," Dave replied.

"Then why were you speaking to my client?" Warlock asked again, speaking deliberately slowly.

He avoided eye contact with all of us. His gaze fluttered everywhere in the room except at us. Dave touched his lips, and I was about to ask the same question again when he spoke.

"I know Gig from the streets. I've used him as a CI once or twice. I was just chewing his ass for being such a dumbass and getting arrested."

Shep stepped forward and cocked his head. "He's not in the system as an official Confidential Informant."

He rolled his shoulders and shrugged. "I haven't made him *official* yet. He gave me some information, and I bought him lunch. I was going to put him on the payroll but seems like that won't be happening."

"Is that it?" I asked.

"Uh, yeah." He glanced around. "Well, I gotta go." He turned and strode away.

Shep and I exchanged confused glances and led Warlock in to see his client.

"I need to talk to my attorney alone," Gig said immediately, and Shep and I backed out of the room.

Less than three minutes later, Warlock waved us back in and sat beside Gig. "My client has information you might find useful. He is willing to share what he knows with you provided you make a deal on this case."

"He's not going to skate on this case, no matter what he tells us."

"Mr. Hewitt is aware prison time will happen, regardless. However, he's willing to testify to what he knows in another case. I think you'll find what he has to say fascinating."

"Okay," I replied. "You talk and if it's as earth-shattering as you say, we'll go to the DA and take care of you."

Gig glanced at his lawyer, who nodded. "You know why I'm called Gig?"

"No idea," Shep replied.

"It's short for Gigabyte. I'm a computer whiz. It comes naturally to me. Probably better than most of the cops you got working for ya."

"Get to the point." I leaned over the table and glared at him.

"That Po-Po that just left, he's a crazy mo-fo."

"Officer Gomez?" I asked.

"Yeah. Some months back he busted me with some heavy shit."

"Drugs?"

He nodded. "Not just weed. Meth. 'Nough to send me away for years."

"But he didn't arrest you?" I pulled out a chair and sat backwards on it.

"Nah. He told me he'd forget what he saw provided I do him a favor."

Making deals with gang bangers and druggies wasn't unusual. Cops did it all the time to get the next person in the criminal food chain.

"What did he ask you to do?"

"He said he'd heard about my technological skills and needed me to check out something on a computer site."

"What site?" I asked.

"I forget what it's called. Got a chick's name. Where married men go to cheat on their bitches."

I leaned back. "*Ashley Madison*?"

"Yeah, that's the one. I got proof that one of the ladies he was chatting up was larger than she was saying. She claimed to be like one twenty and she was more like two fifty."

"Anything else?" I asked.

"Not right then. But later he had a bigger job for me. This is what you really want to hear about."

I waited for him to continue, practically holding my breath in anticipation.

"I got on his wife's laptop and changed a bunch of shit in some diary. He told me exactly what to add and take out and where to put it. He also had me create a new profile on that same site and make it appear like it was his wife's. He gave me other dudes' profiles and said it had to look like she had contacted them. I faked a whole bunch of shit for him."

Holy damn! This was what I needed. The final clue.

Dave Gomez had framed his wife. Diana Gomez was *not* the killer.

Gig talked for a bit longer before Shep and I left the room.

"Does this mean what I think it does?" he asked.

I didn't answer him directly. Instead, I said, "I need to speak to the chief right now."

"Want me to go with you?"

"No. You need to stay here with Gig. Make sure Dave doesn't get anywhere near him." I marched to Slight's office and shut the door behind me.

"What do you want?" she demanded then waved a hand. "Never mind. It doesn't matter. I don't have time. I'm on the way to see the commissioner."

"Pardon me for being blunt, Chief, but you *need* to hear what I have to say."

"This better be damn good, Detective. I'm in no mood for bullshit."

I remained standing and began. "Diana Gomez was innocent. She wasn't the killer."

That certainly got Slight's attention. She put down her phone, closed a folder in front of her, clasped her hands together, and said, "I'm listening."

I chose not to bury the lead and worked my way backwards. First I told her about what Gig had just told me, then explained the other things I'd found out thanks to Molly and Aza. I said nothing about Shep since it wasn't necessary yet. Right then, it wasn't about finding the killer, it was about proving Diana had been framed by her husband.

When I was done, Slight grabbed her phone and punched in a number. "Doyle, I need to talk to Gomez right now." She paused. "He what? Damn it." She hung up and scowled. "He just left. Claimed he needed a personal day."

"He's making a run for it, Chief."

"Well, go stop him."

I dashed out the door without hesitation and hightailed outside, grabbing as many officers as I could. "Do not let Officer Gomez leave the parking lot," I ordered. "Use deadly force if required."

We spread out and began the search. I heard an engine start near the exit to the parking lot and ran over there as Gomez pulled out in a police cruiser. I stood in front of the car, pulled my gun and aimed.

"Get out of my way, Tao. I *will* run you down."

"That's what you're gonna have to do, Dave, because I'm not moving."

He revved the engine but didn't put it into gear.

"It doesn't have to be this way," I shouted. "Just turn off the car."

"I am not going to prison. No way in hell."

He put the car in gear and accelerated toward me as I fired my pistol again and again. I emptied the magazine before I leaped to the side just narrowly missing being hit by the car. It swerved to the side and crashed into another vehicle. I bounded back to my feet as other cops came running up with their guns drawn.

"There's no movement in the car," I yelled. "I don't know if I got him or not." I was pretty sure I had, judging by the way his head lolled to the side.

Two officers stood on the passenger side while another two approached the driver side. One reached in and felt for a pulse.

"He's dead," the cop called out.

So much was a blur after that. I was checked out for injuries, but I had nothing but a scraped knee and elbow from hitting the ground. My badge and gun were taken from me, which was standard protocol in an officer-involved shooting. I'd have to be cleared by Internal Affairs before I returned to active duty. IA wasn't like it was shown in TV and movies. They were an outstanding group of cops who were out to get to the truth. They weren't out to hang every cop who got in trouble. The only cops who should be afraid of IA are the dirty ones.

I gave my statement several times to many different people. Chief Slight assured me it was a good shoot, and I likely wouldn't face any disciplinary charges. She swore she would back me up every step of the way, and I believed her.

Despite being on paid leave for the next couple days, I was kept up to date on the case by Shep, Molly, Aza, and Chief Slight.

Aza recovered the parts of the diary Gig had deleted. In it, Diana talked about her activities, including going to Sinner's Row and talking to Warlock regarding a divorce. She had indeed contacted Jamey through *Ashley Madison* and had recognized his picture. She'd seen him the night he was murdered to talk to him about why he'd cheated on his wife. Diana had hoped to get some sort of insight into her husband's mind, but Jamey hadn't helped.

Aza also figured out Dave had been accessing the case files despite not having permission to do so. He had used the information I had gathered to set up his wife. Aza also found a credit card receipt for a set of Victorinox knives. He apparently bought a set and threw away two of them to strengthen the case against her.

With Dave dead, we didn't have a signed confession, but his actions and the proof we had were more than enough to close that part of the case. Diana Gomez was not the killer. There was no doubt about that.

Marnie, the young woman carrying Dave's child, was first incredulous then furious when Molly told her the truth. I just prayed that child never learned who its father was. That would be a horrible legacy to have.

My other case was also put to bed. The DA made a deal with Gig for the information he'd provided. As much as I didn't like the mouthy punk, I did argue that he deserved a decent arrangement. Gig ended up going to prison for twenty years to life. Weasel Boy went away for fifteen to twenty, and Dice got ten.

Two cases closed wasn't a bad thing. Even though proving Diana innocent meant the hacked-up case was back open. There was a killer out there, and I needed to find her. With all the information I had, I still believed it was a woman.

I was curious why the murderer hadn't struck again. Had she only planned to go after those five men? She'd killed four but failed with Bryce. Would she come after him again? Was she lying low since everyone believed Diana to be the killer? So many questions and not enough answers. I was right back where I was a few days before: without a suspect.

Technically, I did have a suspect—Shep. My plan once I returned to work was to find alibis for Shep. I prayed he wasn't my guy. Not just because I'd worked with him and liked him, but because I wasn't sure I could handle another dirty cop. Dave framing his wife was horrible, but having a cop as a serial killer would be even worse.

TWENTY

Normally, being forced to take days off was a punishment, but I was confident I'd be cleared and chose to enjoy my time. I spent a great deal of time with Bryce, both just chilling as well as listening to his plan on how to get back into SeattleCarrick.

The Monday after the shooting, I was called into work for a meeting with Internal Affairs. Even knowing I'd done the right thing, it was still a nerve-wracking event. Being on the other side of the interview table in a low-lit room felt wrong, and for a moment, I felt the need to confess to something I hadn't done.

Inspector March sat across from me, flipping through a file folder as if he hadn't already made his decision. He was no doubt torturing me on purpose but calling him on it would just extend it so I kept my mouth shut.

Finally, March cleared his throat and said, "It is my pleasure to tell you that we found the shoot was a clean one." He rose and extended a hand. I shook it firmly.

"Thanks, Inspector."

"You're welcome. Now get your ass back to work."

A few minutes later, I strode into the squad room with my head held high and received plenty of congratulations.

"Tao! Get your ass in my office now," Slight yelled from her doorway.

I marched in and stood at attention with my arms at my side.

She glared at me and crossed her arms. "They cleared you, huh?"

"Yes, ma'am."

"Now you need to get your ass back to work and find the real killer. No more chances on this one."

"I understand."

She finally smiled and held out a hand. "Congratulations."

I took it and thanked her.

"Do you have a plan on how to proceed?"

"It's tough because I don't have any suspects," I admitted. "I just have to go through every last scrap of evidence and keep digging."

"I assume you'll need help. Any idea who you want to work with?"

"I'll need Aza for sure, and I'd like to be able to use Molly when needed."

"What about a detective? Maybe Adley?"

"Nah, I think I'll be fine with who I have." I couldn't tell her there was no way I could let Shep work the case, not until I cleared him.

She shrugged. "Your choice. Just let me know."

"I will." I turned and strode out of her office, more than ready to get back to work.

Aza was sitting at Jamey's old desk wearing a shit-eating grin. "I was hoping you'd need me again."

I chuckled. "Yes. I do. We have some work to do."

"I'm ready," he replied. "I've been searching through all the local *Ashley Madison* profiles. Just searching for anything that stands out."

"Did you find anything?"

"There's an account owned by a woman named Loretta Roach. She was a *very* active member and messaged at least a hundred men. Mainly the guys in the wealthy range but also tons of other dudes as well."

"Did she reach out to our victims?"

"All of them," he answered. "Including Bryce Carrick."

"She went into the down low section as well?"

"Yeah, her message to him was basically 'Are you sure you want dick? My vagina will make you scream.' Only she didn't use the term vagina."

"Sounds like a classy woman." I snorted. "The fact that she spoke to our victims could just be a coincidence."

"It was statistically likely considering how many guys she communicated with."

"You got a picture?"

He nodded and punched a few buttons on his keyboard. I ambled over to his desk to take a peek at the DMV photo. Loretta Roach most certainly did not match the profile of our killer. She was tall and blonde with a little extra weight. Regardless, I'd still have to talk to her.

"Any luck with the Adult Friend Finder assignment?" I returned to my desk and sat.

He screwed up his face and shook his head. "Not really. The AlphaDog profile is closed and deleted. Unlike *Ashley Madison*, AFF removes and eliminates all traces of the account."

"So you can't get his real name?"

Aza held up a finger. "I didn't say that. I can do it. It'll just take a bit more work." He paused and tapped his teeth. "Can you tell me what Detective Adley has to do with the case?"

I glanced around to make sure no one was nearby who could hear us. "He was at the scene of the first crime. AlphaDog could prove his alibi."

"Oh my," he gasped. "What about the other murders?"

"I was just about to check on that," I replied. Thanks to the many reports we had to write, it was fairly easy to find out exactly what any detective was doing on a given date. I hoped Shep had been working the nights of the murders and his activities would prove he couldn't have done it.

He had indeed been working. However, it was on a solo stakeout. He had been alone the whole night. It was entirely possible he could've left his assignment to kill the three men and attack Bryce. He was off the afternoon of Tanev Singh's murder. Hopefully, he had a decent alibi for that date.

I didn't see Shep at his desk when I left to pay a visit to Loretta Roach but I ran into him in the parking lot.

"I still haven't located this AlphaDog guy," I said. "But I'm still working at it."

"Thanks," he said.

"Unfortunately you were on stakeouts the nights of the other murders."

"Yeah, I was by myself. Guess that doesn't help."

"What about the day Tanev was killed? You were off. Don't suppose you saw anyone, or, better yet, a *bunch* of people."

He huffed. "I wish. I was home alone. Spent the day watching a *Walking Dead* marathon."

"Damn." I ran a hand through my hair.

"I swear, man, I did *not* do this."

I chucked his shoulder. "I believe you. But I *need* proof. If I don't find any soon I might have no choice but to go to the chief."

He hung his head and sighed. "I understand. You gotta do what you gotta do."

"Thanks for understanding."

AFTER LESS THAN A MINUTE WITH LORETTA ROACH I was convinced she couldn't be a killer or even involved with the murders. She was after one thing and was open about it.

"I want a sugar daddy," she said unapologetically. We were in her living room in a small apartment. "I don't want a man in my life every day. I like the idea of being the other woman."

I asked several questions about her location on the nights of the murders and I got names and numbers of men she'd been with. I was sure her alibi would pan out and I could erase her from my list of suspects.

I spent the day making phone-calls to men who didn't want to hear from me but ultimately admitted they had gone out with Loretta. I was able to clear Loretta as a suspect—at least it was progress.

I MET BRYCE FOR DINNER THAT NIGHT AND asked if he remembered being contacted by Loretta Roach.

He nearly choked on his bite of steak and coughed to clear his throat. "Yeah, I remember her. I kindly thanked her for the offer but said I was only interested in men."

"Yeah, she was a piece of work."

"Have you considered checking out other sites married men use to cheat?" he asked.

"Like Adult Friend Finder?"

"Exactly."

"Did you ever use it?"

"Years back," he answered. "I didn't have much luck meeting halfway decent guys. *Ashley Madison* had fewer tweakers and scumbags. Plus, the men there are mostly married so I wasn't as worried about my secret coming out."

I excused myself and called Aza to have him look at Adult Friend Finder. When I came back, I asked Bryce about his day.

He shrugged. "I checked out a few houses and had lunch with Zach. That was nice. He's still withdrawn and didn't talk much. I think he's afraid he's going to lose me."

"You'll just have to prove that you're not going anywhere."

"Yeah, once I get a permanent residence and set up a room for him things should be better."

"Any headway on getting your job back?"

He set his fork down and leaned back in his seat. "I've reached out to several people on the board. I thought I'd have more support but it's turning out people I thought were my friends aren't as loyal as I'd hoped."

"I'm sorry," I reached out and touched his hand briefly. "What are you going to do?"

"Honestly? I'm not sure. SC has been my life for so long I'm having trouble imagining anything else."

"Yeah, I have no clue what I would do if I couldn't be a cop."

"That is an option now that you have the money from Jamey."

I'd been so focused on the case I hadn't thought about that much at all.

"Any idea what you're going to do with it?"

I gave a one-shoulder shrug. "I'm going to pay off my parents' mortgage. Not sure what else."

He put down his fork and regarded me with a slight smile.

"Why are you looking at me like that?"

"You're a good person."

I waved a hand. "Whatever. Just a regular guy."

"You just got two million dollars and your first thought is to take care of your mom and dad."

"They've done a lot for me. Gave up their lives in Korea so I could be born in America. I wouldn't have had near as many options there. Taking care of them is the least I can do."

"What about buying something for yourself?"

Another shrug. "I would like to have my own place. A house instead of an apartment. In a better neighborhood."

"You want the two point five kids and white picket fences?" He arched an eyebrow.

I chuckled and said, "I wouldn't mind a nice house with a yard and a dog."

"And kids?"

"I never saw that as an option. Not just because I'm gay but because of my job."

Bryce's face darkened and he stared off into the distance. Oh, I'd forgotten about Zach.

"Hey," I waved a hand in front of his face to get his attention. "Just because I never thought kids would happen doesn't mean I wouldn't date a guy who had one."

He brightened. "You'll like Zach when you meet him. Not sure when that'll be. Probably not until things calm down a bit."

"That decision is totally up to you," I replied. "I'll follow your lead."

We said good-night to each other at our vehicles. Bryce pressed me against my driver-side door and kissed me. His erection ground against mine, and I let myself enjoy the contact until he lowered his lips to my neck and bit.

"Hey, no hickies." I shoved him away.

"Sorry, not sorry," he said with a snicker. "It's so hard to control myself."

I kissed him again, this time keeping our groins apart. But soon, he was up against me again. Pushing, rubbing, caressing. He slipped his hand into the top of my pants, and I was so close to letting him go for it until the right head re-engaged. I grabbed his wrist and pushed him away.

"I think it's time to say good-night."

"Yeah." He nodded. "I guess so."

After one more gentle kiss, he got into his car and drove away. I was still painfully hard. I'd have to take care of it at home or I'd never get to sleep.

TWENTY-ONE

WHEN I ARRIVED AT WORK TUESDAY MORNING, THE first thing I noticed was that Shep was in Chief Slight's office, and the chief did *not* look like a happy camper. When she spotted me she pointed at me and gestured for me to join them.

"Shit, what did I do now?" I murmured.

I entered the office, shut the door behind me, and stood next to Shep.

"I don't know if I should scream at you for keeping something from me or commend you for having your co-worker's back."

"Excuse me," I said, "I have no idea what you're talking about."

Shep glanced at me. "I came clean to Chief Slight about being at the scene of the Julian Ramsey murder."

Shit! "Chief, I'm…"

She cut me off with an icy glare. "I understand why Detective Adley was hesitant to say anything since it involved his sexuality. So perhaps I should make something clear to the both of you." She stood, came around, and leaned against the front of her desk. "I don't care if you like men or women or both. I don't care if you're a drag queen or if you wear women's clothes at home. For fuck's sake, there's a transgender detective in my precinct."

"There is?" My jaw dropped. "Who?"

"I'm not going to tell you. Just like I'd never tell anyone that you're gay, Detective Tao."

"Oh, you know."

She rolled her eyes. "Of course I do. Just like I knew Detective Adley liked to moonlight as Miss Lavish Gloss before he told me."

"You did?" he gasped.

She ignored his question. "I know most of what goes on with my people. Dave was a shock, though. I never expected that in a million years. But that's neither here nor there. The point is that you should always trust me enough to come to me with anything."

"I'm sorry, ma'am," Shep and I said in unison.

She pointed at Shep. "The evidence against you is circumstantial and extremely weak. Nonetheless, I have to be careful. You have a ton of vacation time, correct?"

He nodded.

"I'd like you to use a week or two. That'll give us time to get the evidence we need to clear you and I won't have to put you on leave, which would require a reason. For now, I'd like to keep this under our hats."

Shep didn't appear thrilled about the idea but didn't argue.

"I suggest you do that ASAP. Go to HR and put in the paperwork. I'll approve it."

"Thank you, Chief," he said then turned to me. "Sorry. I thought it was best to be honest."

"Probably the best choice." I gave him a one-armed hug before he left.

Once the door was shut behind Shep, Slight scowled. "Do you actually think he's the killer?"

"Not really," I admitted. "I'm hoping we find something to clear him but so far I haven't gotten anything."

"Lord help me if he's guilty. I'd lose my job for not saying something officially. If he is the one, I just gave him time to run."

"Trust me, Chief, I'm doing everything I can."

"I know." She took a few steps away and grabbed her coffee mug. "I'm going to make some phone-calls as well. See what I can find out about Adley's stakeouts."

"I'll let you know the minute I find anything."

Aza was sitting on the corner of my desk when I returned to the squad room.

"What's going on?"

"I got here early and started searching Adult Friend Finder."

"I assume you found something?"

"Yes, indeed. Both Tyrone Osceola and Tanev Singh also had accounts on AFF. That alone wouldn't have helped so I did more. I cross-searched for anyone with accounts on both sites. It's not the easiest thing to do since I don't have as much *legal* access to AFF's database, but I found at least a dozen people with profiles on both sites."

I sat at my desk and waited for Aza to continue.

"I found one woman who contacted all our victims, minus Bryce. She messaged Ramsey and Detective Nolan on *Ashley Madison* and the other two on AFF."

"What's her name?" I asked.

His face dropped. "Well, I haven't got it yet. She's one of the people who were extra careful, including paying with Bitcoin. Makes it harder for me to get an identity."

"Harder, but not impossible, right?"

He grinned and took his seat. "Exactly. Oh, I don't know if this means anything or not, but I found a profile on *Ashley Madison* that caught my attention."

"Why?"

"He was an employee of SeattleCarrick. Didn't originally catch my attention because of the lower salary range."

"Why did you look at it now?"

"First it was that he worked at SC and the connection therefore to Bryce Carrick. I did a records search and found that this guy lost everything. His wife has filed for divorce and left town with their kids. He lost his job when Bryce Carrick was fired and is close to losing his house."

"Why did he lose his job?"

"He was Bryce's personal assistant and the brother cleaned house of anyone who was loyal to Bryce."

Bryce's assistant? I'd spoken to him. What was his name? "Are you talking about Thomas Grainger?"

"Yeah," his brow furrowed. "How did you know?"

"I met him. We talked about Bryce getting ousted and the *Ashley Madison* scandal but he didn't say anything about being a victim of the hack himself."

"You think it means anything?"

"Not sure." I shrugged. "But I'll pay him a second visit to find out."

I dialed Molly and asked her what she was doing.

"Patrolling at the moment. Why? Do you need me? Chief Slight said you were my first priority."

"I like the sound of that. You are at my mercy, Officer Whitmore," I cracked.

"Don't let the power go to your head." She giggled. "I am not afraid to put you in your place."

"I'll be good. I promise," I replied. "I need to re-interview someone, and I'd like you to join me."

"I can be there in five minutes."

"Meet you outside."

She pulled up right on time, and I hopped into her cruiser.

"Where we going?" she asked.

I gave her the address and she took off.

"Who are we visiting?" she asked.

"His name is Thomas Grainger. Former personal assistant to Bryce Carrick. I spoke to him before we located Bryce."

"Why are we going back?"

"He neglected to tell me that he was an *Ashley Madison* user as well and that his wife left after the site was hacked. Might not mean anything, but I wanted to be sure."

"Just tell me what you need me to do."

"I'll take the lead but you should feel free to jump in with any questions. Otherwise, listen and take note of anything that strikes you as odd."

"Got it."

Thomas Grainger took longer to answer the door than the first time. And when he did get there, I was sure a dark scowl took over his face before he replaced it with an obviously fake smile.

"Detective Tao? What do you want?"

I cocked an eyebrow at his brusqueness, but before I could respond he said, "Sorry. I've been trying to find a job and not having any luck. I'm just stressed out. Please, come in."

I introduced Molly. He offered drinks but we declined. There was now a couch in the living room but it was obviously second, or third, hand. Molly sat on it while I remained standing, and Thomas rested on the edge of his recliner.

"What can I do for you?" he asked.

"When we spoke the first time, why didn't you mention that your wife had left you?"

He shrugged. "I didn't think it mattered. You asked about Bryce."

"You didn't think it was important?" Molly asked. "Even though both you *and* your former boss went through the same thing? One of the reasons Bryce was missing was because of the scandal with *Ashley Madison.*"

"Sorry," he replied. "I guess I should've told you."

"It appears your wife hasn't come back," I said.

"No, she isn't ready to forgive me…yet." He scrubbed at his face. "I'm not giving up though."

Changing the subject, I asked, "Have you had anything unusual happen to you lately?"

"Nope." He shook his head. "Is this in regard to the recent murders of those wealthy guys?"

"Yes. Since the killer is going after males who had *Ashley Madison* accounts, we're checking in on as many as possible," I lied.

"I thought only rich dudes were being targeted."

"So far," Molly replied. "But we're just being cautious."

"I was sorry to hear about your partner, Detective Tao. Must've been tough, finding him like that."

"Yes, it was. Thanks."

We asked a few more questions and took off.

Back in the car, Molly chuckled. "He shaves his eyebrows?"

"No," I said. "His body doesn't grow hair. Condition called Alopecia."

"Okay. He's an odd duck, regardless."

"That's the truth. Not sure that it means anything though. He doesn't fit any part of the profile of the killer."

"Not female and definitely *not* a redhead."

"I WANT A FILE ON EVERY WIFE WHOSE husband was on *Ashley Madison* in the local area," I told Aza.

"That's a huge list. In the thousands. Any other parameters?"

"Eliminate anyone over the age of forty-five."

"That's it?" he asked, exasperation evident in his voice.

"Start with the rich guys," I said. "And we'll work our way through them." I glanced at Molly. "I suggest grabbing some coffee. We're going to be here for a while."

She sighed then shot me a grin. "Let's do it."

Hours later, we gone through dozens of files, eliminating women one-by-one for various reasons. Hair color was the main reason, but we did account for the possibility of hair dye and wigs. We did preliminary location searches and excluded women who were obviously near Seattle.

I called a halt to work at seven and told them both to go home. As soon as they were gone I dialed Bryce.

"You available for a late dinner?" I asked.

"I'd *love* that." He sighed loudly. "I've been on the phone all day trying to secure supporters to get back into SC."

"Any luck?"

"I think so, but let's discuss it in person. I know we just ate at Changes but I'm craving their burgers again."

"That works for me. I'll meet you there in thirty minutes."

IT WAS FORTY-FIVE MINUTES BY THE TIME BRYCE arrived, but I'd already ordered the burgers and had a drink waiting for him. He greeted me with a big kiss that made my feet tingle.

"It's nice to see you," he said as he sat.

"Definitely."

He took a swig. "Thanks for this. I needed it."

"Rough day?" I asked.

He rested his elbows on the table and rubbed his forehead. "Just a lot of talking. Felt more like I was campaigning than trying to get *my* company back. Brendan doesn't have the sense God gave a billy goat. He's going to run it into the ground."

"You'll do it. I don't have a doubt. You are a very persistent man."

"Thanks. I wish I had as much faith as you."

The bar wasn't full but there were a few guys dancing and a couple practically making out in the corner. The few women present seemed to be with their gay buddies. Best of all, it was quiet, and I could touch Bryce's hand without worrying about someone freaking out. Seattle was fairly liberal but there were places queers couldn't so much as exchange friendly glances for fear of getting beat up.

Our burgers arrived, and I'd just taken a bite when someone sidled up beside me. I glanced up but his eyes were solely on Bryce.

"I was wondering if you'd like to dance."

Bryce nearly choked on his food, swallowed hard, and put a hand on his chest. "You're asking me?"

"Yeah, I just *love* silver foxes." The kid couldn't have been a day over twenty-one, though he appeared closer to fifteen or sixteen. He wore a painted on pair of white skinny jeans and a bright green T-shirt that showed off his trim figure. He had longish blond hair, and he twirled a lock as he winked at Bryce.

"*Excuse* me?" I snapped. "What makes you think he's available? We are sitting together."

Twink boy glared down at me. "No offense," he said, obviously lying. "But you two are totally mismatched. Anyone can see that." He swaggered toward Bryce and put a hand on his shoulder. "I am much more your type."

I rose swiftly making my chair scrape across the floor and was about to tell the kid off when Bryce held up a hand. "I can handle this, Peter."

Holding in my irritation, I took a deep breath—three actually—and returned to my seat. The twink smiled at me as if he'd won, but I kept my calm. Bryce took the kid's hand off of his shoulder and patted it once before dropping it.

"I appreciate the offer, young man, but I am here on a date. And I couldn't care less what you think of our incompatibility. I happen to believe that we are *very* well-suited for each other."

The boy harrumphed and said, "Your loss" before turning away and swaying off.

"Some fucking nerve," I mumbled and returned to eating. Feeling Bryce's eyes on me, I glanced up. He wore a shit-eating grin and his eyes twinkled.

"What?" I asked.

"You were jealous." It was a statement and not a question.

Shooting him a scowl, I shook my head. "I was not! I just

thought it was rather rude for him to come up to you when we're here together. He had no idea if we were together or not."

"Nope," he said insistently. "You were definitely jealous. That green-eyed monster was more than obvious."

"If you want him, go for it," I growled. "It's not like we have a commitment. Not at the moment."

His face darkened, and I saw hurt. Instantly, I regretted what I said. Causing him any sort of pain wasn't anything I ever wanted to do intentionally.

"I thought we did have a commitment," Bryce murmured. "One to wait until we could be together. I care about you, and I thought you felt the same."

I reached across the table and took his hand. "Of course I care about you. I want you so much I can fucking taste it. It takes every bit of my strength to turn you down. I want to take you to bed and fuck you harder than you've even been fucked, but I know I would regret it. Not because I don't care about you or you don't care about me. Regardless of how fucking much I want to be with you, you would still be a married man, and I would be your side piece."

He laughed. "You'd never be *just* a side piece."

"But I would be having sex with a married man. I know you're not Darren. Not even close. But when I walked away from that relationship I swore never again. If I break my word, then what kind of man am I?"

"A sexually satisfied man?"

I tried to remain stoic but quickly smirked.

"Relax," he said. "I said I'm willing to wait, and I mean it. It's our commitment to each other, and that isn't one I take lightly. I may be horny as a rabbit on Viagra, but I'm not going to sleep with anyone. You're the only man I want. In my bed and in my life."

"Damn, you sure know what to say to get what you want."

"Obviously not, if you insist on waiting until my divorce."

I shrugged. "It's important to me."

"Then it's important to me. Now, enough serious talk. I want to enjoy the rest of my evening. I'd like to make the night last as long as possible."

"Is that your way of asking if you can spend the night?"

He grinned and shot me puppy dog eyes. "Please?"

"As if I could resist that face."

"I promise I'll be a good boy. I just want to hold you."

"Well, as long as you can maintain control."

"Scout's Honor."

There was nothing comparable to sleeping with Bryce's arms wrapped around me. I'd never felt such peace. I wished we could do it every night for now and for the rest of my life.

TWENTY-TWO

BRYCE WOKE ME EARLY, MUCH EARLIER THAN I would've preferred. But he did it with a sweet, romantic kiss so all was forgiven.

"Your cupboards are bare, and I'm starving. Want to go out for breakfast?"

"Sure, but I'm buying."

He raised his hands. "No argument here. I'm the one without a job."

"Yeah and a mere, what, fifteen million in your accounts?"

"Twenty, but who's counting?" He chuckled and kissed me again. "Now get your pretty ass up and in the shower so we can get going."

I swung my feet to the floor and stood. "How do you know I've got a pretty ass? It's not like you've seen it."

"Maybe not bare, but it looks mighty fine in those boxer briefs." He reached over and lightly smacked my butt.

"Hands off, mister," I ordered. "It's not yours to touch."

"Not yet, but soon. And I *cannot* wait."

The sexy tone of his voice sent shivers down my spine. Damn, I was also hard as a rock. As much as I enjoyed sleeping with Bryce it also meant I didn't have the privacy to jack off. I considered doing it in the shower but decided against it because Bryce was waiting for me.

WE CHOSE A GREASY SPOON DINER MAINLY BECAUSE of the location. I had a ham and cheese omelet while Bryce chowed down on biscuits and gravy.

"Gawd," he groaned halfway through the meal. "We've been eating like shit lately, and I haven't been working out."

"I just figured you were a chubby chaser and trying to get me fat," I cracked.

"You could gain two hundred pounds, and I'd still want to be with you."

"Aww," I cooed. "So sweet. And so full of shit."

He pretended to be offended. "Honestly, I'm not just attracted to your body. It's your mind I like as well."

"Hmm, not sure I buy that, but I'll let it go."

"Seriously though, I do make a stellar Chicken Caesar Salad," he said. "Why don't you come over to my place tonight, and I'll make it for you."

"It's a date," I replied.

"Excellent."

I glimpsed over at the guy next to us, who was reading a paper, and spotted Bryce's face on the front page. When he set it down and left I reached over and snagged it.

Oh, damn! The article was about SeattleCarrick and whether or not Bryce would be returning. Brendan was quoted as saying, "Absolutely not."

"What's that?" he asked and snatched the paper out of my hand before I could hide it. I watched him as he read the story, his face gradually getting darker and darker until his lips set into a firm scowl.

"You still have a chance, don't you?" I asked. "He might not know your plans."

"Apparently he does. He says that I've reached out to many shareholders and members of the board but he's swayed them to his side. A couple of the people I thought I had on my side were interviewed and said they're happy with Brendan and have no plans to change anything." He pushed his half-eaten food away and rubbed his brow. "Damn, this isn't good. I need to make some phone-calls right away. I need to go. I'm sorry." He stood and grabbed his coat.

"Absolutely. Don't worry."

He leaned over and kissed me. "I'll call you later." Then, he strode out the door, already pressing his phone to his ear.

AZA WAS AT HIS DESK WHEN I ARRIVED at work but jumped to his feet the moment he spotted me.

"Looks like you have news," I said.

He beamed and nodded. "I identified AlphaDog. His name is Antwan Becker, and he's a preacher at a small church in Newcastle."

"A minister, huh? That might explain why he's so secretive."

"Yup." Aza handed me a slip of paper. "This is his phone number and the address of the church. He lives in a house on the same property."

"Anything I should know about him? Married? Convictions?"

"Single and not even a parking ticket as far as I can tell."

"All right. I think I'll pay him a visit," I said. "I want you to keep working on those files of the scorned women. Where's Molly?"

"She got called away for a raid. Didn't figure you'd mind."

"I'd never stand in the way of an officer getting some action like that," I said before I left.

I decided to call Becker ahead of time but wasn't specific about why I needed to speak to him. We agreed to meet in his office at the church.

When I stepped into Newcastle Church of Christ I entered a narrow hallway that curved around to the left. To my right was a set of large double doors that most likely led to the sanctuary. I strode down the corridor and spotted several more doors. They were all labeled: *Daycare, Youth,* and finally, *Pastor's Office.* I opened the door and was greeted by a middle-aged woman with red hair that was obviously a wig. A nameplate on her desk said Marjorie.

"You must be Detective Tao," she said cheerfully. "Pastor Becker told me to send you back." Marjorie motioned to an open door a few feet away.

I thanked her and headed into Becker's office. He smiled when he saw me, stood, and shook my hand with a firm grip. Becker fit the bill of how Shep had described AlphaDog55. He was African-American and tall. I'd say at least six five.

"How can I help you, Detective?" he asked.

I shut the door before taking a seat across from him. "This is a delicate matter," I began. "But I want to assure you I am not here to expose any of your secrets. I simply need the truth."

He furrowed his brow and fingered a silver cross necklace that hung around his neck.

"Do you know a man by the name of Shepherd Adley?"

"Doesn't sound familiar." He shook his head.

"You might know him as Spicy Ginger Bottom." Shep's actual screenname had been SpicyGngrBtm0016.

He gulped audibly and tucked in his upper lip. "I'm sorry but I don't know what you're talking about."

I leaned forward, put my elbows on his desk and stared directly into his dark brown eyes. "Pastor Becket—Antwon—I am not here to expose you to your church members. I don't care what your sexuality is. This won't leave this room. I promise you."

He sighed dejectedly and slumped his shoulders. "Yes," he admitted in a low whisper. "I know him."

"Did you meet him around midnight two weeks ago at the Elliot Bay Harbor? It was a Monday night."

Becker answered with a small nod.

"How long were you with him?"

"A couple hours. Three at the most." His eyes had become dull and sad.

I felt for the guy, because I knew what it was like to hide

something major. He had it worse than I did. I only lied to my parents while he was deceiving an entire congregation of people.

"Thank you, Pastor." I sat back in my chair. "I know this was difficult but your statement has helped me clear this man of murder."

His head hung low, and he let out a long exhale. "Glad I could help."

"If you don't mind me asking, why don't you lead at a church that accepts homosexuality?"

Becker sat up and made eye contact. "My church *does* accept homosexuality. I could date and marry a man if I wanted."

"Then why the secrecy?"

"It's the promiscuity that's frowned upon. And that also happens to be my vice. I don't enjoy committed relationships as much as one-nighters."

The opposite of me. I generally disliked sex with men I didn't know and preferred a strong connection with a guy before we went to bed together.

"I've fought my desires and prayed for help. Marjorie has helped me stay strong, but I slipped. I regretted it shortly afterward. That's why I deleted my account."

Tears dropped down his cheeks, and he quickly wiped them away. I wished I could help him but I'd never been a religious man. I wasn't sure I believed in God. "I don't have any advice for you, Pastor, though I do understand what it's like to have secrets from people you love. All I can say is follow your heart." I stood, and he did the same.

"I really am glad I could help," he said as we shook hands.

As soon as I stepped out of his office I saw Marjorie shift nervously away from the phone.

Had she heard our entire conversation?

Judging by the stern scowl on her face, I was sure the answer was yes. She was not happy that Pastor Beckett had had random sex with a man he barely knew. Marjorie pasted on a fake smile for me, but I could see the anger boiling behind the pretend visage. I ran the profile of my killer through my head. Female, small, redhead. Marjorie fit the description though she was older than I'd originally thought the killer would be.

"Thanks for lending me your boss," I said.

"Oh, no problem at all." She cocked her head and grinned at me.

I held out my hand and she took it. "I didn't catch your name. Mrs…?"

"Croft," she said. "Marjorie Croft."

"Well, thank you again," I said before leaving the room. I could feel her staring at me until I sauntered out of sight. As soon as I was in my car, I was on the phone with Aza.

"I need you to run a background check on a Mrs. Marjorie Croft. Give me everything you can."

I ran a scenario through my head. Playing *What If?* often helped me figure things out. Maybe Marjorie already knew about Becker's activities that night or at least knew about them ahead of time. What if she'd gone to Elliot Bay and saw Julian Ramsey waiting around and assumed he was the guy Pastor Becker was meeting? She could've attacked him, hoping it would put a stop to Becker's promiscuity.

It didn't explain the other victims, but I could figure that out later. Several serial killers began with accidentally murdering someone or doing it spur of the moment. Unplanned. Then they realized how much they enjoyed it. They love the thrill of it, and they get the taste of blood in their mouth, so to speak. After that, they'll find any reason to kill again. Maybe Marjorie chose to go after men who cheated on their wives. She would've figured out Julian wasn't the guy Becker was meeting but he was still an adulterer. So she killed more unfaithful husbands.

I was onto something. I was sure of it. Marjorie wasn't the wife of a cheater, but perhaps she had been. Her anger at Becker's slutty ways bled over into a fury regarding infidelity.

On the drive back to the station, I placed a call to Bryce to see how he was doing.

"Not very well," he said. The stress level in his voice was obvious. "Everyone who promised to support me has changed their mind. My chances at getting back into SC are disappearing right before my eyes. I think it's time to admit defeat."

"I'm sorry." I wished I could say more.

"I'll be fine. I'm going to start a new business. I don't know exactly what yet, but I'll figure it out."

"Yes, you will. You're one of the smartest men I've ever met."

"Maybe you can help me brainstorm ideas over dinner tonight."

"I'd love too."

"Okay, I gotta go. An old friend called me today, and I'm getting together with him for lunch."

"Okay. See you later."

"Can't wait."

BOTH MOLLY AND AZA WERE BUSTING AT THE seams to tell me stuff the minute I arrived. I held up both hands and said, "Wait, I get to go first." I then made them wait until I took off my coat and placed my gun in a drawer. I sat, leaned back, and interlaced my hands behind my head. They were like impatient children bouncing from foot to foot.

"Shep is not Julian Ramsey's killer. Pastor Becker confirmed he was with Shep that night."

"That's excellent. Goes right along with my news," Molly said. She eyeballed Aza, and he motioned for her to go ahead. "The raid I was on this morning was at Emerald City Automotive. It was really a front for a major chop shop. This place dealt with hundreds of stolen vehicles."

"And they're out of business. That's outstanding," I said, wondering what this had to do with Shep.

"A guy by the name of Rico Pitts worked for Emerald City. He's an excellent car thief."

"Are you ever going to get to the point, Officer Whitmore?" I scowled.

"Just making you wait like you did to us," she cracked.

"Smartass."

"The nights in question, Shep was on a stakeout; he was following Pitts. He liked him for the murder of an elderly fellow who was killed during a carjacking. Shep was right, by the way—Pitts already copped to it. He's not the brightest bulb."

"Anyway…" I said impatiently.

"Anyway…Emerald City Automotive has hidden cameras everywhere. We had no idea until we busted the place. They save *all* their footage. As soon as I learned that, I went to the dates of the murders."

"And?"

"He was there," she said. "Hours of footage showing Shep on stakeout. It's no wonder he never got anything on Pitts. The dude knew he was being tailed thanks to the cameras."

"That's certainly enough to clear Shep of any suspicion." I stood. "I better go tell the chief."

"Don't you want to hear my news first?" Aza asked, his voice high-pitched.

"Does it have to do with Shep?"

His shoulders drooped. "No."

"Then you'll have to wait." I marched to the chief's office and knocked on the open door.

She waved me in, finished her phone conversation, and said, "Please tell me you have good news."

"I have good news."

"Thank God." She sighed loudly. "What is it?"

"I've cleared Detective Adley of any involvement in the murders. I have proof he was nowhere near the scenes of three of the murders."

"Excellent!" She clapped her hands together. "I'll call him right away. Unless you'd like to do it yourself."

"I'll make the call. Do I have permission to bring him aboard the case?"

"Absolutely." Her phone rang, and she shooed me out.

In less than a minute, I had Shep on the phone.

"You ready to get your lazy ass back to work?" I asked as soon as he answered. "Or are you enjoying your mandatory vacation?"

"Oh, hell no," he retorted. "I'm bored to death."

"The chief has cleared you to come back *and* to join me on the case. If that's okay with you."

"Definitely. I'll see you in an hour."

"Excellent."

"Thanks, Peter," he said before disconnecting.

When I returned to my desk, Aza asked, "Can I tell you now?"

"Go for it."

"Marjorie Croft has been married—and divorced—twice. Both times her husbands cheated on her."

"Definitely not a fan of adulterers then."

"Not at all," he said. "I also did a preliminary location search for her, but she's not active on social media. No tweets or posts about where she goes. It appears she spends most nights at home alone with her poodle, Mad Max."

"So we can't prove she was or wasn't near the murders."

"Right, but I'm working on getting access to her cellphone."

I turned to the stack of files on my desk. "You keep working on her while I sift through these files."

Shep was at the station in less than forty-five minutes, eager to get to work.

"Any suspects?" he asked.

"Nothing solid," I replied. "We're digging into as many of the scorned wives as we can." I told him about Pastor Becker and his assistant.

"You're thinking it could've been her?" he asked.

"Something about her struck me as odd. It's just one of those gut instincts."

He shrugged. "Well, your gut told you I was innocent so I wouldn't discount your feelings. Not yet anyway. Thanks again."

"Don't mention it. We're partners after all."

He glanced at me and cocked an eyebrow. "You want to keep working together? Even after this case?"

"Yeah, I think we work well together. You need to loosen up a bit on the job, and there are times I need someone to keep me from running off half-cocked."

He gave me a one-armed, manly hug. "Sounds great to me." He straightened his shirt and tucked in part that had come out. "I'm going to read over your reports so I can get caught up."

I gave him the thumbs-up sign, and he strode to his desk on the other side of the room. He'd take over Jamey's desk as soon as Slight approved our partnership.

The day was spent poring through file after file of women who had been cheated on. Many, multiple times. I felt for them and almost understood why one of them might've gone after these guys. I wondered if Darren's wife ever discovered how many times he'd cheated. I'd considered telling her after I left him, but decided it was better for my emotional health to make a clean break.

None of the women stood out, and my mind kept going back to Marjorie Croft. There was something off about her, though I couldn't put my finger on what it was. She bugged me, but I had no idea why.

Nothing Aza found on her helped us. We couldn't label her as a person of interest but I wasn't ready to discount her either. I knew that if we dug far enough something would click.

Before I knew it, the clock read six-thirty p.m., and I called an end to the work for the day. Aza and Molly were relieved, but Shep insisted on staying longer.

"I want to make sure I'm completely up on everything so we can hit the ground running tomorrow."

I said good-bye and headed for my car. I was surprised Bryce hadn't called me yet to ask me where I was. I'd been looking forward to spending time with him and his Caesar Chicken Salad. I called him, but it went right to voice mail.

"Hey, it's me," I said. "I'm heading home to take a shower and change. Call me when you're ready for me to come over."

However, by the time I was clean and ready to go out, he still hadn't called. I left another message before flopping down on the couch.

By ten p.m. I'd left three messages and was alternating between worry and anger. I didn't see him flat-out ignoring me, so I was sure whatever was going on had to be important. I gave up around midnight and went to bed, sorely missing Bryce being next to me.

TWENTY-THREE

Bryce still hadn't returned my call by morning time. I dialed him again but didn't leave a voice mail. Whatever was going on, he better have a damn fine reason for standing me up. If this was how it was going to be when we were in a real relationship, then I would have to re-think everything. I understood he was a busy man, but communication was important. If he couldn't make our date, the least he could've done was call.

It wasn't until I got to work that my cop brain kicked in, taking over for my boyfriend brain. The killer was still out there. What if she decided to finish what she started and kill Bryce? The worry on my face must've been evident when Shep spotted me.

"What's wrong?" he asked.

It was still fairly early so the squad room wasn't full of cops just yet. That helped me speak openly without the worry of someone overhearing me talk about my boyfriend. "Bryce and I were supposed to get together last night, but he hasn't returned any calls."

"When was the last time you talked to him?"

"Yesterday afternoon. I'm afraid the hacker might've decided to go after Bryce again. He's a smart man, and an excellent fighter, but she's proven herself excellent at surprise attacks."

"What do you want to do?" he asked.

I wiped my sweaty brow. "I can check with the hotel he's staying at. Find out if he's there or not."

"Why don't we do that together?" He rose from his desk and put on his coat. "Where's he staying?"

"Tucker's Point Resort."

"Same place you originally found him?"

I nodded.

"So they already know you there. That should help with getting in." He put a hand on my shoulder. "Don't worry. I'm sure nothing awful has happened to him."

"I hope."

Before Shep and I left, I gave Aza and Molly their assignment for the day. "Focus on Marjorie Croft. Dig as deep as you can. Break as many rules as possible without getting caught."

Shep coughed and pretended to cover his ears.

"I *need* to know where she was the nights of the murders. And last night."

"Why last night?" Molly asked.

"I'll explain later. Just do it."

She saluted and returned to her computer.

"We're on it," Aza said.

Shep insisted on driving to the hotel, and it was a wise choice. I undoubtedly would've broken a few speeding laws, which would've sent Shep into a tizzy. I didn't feel like getting a lecture on how important following the rules was.

The concierge at Tucker's Point remembered me. "I haven't seen Mr. Carrick since yesterday," he said. "He left around three in the afternoon and hasn't returned."

"How do you know?"

"He's a high-profile guest," he replied. "I searched the computer and read the records of his key swipes. Nothing past the morning when he came back after spending the night out."

Shep shot me a glance, and I nodded, telling him it had been me Bryce spent the night with.

"We'd still like to take a peek inside his room," Shep said.

"Of course."

A few minutes later we had a key and were heading to his room.

"This is a nice place. I wouldn't mind spending time here."

"I haven't been here except for that one time. Bryce and I usually hang out at my place."

"Your apartment is a bit homier," he said. "I assume so, anyway."

I slid the key card in, unlocked the door, and we entered with our hands on our holsters. "Hello?" I hollered. "Bryce, are you here? It's me, Peter. Shep is here with me."

There wasn't an answer so we continued forward. I ambled one way and Shep the other. There was no sign of Bryce. The bed was made so he hadn't slept in it. It didn't appear he'd been there for at least half-a-day.

"Where the hell could he be?"

"Pardon me for saying so," Shep said, "but do you think it's possible he's with his wife?"

I shook my head insistently. "No way. You don't know the whole story. It's a loveless marriage. One of convenience."

"She's his beard, right?"

"It's more than that," I replied. "She blackmailed him into marrying her."

He raised his eyebrows. "Are you sure he's telling you the truth?"

Anger and annoyance rose up but I held it back. "Let's just concentrate on finding him."

Shep raised his palms. "Sorry. I like you. I don't want to see you get hurt."

"Thanks, but I know what I'm doing."

The ride back was a quiet one. Not only was I annoyed Shep was sticking his nose into my personal business, I was also trying to concentrate on how to locate Bryce and how to identify the killer.

"Don't ask me how I did it," Molly said, "but Marjorie was definitely in Seattle the night of Julian Ramsey's murder. I can't narrow it down further than that, however."

"We need to find out why she was here," I said.

"Why don't Molly and I head over and talk to her?" Shep offered. "We can handle this while you work on shit here."

"That works for me." I sat at my desk and took a deep breath. I was about to open a file when Aza called out.

"Holy shit, I got her."

"Got who?"

"I have a name for the lady who had accounts on both Adult Friend Finder *and Ashley Madison and* who reached out to all our victims, except Bryce."

"Is it Marjorie Croft?" I dashed to his desk and read over his shoulder.

"No, but you might recognize her last name. Grainger. Sarah Jo Grainger."

"As in Thomas Grainger?"

"I'm checking on that right now." He tapped at several keys, and pages flew onto his screen. "Yes. They are siblings. They grew up in Seattle, but she lives in Michigan. Has been there for three years."

"How do you know the account belongs to her?"

"I traced them both to credit card accounts in her name."

"Give me her number."

He scribbled it down, I grabbed it and dialed her number the minute I was at my desk.

"Hello," she answered.

"Is this Sarah Jo Grainger?"

"Yes." She spoke with a slight lisp as if she had trouble making the S sound.

"This is Detective Peter Tao with the Seattle Fraud Department." The fact that no such section existed didn't matter.

"Did I do something wrong?" she gasped.

"Not you, ma'am, but we believe you could be a victim of fraud. Were you ever a member of a website called *Ashley Madison*?"

"I've never even heard of it."

"What about Adult Friend Finder?"

"Absolutely not!" She must've recognized that name.

"We've traced accounts on both those sites to a credit card in your name."

"That is not me," she insisted. "I don't have a credit card. I don't like owing anything."

"Do you have any idea who might've forged your name? Maybe someone who might've gotten your mail with credit card applications?" I was fishing but was sure I was going to hook something.

"The last person I lived with was my brother…Thomas."

"Would he do something like this to you?" I asked.

She sighed before answering. "I'm afraid so. We were never that close. He was never close to anyone. Only had one friend his entire life. Chip. His wife just left him. He's a total mess right now. I wouldn't put anything past him right now."

"I assure you, Miss Grainger, we will take care of this. If you just please type up a statement saying that you never signed up for this credit card, I can see what I can do to prove whether or not it was your brother."

"Will he get in trouble? I don't want anything bad to happen to him."

With the way things were pointing, Thomas was going to be in a great deal of trouble but I couldn't tell her that. "I will do my best to lessen any punishment," I assured her.

I gave her my email to send the statement and ended the call.

Shit, shit, shit. Had I been seeing this all wrong? With my insistence the killer was a woman, had I overlooked the real murderer? Thomas Grainger was an odd duck for sure, but was he a serial killer? I couldn't fathom a motive for him doing such a thing but if he was insane he didn't need a reason.

I read over my report that I had written after both interviews with Thomas. There was something I hadn't written down because it wasn't relevant to the case. What was it? He apologized for something. I wracked my brain trying to remember and then it came to me.

He'd said, *"I was sorry to hear about your partner. Must've been tough finding him like that."*

I avoided newspaper articles and news reports on my cases because they tended to mess with my brain. I could get too focused on what the reporters said or conjectured and lose track of the facts. I left all that to Len Pratt, the Public Relations Officer, though he was provided with what to release to the media. Jamey usually did that with our cases, but I didn't remember doing it this time.

A quick call to Pratt told me two things. The first was that the chief had spoken to him about media coverage. The second was that the fact that I was the one who found Jamey's body had *not* been released. If Thomas knew, he either had insider knowledge or he was there himself.

"Bryce and Thomas!" Had I said that out loud? Judging by the odd expression Aza was giving me I had.

I strolled over to Aza's desk as nonchalantly as possible. "I need you to hack into somebody's phone," I said. "Now. And don't ask questions." I scribbled down Bryce's number and handed it to him.

Aza didn't even look at me askance when he saw whose information we were accessing.

"I need the names of all incoming callers."

"He was a busy guy that day. There are a ton of outgoing calls but just a handful of incoming."

A list of names popped up on the screen, and I spotted the one I was searching for. Thomas Grainger.

Bryce had said an old friend had called and wanted to catch up. Thomas had been Bryce's personal assistant for years. Thomas could've lured Bryce to his place to finish the job he failed at weeks ago.

"What kind of car does Grainger drive?"

A moment later, Aza responded, "2009 Honda Accord. ACG8073."

Just like the car from the funeral.

"If it was Thomas using his sister's credit card," I conjectured, "then he spoke to the four dead men online pretending to be a woman to set up dates."

"Right," Aza said. "But he didn't message Bryce."

"He wouldn't have had too. As Bryce's PA, he might've had a way to track Bryce down."

Aza snapped his fingers. "You're right."

"That's *gotta* be enough for a warrant." I marched into the chief's office and spelled out what I'd just discovered. She made a call to the DA, who set the wheels in motion.

While waiting for the warrant to be signed, I got organized with the SWAT team.

"He's most likely holding a hostage," I said. "We can't just bust in until we know he's safe."

"What's the plan?" an officer asked.

"I'm going to go in under false pretenses," I replied. "I'll ensure the hostage's well-being before I make the call for you guys to come in. Until then, you'll be in hiding and be able to hear everything that's going on at my end. The go word is *lighthouse.*"

"What's going on?" Shep asked as he entered the conference room. "Aza said we had a lead on the killer?"

I'd spaced the fact that Shep and Molly had gone hunting for information on Marjorie Croft. I pulled him aside and gave him the down low on the situation.

"Wow. I was going to say it appeared like you were right about Marjorie. She acted extremely nervous. She's definitely hiding something."

"Whatever it is, she's not our killer," I said. "Grainger's our man."

"I don't like the idea of you going in alone. Why don't I go with you? That way I can distract Thomas while you make an excuse and look around."

Not a bad plan. "If you're sure."

"Couldn't be more sure that this is what I want to do. You know I got your back."

"Thanks."

I returned to the squad room to check on the status of the warrant, and Molly motioned me toward her. I was headed her way when Chief Slight stepped out of her office and announced, "We got the warrant. It's go-time."

The SWAT team loaded up, and every officer coming to the scene picked up an extra magazine of ammo. Chief Slight even slid on a bullet-resistant jacket so she could come to the scene. Molly kept wanting me to speak to her but there was too much hustle and bustle for me to get to her.

Shep and I put in earbuds so other team members could speak to us and slipped wireless mics into our pockets so they could hear us. He and I went over the plan several times on the drive over. My phone rang, and I checked in case it was Bryce. It was Molly again so I let it go to voice mail. Couldn't figure anything she had to say was as important as what I was about to do.

We'd just pulled up the car when my phone buzzed again. This time it was a text message from Molly. I read it quickly:

Spoke privately with Pastor Beckett. Made mistake about time. Hour late.

I didn't even process the message before shoving it back in my pocket so I could focus on saving Bryce.

Thomas appeared even more pissed when he saw me at the door. He grimaced and tilted his head to the side when he looked at my partner.

Shep stepped around me and extended his hand. "I'm Detective Shep Adley, Detective Tao's partner. We're here to ask you a few questions."

"Ask me questions?" Thomas repeated and narrowed his eyes.

Shep nodded. "Can we come in?" But he didn't wait for permission. He stepped past Thomas and marched into the living room.

I waited until Thomas shifted to the side before I entered. Shep had sat on the edge of the recliner so I remained standing and gestured for Thomas to sit on the couch.

"What is this about?" He glanced first at Shep then at me.

"Bryce Carrick is missing," Shep said before I could. "I hear you guys used to work together for years."

"Yes, that's true."

"Have you seen him recently?" Shep asked.

We'd decided I'd take the lead in the questioning, but Shep was probably just overexcited. It worked just as well this way. It would allow me to get away earlier than we'd planned.

"Can I use your bathroom?" I questioned.

"Oh, umm, uhh…" Thomas mumbled and checked us both out before he said, "Yes. Through the kitchen, down the hallway. First door on the left."

I followed his directions and spotted a set of Victorinox knives, missing two, on the way through the kitchen. I traipsed to the first door on the left, turned on the light and the fan, then stepped back out, shutting the door behind me.

I silently creeped down the corridor and tried the first of three more doors—two kids rooms and the master bedroom. The master had an ensuite bathroom and a walk-in closet. In the closet was a shelf of Styrofoam heads displaying a number of wigs, including a red one.

The first kid's room had been a boy's, and a girl's was right next door. Neither one had any signs of having been used for some time.

Where was Bryce? He had to be there. I was one hundred percent positive of it. Maybe there was an attic or a basement or some sort of hidden room. Back in the hallway I checked out the space between the two kids' rooms. They were opposite to the TARDIS from *Doctor Who*—It was bigger on the inside, but these were smaller on the inside. There was unaccounted for space, which led me to think there had to be some sort of secret room.

Shep and Thomas were still speaking, so I was assured I had more time to continue my investigation of the house. I returned to the girl's room and took a closer examination of items on the shared wall: a dresser, a bookcase and a large, full-length mirror. I pulled both pieces of furniture away from the wall—nothing. I was about to check out the boy's room when I pushed on the top right corner of the mirror and it popped open like a door.

Whatever was on the other side, it was totally dark so I retrieved my flashlight and gun, flipped on the beam and stepped inside. It was a small room with no decorations. However, six feet away, Bryce was bound and gagged and behind him, holding a knife to his throat, was Thomas. Bryce's arms extended from his side and were tied to bolts on either side of the room. He hung limply and I would've thought he was dead except for the fact his chest lifted slightly as he breathed.

I only then realized that my earpiece had been silent for too long. If Thomas was here, he must've done something to Shep.

"Lighthouse," I said loudly, giving the crew the word to move in. There was no response so I repeated it even more forcefully. Still nothing. I was about to say it one more time when cold steel pressed against my head.

"Don't waste your time. I disconnected the communication. You have no way to reach them."

I didn't have to look at him to know who it was, but seeing his face made it all real.

"What the fuck is this, Shep?"

"I'm surprised you didn't figure it out sooner, Peter. You really are rather smart. More intelligent than I originally gave you credit for."

My mind reeled with the facts. How could this possibly be? What had I missed? Then a few things fell into place. Sarah Jo Grainger saying Thomas's sole friend had been a kid named Chip. She'd said Shep, but I'd misheard her because of her speech impediment.

And Molly's text. Becker had met Shep an hour later than we'd thought.

"But the video surveillance from Emerald City Motors showed you on stakeout," I said. "You couldn't have been the killer."

He chuckled, whatever warmth in his voice now entirely gone. "I didn't kill Osceola or your precious Detective Nolan. And I wasn't the one who attacked Bryce. That was my buddy Thomas."

Two killers! I'd never seen that coming. The deaths had been exactly the same so I had no reason to suspect otherwise.

"Slowly put your flashlight and pistol on the ground," Shep ordered. "And kick them away."

I did as instructed but didn't shove them too far. The torch rolled away but my Glock was only a couple feet away and between me and Thomas.

"Why did you do this?" I asked Shep.

"Rules are *not* made to be broken, Peter. Laws are as important as marriage vows. I wanted to make an example of these men. So maybe other married guys would think twice about cheating after seeing what happened."

"My reasoning is a little different," Thomas said. "I know the hurt these guys suffered. They lost everything, and I wanted them put out of their misery. I was going to leave Bryce alone because it seemed as if he was better off now that he was out of the closet. But

I saw the article about the company. I know how much SC means to him. He can't be thrilled about losing any chance of getting it back."

"Thomas," I said softly, "please don't kill him. He'll get over losing his company. Think about his son and how much he'll miss his dad."

He didn't waver and pressed the knife harder against Bryce's throat. Bryce grunted, and he darted his eyes from me to Thomas.

"Please," I begged again. "I love him. I want a life with him, and he wants one with me."

Bryce's eyes widened, and he flinched slightly. Thomas peered at me but pulled the knife away slightly. He appeared at least somewhat moved by my confession. Shep, however, was not. He pressed his pistol harder into my neck.

"You're as disgusting as the adulterers," he snarled. "You deserve to die as much as your married boyfriend does. You both make me sick. Men and women like you are the reason my mother killed herself."

"But I just wanted them to be out of their misery," Thomas whined as he slumped his shoulders. "If these two can be happy together, I don't see…"

"They know who we are, dumbass. We couldn't let them go even if we wanted to. Now kill him. I want Peter to see his boyfriend die."

Thomas bit back a protest then straightened his body. "Once a cheater, always a cheater, right? If he did it once he'll do it again."

"Exactly," Shep replied. "Do it. Now!"

He put the blade to Bryce's throat and was about to slice when both he and Bryce glanced behind me. "What the fuck?" Thomas mumbled.

I heard the click of a trigger but instead of a bullet I heard the electric buzz of a Taser. Shep's body jolted, and he dropped to the floor. I didn't take time to see who my savior was. I didn't have time because Thomas was ready to kill Bryce, and his partner going down wouldn't stop him. I dropped down, retrieved my gun, and fired at Thomas's only visible body part—his head.

Unlike what is shown in TV and movies, it's not *that* easy to hit a guy square in the forehead. Cops are trained to shoot center mass because it's the largest target area and you're likely to hit something even if you're off by a bit. The head is a smaller target, and if I was off by even an inch the bullet would miss him, and he'd have time to slice Bryce's jugular.

I aimed for his temple but because of my angle I hit lower than I wanted, but it did the job. The bullet entered his head just above the jawline on his left side and came out the right side of his skull. His head exploded like a smashed pumpkin. Brains and bones flew everywhere. Bryce cringed and closed his eyes. As much as I wanted to run to him, I had to make sure Shep was secured.

I got up on one knee with my pistol aimed. Molly had the Taser still in her hand and was slowly making her way toward Shep, who was on his side. It appeared the prods had hit him in the ass. Normally cops aim for center mass with both a Taser and a gun, but Molly had been smart enough to avoid that body part because he was wearing a vest. The butt was the next best choice. I rose and put my foot on Shep's pistol before kicking it to the back of the room.

Molly got to Shep first, but I didn't see him move in time to warn her. He grabbed her foot and tossed her to the ground. Before he could get on top of her, I ran over and kicked him in the face, sending him rolling away. He leaped to his feet and tackled me in the midsection. I went sprawling backward but I kept hold of my gun. I wanted Shep to pay for his crimes. It would be sweet justice for the laws he claimed to believe in so strongly to be used to send him away to prison for the rest of his life. But I wouldn't hesitate to kill him if I had no other choice.

He straddled me and used both of his hands to grab my right arm in an attempt to get my pistol away. I punched him in the ribs with my left hand, but his adrenaline was flowing so high he didn't feel the pain. I tried to roll to the side to get him off me, but he was positioned so high on my chest I couldn't get the right momentum.

That was when I spotted Molly. She still had the Taser in her hand but it wasn't shocking Shep because the barbs weren't in contact with his skin. They were, however, still hooked in his pants. I reached up and grabbed Shep's ass, slamming my hand down on the Taser prods. "Now, Molly!"

Shep's body shook as fifty thousand volts ran through his body. My body jolted as well. Since I was touching the prods I was getting as much juice as he was. I didn't care as long as Shep was incapacitated. I just hoped I didn't piss myself. I remained conscious long enough to feel Shep collapse on top of me.

When I opened my eyes, at least a minute had passed. The room was full of officers but most importantly, Shep was handcuffed. I bounded to my feet and pushed away the wave of nausea that hit me. I ran to Bryce, who was being released from his bindings. I held him as he was freed, and he wrapped me in his arms.

"I love you, too," he said before he passed out.

TWENTY-FOUR

Despite insisting I was fine and begging to stay with Bryce, Chief Slight demanded I let the EMTs check me out. The hand I'd used on the Taser had two marks on them from the barbs, but I was otherwise fine. When they released me, Chief Slight pushed a bottle of water in my hand and demanded I drink it.

"You're not going anywhere until it's gone." She was dead serious, so I cracked it open and took a big drink.

"I really want to go see Bryce," I said.

She narrowed her eyes at me. "You're involved with him, aren't you?"

"I know it's against the rules," I replied. "But I tried to follow the regulations. I didn't pursue anything with him until after the case was closed. Well, when we all thought it was done. By the time we learned Diana Gomez *wasn't* the killer it was too late."

"We can talk about this later," she said. "You're the least of my worries. I have to talk to the commissioner, the mayor, and the press about how I allowed two psychotic men on my police force. I'm going to have to do some damage control. Not to mention you'll be on suspension—*again*—until IA clears you for killing Thomas Grainger."

I held up a hand. "I had no choice."

She patted my shoulder. "Officer Whitmore's report supports you. I'm sure you'll be cleared."

"How is Molly?" I asked.

"Freaked out," Slight said with a chuckle.

"She did a great job. I'm glad she used less than lethal force on Shep, though she would've been justified in killing him."

"It'll be terrific for the public to see Detective Adley pay for his crimes. You and Whitmore might just get medals of commendation out of this."

I didn't do this job expecting to be patted on the back, but it didn't hurt to be praised for a job well done.

"By the way, you may have been wrong about Marjorie Croft being the killer but you were right to be suspicious. Turned out she'd been stalking the pastor. She had some kind of odd fixation on him."

I was glad I hadn't been too far off base with the woman but that wasn't my worry right then. "Can I go now?" I asked. "I'd really like to see Bryce as soon as possible."

She sniggered. "You got it bad, don't you? Fine. Go see your man. But I want you to make your official report on the incident today."

"Yes, ma'am," I saluted her and reached for my keys. "Shit, Shep drove."

Slight glanced around, hollered at a uniformed officer, and waved him over. "Take Detective Tao to Harborview Medical Center, then get your ass back here."

BRYCE WAS BEING CHECKED OUT BY A DOCTOR when I arrived, but I left instructions to tell Bryce as soon as possible that I was there. I paced the waiting room for thirty minutes, unable to sit still for long, until a nurse escorted me to Bryce's room.

I kissed him immediately, not caring what the doctor or nurse thought. I was so grateful he was alive I couldn't keep my hands off him. "Did he hurt you at all?" I asked.

"He was drugged," the doctor said. "Rohypnol, standard date rape drug."

"Oh, my God, did he…"

Bryce squeezed my hand. "No, he didn't hurt me physically at all. Other than to tie me up."

"He has some slight injuries to his arms from being tied up as he was," the doctor added. "It's not major and should heal fairly soon."

Once the doctor and nurse left the room, Bryce said, "There wasn't any physical torture. Just verbal, mainly. He called me names and screamed at me. Threatened to use the knife on my cock and balls. I was pretty sure I was going to die until you came along."

"Yeah, with Shep right behind me."

Bryce rubbed his forehead. "I did not see that coming."

"Me either," I huffed. "I worked hard to prove he wasn't the killer. Played right into his hands. I can't believe I fell for his lies."

He pulled me toward him, and I lay down on the bed. My back to his chest with his arms wrapped around me. "He's a master manipulator. He fooled a lot of people. Think of how Ryan is going to feel."

"Poor kid."

Bryce and I lay there in silence for several minutes. It always felt amazing to be with him, but this moment was special because there had been a chance it would never happen again.

"Did you mean it?" Bryce whispered in my ear.

I knew what he meant but I still asked, "Mean what?"

He sighed. "When you told Thomas that…you loved me. Did you mean it or were you just trying to get him to second guess killing me? It's fine if it wasn't the truth. I just want to know. I *need* to know."

I paused, unsure how to answer. I knew what the truth was but wasn't sure I was ready to be that open. But one thing a near-death experience does is make you realize you don't have forever.

"Yes, I meant it. I love you, Bryce Carrick."

He squeezed me tighter and kissed the back of my neck. "That's good, because I love you, Bae Peter Tao."

"I'm still not going to sleep with you until you're divorced."

Bryce chuckled, then it became louder, and soon he was chortling loudly. And I laughed right along with him.

THE END

ETHAN STONE
ROMANCE ON THE EDGE

Ethan Stone doesn't write your typical boy meets boy stories. With a combination of love and suspense he makes his characters work hard for their HEAs. If they can survive what he puts them through, then they can survive anything. He enjoys Romance with an Edge.

Ethan has been reading mysteries and thrillers since he was young. He's had a thing for guys in uniform for just as long. That may have influenced the stories he writes.

He's a native Oregonian with two kids. One of whom has made him a grandfather three times over; even though he is way too young.

READERS CAN FIND ETHAN ONLINE.

WEBSITE: WWW.ETHANJSTONE.COM
FACEBOOK: WWW.FACEBOOK.COM/ETHAN.STONE.54
TWITTER: @ETHANJSTONE
PINTEREST: WWW.PINTEREST.COM/ETHANJSTONE/
TUMBLR: WWW.TUMBLR.COM/BLOG/ETHANSTONE
EMAIL: ETHANSTONE.NV@GMAIL.COM

OTHER BOOKS BY ETHAN STONE

STANDALONES

HACKED UP

SUBJECT 13

BARTENDER, PI

DIRTY

TRANSPARENCY (WITH SARA YORK)

WOLF MOON

BEING TAUGHT

STARTING OVER

SMALL CLAIMS

HIJACKED LOVE

TALES OF A PRISON BITCH

RACING HEARTS (MULTI-AUTHOR ANTHOLOGY)

LOVE, VEGAS STYLE

MUSE

LIES & DIAMONDS & BEARS

ONE MORE TIME

SEASIDE SHIFTERS

WILD RETALIATION

WILD INSTINCTS